On the viewscreen, the glowing red fighters swept in on the militia fighters. One by one, the green holographic fighters of the militia peeled away, most of them tailed by the enemy. In a matter of minutes, the green lights simply did not exist. Rhonda looked at the palm communicator lying on the desk, then back at Count Fisk, who shook his head.

"I know what you're thinking, Colonel," he said. "You want to call back my unit. Just so you don't waste your energy, I've given Captain Malcolm strict orders to obey only my commands."

"They'll be massacred if they rush that regiment with only a company," she said angrily. "You're killing them."

"*Au contraire,* Colonel. *You* will have killed them, or your inaction will have. They were doing their duty—that's how the public will see it. And they will view your irregulars as traitors who refused to save the planet's defenders from certain death."

"This is blackmail," Rhonda hissed.

"No, my dear Colonel," Fisk returned, letting his own anger bleed into his words, "this is war."

BATTLETECH®

CALL OF DUTY

Blaine Lee Pardoe

A ROC BOOK

ROC
Published by New American Library, a division of
Penguin Putnam Inc., 375 Hudson Street,
New York, New York 10014, U.S.A.
Penguin Books Ltd, 27 Wrights Lane,
London W8 5TZ, England
Penguin Books Australia Ltd, Ringwood,
Victoria, Australia
Penguin Books Canada Ltd, 10 Alcorn Avenue,
Toronto, Ontario, Canada M4V 3B2
Penguin Books (N.Z.) Ltd, 182–190 Wairau Road,
Auckland 10, New Zealand

Penguin Books Ltd, Registered Offices:
Harmondsworth, Middlesex, England

First published by Roc, an imprint of New American Library,
a division of Penguin Putnam Inc.

First Printing, October 2001
10 9 8 7 6 5 4 3 2 1

Series Editor: Donna Ippolito
Designer: Ray Lundgren
Cover art by Ed Cox
Mechanical Drawings: Duane Loose and the FASA art department

ROC REGISTERED TRADEMARK—MARCA REGISTRADA

BATTLETECH, FASA, and the distinctive BATTLETECH and FASA
logos are trademarks of the FASA Corporation, 1100 W. Cermak,
Suite B305, Chicago, IL 60608.

Printed in the United States of America

PUBLISHER'S NOTE
This is a work of fiction. Names, characters, places, and incidents either
are the product of the author's imagination or are used fictitiously,
and any resemblance to actual persons, living or dead, business
establishments, events, or locales is entirely coincidental.

BOOKS ARE AVAILABLE AT QUANTITY DISCOUNTS WHEN USED TO PROMOTE
PRODUCTS OR SERVICES. FOR INFORMATION PLEASE WRITE TO PREMIUM
MARKETING DIVISION, PENGUIN PUTNAM INC., 375 HUDSON STREET, NEW
YORK, NEW YORK 10014.

As always, this book is dedicated to my wife, Cyndi, my son, Alexander, and my daughter, Victoria. It is also dedicated to my alma mater, Central Michigan University, and to my good friends and coworkers, who provided me with a wealth of character material without ever realizing it.

I extend a special dedication to the folks at FASA: Donna, Bryan, Randall, and the other authors in the series.

Finally, special thanks go out to Alan Andrews, who, when I was just a kid, introduced me to war gaming. I devoured the works of James F. Dunnigan and the old SPI and Avalon Hill game companies. Without those roots, I doubt I would ever have ended up writing these books. To this date, those old war games still pack a hell of a punch, and without them, there would not be a gaming industry—not as we know it, anyway. Role players, card gamers, and PC-game players owe a lot to those early days of the industry.

This novel, indeed much of my writing career, never would have happened without the help of L. Ross Babcock III. I had only a few books under my belt with the fledgling FASA Corporation in 1986 when Ross sent me a one-paragraph description for a scenario pack called *Cranston Snord's Irregulars*. I still have that one-pager tucked away in a binder. He asked me if I could write it. Sure, how hard could it be? And in that moment, Snord's Irregulars was born. I am one of the handful of people that know the truth of where the name came from—an old BC comic.

Eight years later, the fans were clamoring for more of Snord. Sam Lewis gave me the green light to answer their calls. Thus was born the supplement *Rhonda's Irregulars*. But that wasn't enough. Out of all of the materials I've written around BattleTech® over the last fourteen years, Snord's Irregulars remains one of the most popular subjects. So for you die-hards, this novel's for you.

I want to thank my neighbor, John Gramache, who provided the incredibly loose basis for the mysterious Sergeant in the book. Thanks to John Kendrick for getting me out for our Civil War relic-hunting/stress-relief trips. And I want to thank my in-laws for putting up with me writing this on the family vacation in MI. Thanks to loyalist fan Camille Klein and Solarmech who helped me sort through the epilogue.

And finally, to the Little Fork Rangers, CSA. I got the idea for this book when reading the inscription on their monument, hidden away in upper Culpeper County, while doing some local Civil War research.

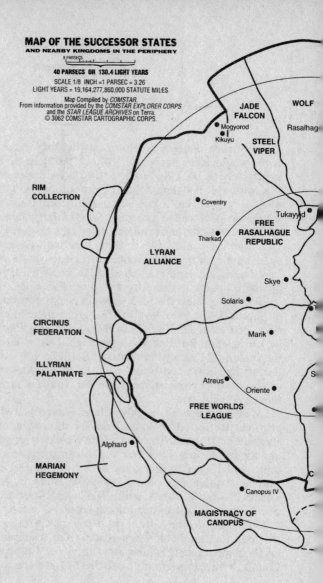

MAP OF THE SUCCESSOR STATES
AND NEARBY KINGDOMS IN THE PERIPHERY

8 PARSECS

40 PARSECS OR 130.4 LIGHT YEARS
SCALE 1/8 INCH = 1 PARSEC = 3.26
LIGHT YEARS = 19,164,277,860,000 STATUTE MILES

Map Compiled by *COMSTAR*.
From information provided by the *COMSTAR EXPLORER CORPS*
and the *STAR LEAGUE ARCHIVES* on Terra.
© 3062 COMSTAR CARTOGRAPHIC CORPS.

JADE FALCON

WOLF

Rasalhag

Mogyorod
Kikuyu

STEEL VIPER

RIM COLLECTION

Coventry

Tukayyid

FREE RASALHAGUE REPUBLIC

Tharkad

LYRAN ALLIANCE

Skye

Solaris

CIRCINUS FEDERATION

Marik

ILLYRIAN PALATINATE

Atreus

Oriente

FREE WORLDS LEAGUE

Alphard

MARIAN HEGEMONY

Canopus IV

MAGISTRACY OF CANOPUS

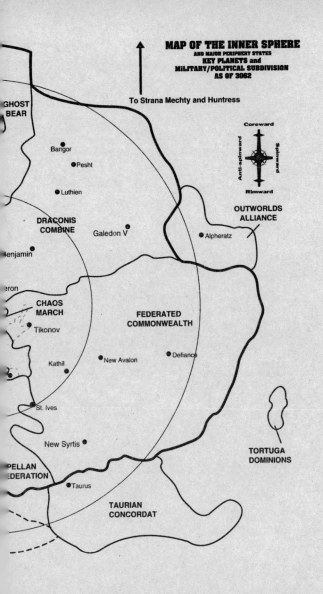

MAP OF THE INNER SPHERE
AND MAJOR PERIPHERY STATES
KEY PLANETS and
MILITARY/POLITICAL SUBDIVISION
AS OF 3062

To Strana Mechty and Huntress

Coreward

Anti-spinward

Spinward

Rimward

GHOST BEAR

Bangor

Pesht

Luthien

DRACONIS COMBINE

Galedon V

OUTWORLDS ALLIANCE

Alpheratz

Benjamin

eron

CHAOS MARCH

Tikonov

FEDERATED COMMONWEALTH

Kathil

New Avalon

Defiance

St. Ives

New Syrtis

TORTUGA DOMINIONS

PELLAN FEDERATION

Taurus

TAURIAN CONCORDAT

Prologue

Davion Memorial Park
Avalon City, New Avalon
Crucis March, Federated Commonwealth
3 February 3063

Katrina Steiner-Davion gazed up at the granite statue guarding the entrance to the Davion tombs on New Avalon. Its proud face seemed to scan the wide blue sky, which was crystalline and almost cloudless today. The figure was three times her size, yet it still did not reflect the true scope of the man who had been her father.

She adjusted her light jacket against the chill morning air. In the past few weeks, she had found herself coming here often. Though press members were never allowed to get too near, she always made sure they got a good look at her in solemn contemplation. To the public, she would seem the good daughter, seeking solace in the memory of her dead father. In truth, she was unsure why she came. Perhaps to gloat, perhaps in search of some paternal approval that would never be hers.

"My brother still seeks what you had—what I now possess," Katrina murmured, as though her father could hear her. "The Federated Commonwealth is mine, Father. I hold in my hands the empire you forged. Victor can try to take it from me, but he never will. I have always outfoxed him, and I always will."

And no one could say it wasn't so. Her rule extended across some nine hundred inhabited worlds from one end of the Inner Sphere to the other. Through guile and cunning—and in a few short years—she had become the legitimate ruler of those hundreds of planets. And her people loved her.

She was especially proud that it had all been won through the force of her will and intelligence, without need of military force or a political marriage. Even her father, who had forged the vast empire of the Federated Commonwealth through the wedding bed, could not have made that boast.

Katrina ruled by the affection and consent of her people. She never dwelled on the darker deeds that had paved her way to power. She had only done what was necessary, removing even her mother when she posed a threat. Her mother had been assassinated, yes, and soon after, Katrina walked off with the Lyran half of the Federated Commonwealth when Victor's incompetence set off a war with Thomas Marik's Free Worlds League. Then she'd stepped in to take over the other half of the empire while Victor was away fighting the Clans. Could it have been easier?

She contemplated the medals carved on Hanse Davion's stone chest, and thought scornfully of how men always saw every problem in terms of a military solution. How they loved their toys, their destructive weapons of war. It was the very reason she always beat them at their own game.

While Victor was off playing soldier in Clan space, Katrina had manipulated the polls, making it seem that public opinion had turned against her younger sister Yvonne, Victor's regent on New Avalon. The girl had been only too happy to hand over the reins of power to her big sister. The recent murder of her brother Arthur in the Draconis March had also served Katrina's purposes. With the finger of suspicion pointed at the Draconis Combine, it further tainted Victor, who was still collaborating with the Combine's hated ruler and even bedding the man's daughter.

You would be proud of me, Father, she told him silently. I learned well at your knee.

She had no doubt that Hanse Davion, the Fox himself, would approve of all that she had done. She was his true heir. Always the master politician, he would have seen himself in his daughter's actions were he alive.

Little Victor had surprised her of late, however, showing a vengeful fury she never knew he possessed. Blaming her for Arthur's death, he'd sent out a call to his loyalist troops, demanding that they rally to remove her from power. The weaklings among them had complied. Though she'd tried to black out news of the minor rebellions, the harder she came down, the faster they seemed to spread. Whole regiments had turned against her—she, the rightful heir of her father's legacy.

For now, her prime goal was the Lyran theater, where she was strongest. Her plan was to solidify her dominant position by wiping out the units loyal to Victor, and then shift freed-up units to the Federated theater. Morgan Kell and his ARDC were a slight obstacle to her plan, but that problem—like any other—had a solution. Sooner or later, she would find it.

Katrina wished she could make Hanse Davion's graven face turn to look at her and acknowledge all she had accomplished. She would have to wait till eternity for that, however. Nothing broke the stillness, and her father's eyes of stone continued to gaze up into the New Avalon sky as if she were not even there.

The crunch of footsteps from behind caught her attention. She looked over her shoulder to see a short man in a Lyran Alliance uniform approaching.

"Colonel Lentard," she said, turning on the charm, "thank you so much for coming." Anton Lentard was her most trusted agent in Loki, the Lyran intelligence machine, and she had arranged for their daily briefing to take place here. Her day was so full that even a visit to the cemetery had to do double duty.

"Good morning, Highness," he said, looking around furtively as though the dead had ears.

Katrina turned away from the statue of Hanse Davion. "So, Lentard, I hope you bring me good news on this beautiful morning."

Lentard stood at attention, rocking slightly on his heels. "I trust the news will not spoil your fine mood, Highness, but your brother has been proving himself most resourceful of late," he began.

"Praising that meddling little Napoleon will not curry favor with me, Colonel," she said, fixing him with a stare. "I'd prefer to hear the highlights of the current situation."

"Some of your Lyran worlds are reporting strikes and raids by units loyal to Victor." Lentard shifted to parade rest as he spoke. "We confirm that the situation on Brockway is beyond repair. The Eleventh Avalon Hussars RCT is executing a controlled withdrawal."

" 'Retreat' is the word you are avoiding, Colonel," Katrina said smoothly. Though she could have bitten off his head for bringing her this news, that would get her nowhere. "What about Kathil?"

Fighting had broken out on Kathil in mid-November last year, even before news of Arthur's death had triggered Victor's call to arms. Home to Yare Industries shipyards that produced the powerful WarShips of her fleet, it was a planet she could not afford to lose.

"The fighting continues, with the Kathil CMM still holding us off. It is hard to tell for sure which way it will go. And the list of rebellious worlds is growing. We've suppressed the minor revolts, but only at the cost of saddling numerous regiments with garrison duty. I have ordered the complete file dumped to your command directory for your Highness's review."

"You mentioned raids, Colonel."

Lentard looked glum as he glanced at his noteputer. "Well, none of them were major, but all were enough to require our attention. We're still verifying what units are where, but we have been able to confirm that the First Thorin Regiment has dropped on Alcor and is engaging the local garrison there."

"Archer Christifori's unit?" That was galling news. Despite her efforts to get rid of him, the so-called Archer's Avengers were becoming famous for opposing her in the Lyran Alliance.

"The same," Lentard said. The unit had seized both Thorin and Muphrid in the early days of the unrest. Since then, the Avengers had hit several more planets, reinforcing Victor's supporters and then vanishing without a trace. Christifori was a charismatic man, a Star League Medal of Honor winner who wanted vengeance on Katrina for the death of his sister—a known rebel.

What a waste, she thought.

She cocked one eyebrow slightly. "Why Alcor? You'd think that the 'military genius' they attribute to my brother would have him striking at targets with more strategic value. Alcor is nothing to me."

"The planetary duke was cracking down on Davion dissidents," Lentard said. "The Avengers responded to similar arrests on Milton. It may be more than that, though. This could be part of a larger strategy."

"Explain," Katrina said.

"We cannot be certain, of course, but we believe these raids are aimed at tying down our forces in the Lyran Alliance and sowing the seeds of rebellion on seemingly non-strategic worlds. Once Christifori's forces land, they usually suppress or destroy the local militia, spread Victor's propaganda, and then depart."

Katrina nodded slowly. "And we dispatch forces there, only to find—"

"—that he is already gone. But if we don't send in troops, the local media creates the impression that the war is not going our way. Your popularity on such worlds diminishes, and this encourages unrest on other planets."

Katrina fought to keep the anger and frustration from showing on her face. "My brother and his lies must not be allowed to take root," she said. The outbreak of rebellions had already forced her to deploy troops on many planets that would not normally warrant garrison forces, just to keep the locals in line and show that she was indeed in control of the situation.

"It is more than that, Highness," Colonel Lentard continued doggedly. "These strikes tend to unnerve the nobles who govern these planets. You have seen the messages coming in. The Lyran Alliance nobility want more direct control of some military assets. They believe your brother's strikes are eroding their power and authority."

He did not have to add that those nobles *were* the source of her power in the Lyran Alliance. "I understand, Colonel. However I'm not prepared to hand over Alliance military assets so easily."

Katrina understood the thinking of her would-be peers. Her power base they might be, but she did not really trust them. "Any other bad news, Colonel?"

His cheeks reddened slightly. "Highness, per our discussion two weeks ago, we have redeployed Snord's Irregulars near the Terran Corridor, in hopes of countering some of your brother's recent moves. However, Colonel Snord has opted to exercise a clause in her contract negating the unit's assignment in civil wars or disputes."

Katrina's eyes narrowed. "The Irregulars have always fought on the Lyran side," she said, her tone final. "They are eccentric but effective. You must find a way to get them into the fight. As I recall, their contract expires soon, and I have no desire to see them join the ranks of my enemies."

The thought of Sun-Tzu Liao or Theodore Kurita with such troops under his command—or, worse, her dear brother Victor—was far from appealing. She glanced briefly at the statue of her father, then back at Lentard.

"Tell me, Colonel," she said, "do you have *any* good news?"

"Yes, Your Highness," he said, a thin bead of sweat visible on his brow despite the chill in the air. "The ink is almost dry on the deal you asked me to broker—the absorption of the Wolverton's Highlanders into the Blackstone Highlanders. Colonel Blackstone informs me that he has met with Colonel Feehan and that they have begun to work out the logistics."

Katrina nodded. She had "encouraged" the merger at the end of the previous year after hearing rumors that the mercenary Wolverton's Highlanders might leave the Lyran Alliance in search of greener fields. Now they were locked firmly in place, where she could use them to her advantage.

A shadow swept over the cemetery as a lone cloud momentarily blocked the sun over New Avalon. She wished she could ask her father for advice right now. How would the great Hanse Davion have handled such a crisis?

A thin, almost wicked smile touched her lips as she turned back to Lentard. "You think too small sometimes, Colonel. I'm sure we can turn this whole thing to our advantage, if we are creative enough."

"Highness?"

She pulled her light jacket closer against the sudden chill in the air. "My brother's forces have been raising hell in the interior of the Lyran Alliance, the nobles of my realm want more military control to meet the situation, and now we have mercenary troops who think to disobey my bidding. You see difficulties. I see opportunities."

Colonel Lentard said nothing for a moment, then he too began to smile. "Perhaps I see where your thinking is leading, Highness. We can assign Snord's Irregulars to a planetary noble in the interior. If one of Victor's raiding parties should attack that world, the mercenaries will have to fight, no matter what their contract says."

"Exactly," Katrina said. "I don't intend to give LAAF assets to all my nobles, but by assigning mercenary troops to one, it gives the rest some sense of security that I might do the same for them. However, I want you to attach a Loki operative to the Irregulars' posting. Should my brother refuse to provide the necessary provocation, order him or her to do whatever is necessary to draw Snord's Irregulars into the fight."

"It will be done." Lentard bowed slightly and then checked his noteputer again. "If I read our intelligence correctly, I think the best place to assign the Irregulars is to Count Nicholas Fisk on Odessa. He controls several worlds, and our intel suggests that Odessa may be on the list of Christifori's secondary targets."

Katrina thought for a moment, searching her memory. "Wasn't Fisk's son injured by Christifori on Thorin?"

"Yes, Highness," Lentard said.

"Good, then Count Fisk will be looking for revenge. We must be careful with him, however. I know how he operates, and if you give him a centimeter, he'll take a kilometer."

Lentard pondered for a moment. "We'll still need a way to make Odessa a primary target for your brother—enough that he would send Archer's Avengers there. I suggest that the Count begin a general roundup of suspected insurgents planning to strike a blow for Victor. We'll play up in the media how Colonel Snord is unwilling to fight for our cause. It will make Odessa seem like a low-hanging fruit—an easy target.

"I'll assign one of my best agents as his 'liaison,' Your Grace," the colonel continued. "Perhaps I could also have Colonel Blackstone dispatch Robert Feehan and the Wolverton's Highlanders? Blackstone would probably find that financially appealing, and Feehan will be hungry to prove himself to his new superior officer. We might also post the Loki agent to the Highlanders. If the Avengers or another rebel unit does hit the planet, Fisk may need their additional firepower."

"A very good idea," Katrina said, nodding slowly. She glanced again toward her father's statue. Good enough for Hanse Davion's daughter? she asked silently.

"You will fail," a voice from somewhere seemed to say, but she heard the words more with her inner ear than from without. She could have sworn it was the voice of her father, and a chill of fear shot through her. She spun angrily on Colonel Lentard.

"Highness?" he asked, taking an involuntary step backward.

She mastered her fear. Never showing weakness was her greatest strength. "Did you say something?" she demanded.

Lentard was looking at her strangely, his head cocked slightly in confusion. "Yes, Highness. I said we cannot fail."

Yes, that was it. She had misunderstood, though she couldn't explain how Lentard's voice could have sounded so like her father's. "Good," she told him coolly. "That will be all until tonight's briefing."

Colonel Lentard bowed, then did a brisk about-face, and walked away. Without another look at Hanse Davion's statue, Katrina, too, then started toward the gate in the stone wall that surrounded the Davion area of the cemetery. The chill of a moment before was still in her. When she reached the iron gate, she looked back.

"Victor will fail, Father," she said, softly enough that her bodyguards would not hear. "The boy you raised to rule will lose everything before I am done. His armies will fall, his spirit will be crushed in my hands. He will be left with nothing. When this is over, Victor will be on his knees before me."

Katrina nodded to herself as she turned and walked through the gate. She made a mental note to have this area sealed. After today, she would never come here again.

BOOK ONE

The Blood of Patriots and Tyrants

The tree of liberty must be refreshed from time to time with the blood of patriots and tyrants. It is its natural manure.

—Thomas Jefferson

If men make war in slavish obedience to rules, they will fail.

—Ulysses S. Grant

1

Little Fork, Alcor
Isle of Skye
Lyran Alliance
11 February 3063

Leftenant General Archer Christifori slowed the gait of his *Penetrator* and adjusted his long-range sensors for what seemed like the tenth time that morning. Little Fork sprawled out before him, its rolling hills covered with patches of snow that refused to melt and a thick frost that sparkled in the morning sun. This region of Alcor's northern hemisphere was farm country: sweeping hills and wide-open spaces marked with fence lines of thick trees. But it was more than that: it was home to the Alcor Home Guard, the militia that defended this planet.

He and the battalion of Avengers he'd dropped onto the planet had been fighting the Home Guard for three weeks now, and had found the militiamen to be surprisingly worthy opponents. Archer had hoped to defeat them in a fast and decisive victory, but things hadn't turned out as planned. Every time he thought he had them pinned, they would melt away into the countryside, only to reappear rearmed, repaired, and ready to continue the fight.

Not today, my friends, he thought as he picked up

a fast-moving Guard *Hollander* cutting across the edge of his sensor range. The enemy 'Mechs were running like rabbits—hopefully back to their rabbit holes.

"Ranger One, you've got them moving," he said into his neurohelmet mike as he angled his *Penetrator* to pursue. "Brain—paint me a picture."

The Brain was Katya Chaffee, his second in command and the unit's intelligence chief. She was also his confidante, one of the few people whose counsel he trusted implicitly. It wouldn't have taken much for her to become more than that, but she and Archer had yet to take it any further.

"The Icepicks are in the slot, and two lances of Rangers are running and shooting, heading north by northwest on their flank," Katya reported. "Sledgehammer has her people anchored on their other flank, forcing them to keep moving. You wanted them flushed out, General. I'd say we've done that."

Archer smiled at the slight sarcasm in her voice, and made the adjustments necessary to bring up the rear of the fleeing Guards. Even a single BattleMech, upwards of ten meters tall and master of the battlefield for centuries, carried enough lasers, particle projection cannons, artillery, and missiles to turn a city block into charred rubble in a matter of seconds. His own *Penetrator* was not just the pinnacle of that technology, but a veteran of the Clan wars as well. Outfitted with salvaged Clan technology, it gave him an edge that most MechWarriors only dreamed of.

Archer switched channels. "Icepick One, this is Spector One," he said. "The good news is that the plan seems to be working. We've got the local kids on the run."

The voice that came back was older, gruff, and faintly amused. "The bad news is that the plan is working. You've got them running, all right—right on top of my infantry."

"Be careful what you wish for, old man," Archer said as the *Hollander* he'd spotted earlier swung around slightly for a shot as he closed range.

"I hear that, Spector One," Darius Hopkins said with a chuckle. Hopkins had been a pseudo father to Archer for too many years to remember. When Archer was just a young militia recruit on Thorin, Hopkins had been the one to train him to qualify for the prestigious NAIS military academy. He'd also been the one to attend Archer's graduation, and many years later, had been there to greet Archer upon his return from the Clan wars.

The *Hollander* further slowed its run and fired its only weapon, the massive gauss rifle jutting from one of its shoulders. The silver blur of the deadly gauss slug raced at hypersonic speed toward Archer's 'Mech, missing him by only a couple of meters.

"Your first mistake," Archer said under his breath. "You should've kept running."

With his joystick, he swung the targeting reticle onto the distant *Hollander* and brought his extended-range large lasers to bear. The huge weapons throbbed to life as the cross hairs changed color on the primary display.

He fired, as he had done thousands of times in his career. The brilliant emerald pulses stabbed out like lances wielded by knights of old. One hit the *Hollander*'s right torso, and the other plowed into the left. Both flash-burned, instantly melting away the 'Mech's paper-thin armor.

The Guardsman reeled under the assault. A fissure of steam from its fusion reactor shot into the cool air as the *Hollander* fell backward like a boxer felled by a knockout blow. Archer did not have to maintain a lock on it. The light 'Mech never stood a chance against his. Archer wondered how many others would fall or die for the Archon before this was all over, how many more would pay the price for her power?

The plan he and Katya had come up with was simple enough. They'd decided that the only way to end the sniping games they'd been playing with the Alcor Home Guard was to locate the enemy's base of operations. While his 'Mech forces drove the Guard into retreat, his infantry, under Darius Hopkins, was tracking their movements and direction in order to triangulate the position of their base. Once it was located, the Avengers would capture or destroy it. Either way, the Archon would no longer claim a military presence on Alcor.

He picked up the faint signal of a *Hercules* 'Mech beginning to escape the advancing line of Captain John Kraff's Rangers. The *Hercules* pilot was skilled— running, dodging, and somehow managing to evade most of the attacks aimed at it while still keeping some distance from its pursuers. Archer throttled up almost to a jog as the 'Mech flickered out of his sensor range. Pushing his *Penetrator* faster then, he reached the point where he should have seen it on his secondary display but didn't.

Three long minutes passed. "Ranger One, this is Spector One," he said finally. "Where is that *Herc*?"

"Beats the hell out of me . . . sir," came back the voice of John Kraff, commander of Muphrid's Rangers, for once catching himself before his cursing got out of control.

"This is Icepick One to all commands," Archer heard Hopkins say in his earpiece. "I think we've found them. Coordinates are coming now. Converge on this point."

The coordinates appeared on Archer's secondary display.

"Spector One to all commands," he said. "You heard the man. Everyone get within striking distance of that point. Move to encircle and enclose, but do not engage. If we can end this peacefully, I'd like to."

"You heard the old man," Kraff said, reinforcing Archer's command. "Move in."

"Your call, sir," said Major Alice Getts, Archer's ground armor commander, "but I think Icepick is blowing smoke. I got a visual on those coordinates, and all I see is a little farm. We've chased these bad boys past this place three times since we landed. I haven't seen hide nor hair of a 'Mech there."

Archer heard her words but was thinking about Kraff's reference to "the old man." After years of calling his own superiors by that nickname, he wondered at what point he had become that symbol—the leader, the "old man." It must have been months ago, when he'd been promoted to general in the field back on Thorin. Hearing the words now made him feel both proud but even older than his forty-three years.

As Archer angled slightly to join the rest of his command, Hopkins came back on the line. "Looks are always deceiving," he said. "That's why we've been missing it for the last two weeks. Trust me, this is the spot."

Archer did not contradict him. Darius Hopkins had been both a father and a mentor to him. If he said that was the base, well, that was good enough for Archer Christifori.

When he reached the hill overlooking the spot his commanders had identified as the enemy's armory/base, Archer still didn't see anything more than a farm.

"Sit rep," he said coolly as he brought the *Penetrator* to a stop near a haystack, putting the farm just within long range of his lasers.

"We've set up some seismic sensors and picked up

two tunnels," came back Katya's voice. "Both exits are covered. That barn appears to be the way in."

"One of my scouts moved in close enough for an eyes-on look and close-range check," Hopkins added. "There's a bunker under that barn. From what she could detect, there are at least six BattleMechs in there."

Archer stared at the innocent-looking farm and sighed. The time had come to end the fighting on Alcor once and for all. If the Home Guard tried to break out, they'd be slaughtered. They were outgunned and outmanned at least three to one, not to mention the aerospace fighter support Archer could call in if necessary. These were mere weekend warriors against his seasoned band of liberators-turned-army. They wouldn't stand a chance.

If he could prevent a slaughter, he would. Archer hadn't entered this fight to wantonly kill his fellow countrymen. What he wanted to do was prevent more killing, to convince them that resistance was hopeless.

Opening the broadband channel that all of his troops could hear, he spoke slowly and calmly. "Listen up, Avengers. Hold your fire unless you get specific orders to attack. These people are simply defending their homes and families. The Archon's propaganda has painted us as marauders. The time has come to prove them wrong." He switched to an unsecured channel, one he knew his foes could also receive.

"Alcor Home Guard, this is Leftenant General Archer Christifori. We have your base and all of its exits surrounded. Power down and come out with your hands up, and you'll be treated honorably." He paused, but there was no response.

Time to play his bluff. "I know you have a lot of ammunition in that armory. If we have to fight our way in, you'll be blown to bits. None of us want that." Again, silence.

Archer's eyes narrowed. "Saber Lance, one strafing run," he said reluctantly. "Destroy the building facades. Get their attention. Shake the foundations a little."

"Yessir," said Leftenant Francine Culver from the cockpit of her *Lucifer* aerofighter. She dove in, followed by Andrew Hackley in his *Chippewa*. Bringing up the rear of the diving attack was a pair of *Corsair*s. Lasers and missiles hit the area so fast that the farm buildings were devoured instantly in a burst of light, smoke, and flames. Even through the feet of his seventy-five-ton *Penetrator*, Archer could feel the ground quake.

He glanced up as the lance of four fighters peeled off to return to combat air-patrol. Then he looked back at the holocaust that had been the Home Guard base.

The false superstructures had been gutted. What remained was a ferrocrete bunker, blackened from the assault and covered with still-burning debris. Deep craters gouged out by the barrage had almost penetrated its defenses. But those bunkers were tough, and Archer knew that casualties would mount if he sent the infantry in to take the enemy room by room.

These people deserved better than to die fighting so that Katherine Steiner-Davion could keep her crown.

"Home Guard, this is General Christifori," he said over the open channel. "We've got your exits covered, and your sensors can probably tell you that I've got a battalion of troops here, complete with artillery and aerospace support. This is your last chance. Surrender, and you'll be treated honorably. Refuse, and I'll have to do something we'll both regret."

He waited. This time there was a crackle on the commline, followed by a voice. "General, this is First Leutenant Darren Stump. Do I have your word that no harm will come to my people or their families?"

Archer was stunned. What had they been told about him? That he was some sort of murderer? The thought was a bitter one. He was so proud that his Avengers always fought honorably. The suggestion that he might harm innocent people stung deep.

"You have my word as an officer and a gentleman," he said after a long moment. "By my own Star League Medal of Honor, I swear that no harm will come to your families. We just want this fighting to end."

"That makes two of us."

"Leave your 'Mechs and weapons. Come out slowly."

They emerged from the charred bunker in single file. None had their hands in the air. Surrender showed only in their expressions of bitterness and frustration. Archer had seen it many times before in his career—the signs of defeat.

"Honors, hut!" he ordered. Instantly, all around him, the BattleMechs of his command straightened to attention. Hopkins's infantry troops on the ground also stood at attention, saluting their enemies. At the same time, Getts's tanks raised their turret barrels in another sign of honor.

The slow shuffling gait of the Home Guardsmen slowed almost to a stop at the respect being granted them. One of them, a First Leutenant by rank, stepped up to Archer's *Penetrator,* saluting as he snapped to attention.

Honor given and received. It was a gesture Archer had performed on Thorin, Muphrid, and two other worlds where he'd led the Avengers in fighting for Prince Victor's cause. The Federated Commonwealth might be descending into civil war, but that didn't mean he had to lose his own honor. Perhaps that was why the Prince's media machine had so publicized the deeds of Archer's Avengers. Footage of this scene would probably be broadcasting over holovid screens in a matter of hours.

Archer stared down at the thin rank of MechWarriors and techs filing out of the armory bunker, then he glanced up at the morning sky. Gray clouds were rolling in, briefly blocking the sun. How many more such worlds would have to fall before Katherine realized the error of her ways? How many more men and women would have to die in her name?

"Katya, have our forces secure the bunker," Archer said, unable to hide the catch in his voice. "I want a full inventory. Priority goes to refitting our gear before repairing their BattleMechs."

"Yes, sir," she said. "Anything else?"

"Send a message to the planetary media. Tell them that the Home Guard has been captured and will be repatriated shortly. Let them know that, as of now, Duke Remington is no longer the authority on this world and that his holdings are forfeit property of the state. Tell them this world now belongs to its people."

"With pleasure, General," Katya said, and Archer could almost see the grin on her face.

One more down, he thought wearily, another nine hundred or so to go.

2

Little Fork Alcor
Isle of Skye,
Lyran Alliance
11 February 3063

Archer stood with his arms crossed as the female reporter moved her hand mike in closer. He had purposely chosen this spot out near his base camp for the interview, instead of in the city where crowds might gather. Behind him lay the charred remains of the Home Guard bunkers, frost glinting off the few wood facades that had not burned. Flanking the reporter, Ms. Holly Neuman, the holovid crew were focusing their portable lights and adjusting their imagers to get both her and Archer in view. When they were finally ready, Neuman turned to him with a false and brittle smile.

"Is it true, General Christifori, that you have expelled the ruling family from Alcor?" Her tone was accusatory and faintly hostile. He had come to expect that from the Lyran press. He knew they were part of the solution, but they were also part of the problem. They had been spreading propaganda for Katrina Steiner for so long that they were having a hard time adjusting to their new role as real journalists.

"The Duke and his family have been asked to leave

Alcor, yes," he replied, keeping his tone polite and matter-of-fact. "I thought that having the Duke remain on the planet would cause unnecessary political tensions."

That was actually pretty close to the truth. Duke Remington had come down hard on anyone who had spoken out against the Archon. In one protest by university students, two dozen young people had been killed and another thirty wounded. His hard-line stance was one of the reasons Alcor had made Archer's target list. Letting Remington stay on would only encourage those harboring thoughts of revenge. "In many respects, it was the best way to guarantee their safety."

"Isn't it more accurate to say that the Duke's support of the rightful Archon was the real reason you forced him and his family into exile?" Neuman asked acidly.

Archer gave a slight shrug, keeping his expression carefully neutral. "I'll make no bones about it, Miss Neuman. We're engaged in a struggle to remove Katherine as Archon, plain and simple. If Remington had won instead of us, I'm sure that right now my men and I would be lined up blindfolded against the wall."

She flushed slightly, the faint red of either anger or frustration staining her high cheekbones. "So, General Christifori, what you're really saying is that you attacked Alcor as part of a strategy to put Prince Victor in his sister's place? That your war against the Lyran people is merely a play to put Victor Davion in power?"

Archer gave her a thin smile. He had to admire her for sticking to her guns. How many other people would be so bold in front of a victorious military commander?

"First off, Miss Neuman, I *am* a Lyran. Born and raised on Thorin. This isn't about Lyrans and Davions.

This is about removing Katrina Steiner-Davion from power before she can do more damage than she already has."

"So you claim she doesn't have the right to rule?"

He shook his head. "I do not deny that she has the right to rule by birth. But her actions of late have shown her *unworthy* of the office. This is not about rights but about integrity." He spoke slowly, emphasizing each word.

"And what of the Alcor Home Guard?"

"There is no Alcor Home Guard," Archer said. "The unit has been captured and disbanded. Their hardware is now the property of my regiment. The former officers and soldiers are being held for a few more days."

"And then what—prison camp?"

Archer had had little use for reporters before the civil war, and even less since. "I'm a soldier myself, Miss Neuman," he said, drawing on every ounce of his patience. "No, they will not be held indefinitely. We're paroling them as soon as they sign oaths not to take up arms against Prince Victor."

"So you're asking our viewers to believe that you would release these captives on their word alone? That rather stretches one's credibility, General."

"I'm sure it is hard for someone like you to believe, Miss Neuman," Archer said, finally losing his temper. "You're a member of the official news media, and in your profession, the truth is apparently something that is bought and sold by the politician pulling the strings—whoever she may be.

"I am a soldier, one who has tried to live my life with honor and integrity. My career tells the story of my character. If the former Home Guard personnel promise to behave, I will take them at their word. I know you can't fathom that, but I'm sure it's something the honorable men and women of this world will have no problem understanding."

Neuman drew herself up, preparing to retaliate. "Those are high-sounding sentiments, General Christifori, but isn't your real motive in all this vengeance for your sister's death?" she asked with barely restrained viciousness.

Archer stiffened, surprised that she would stoop to such a low blow. It was no secret that his sister Andrea—all the family left to him when he finally returned home to Thorin—had been murdered by Katherine's puppets because she had spoken out against the Archon. Worse, Katherine had pardoned her murderer after his family leveraged some political favors to save his life. It was Andrea's death that had transformed Archer Christifori from an ex-soldier turned businessman into a general fighting a rebellion.

He drew a long breath, letting the moment stretch out. His eyes welled up briefly at the memory of his sister, so young and idealistic, and he did not try to hide his grief.

"The loss of my sister brought me to this fight, Miss Neuman," he said with quiet dignity. "My integrity and honor are what keep me in it. I'm not fighting alone. Rebellion is brewing all over the former Federated Commonwealth. If my sister's death roused me to fight, how many other innocent deaths are on the Archon's head? How many other men and women have been driven to rise up against the wrongs she brings down on those she is supposed to serve?"

Archer stared at the holocamera for a moment, then thought of something else he wished to say. "And despite the image you're trying to paint of me, Miss Neuman, I pray that neither you nor anyone else on Alcor or any other planet ever has to endure the loss I experienced at the hands of the Archon."

The young reporter didn't look so cocky anymore,

but Archer didn't give a damn about her. He pushed her mike away with the back of one hand, and got out of there as quickly as his feet would take him.

Later that day, Archer sat at his desk in his field command tent and stared at the paperwork spread out in front of him. The fighting for Alcor had taken long days; the bureaucratic red tape would take even longer. He had taken a few minutes to see how his interview had turned out on the local news and was pleased that it hadn't been edited to death.

Dealing with the media did not come naturally to him, but Katya Chaffee had convinced him of its importance and had coached him on smoothing out some of his rougher edges. He had resisted at first, but now he was glad he'd humored her. In the interview with Holly Neuman, he'd been careful enough of his words so that they couldn't be chopped to pieces without becoming incoherent and unusable. It ran in its entirety on the holocasts and let him be seen for who he was.

More important, though, was that Alcor was secure, at least for the time being. Archer was proud to have unshackled another world from the Archon's dominion. Yet, the interview had stirred up painful thoughts and feelings, his memories of Andrea and how and why she'd died. The memories hurt, but they also helped him channel his anger. Out of her death, life had been breathed into the cause she'd championed. As he sat there, staring at the mound of papers, Archer could almost hear her voice in the back of his mind. He allowed himself a slight smile at the idea that she was never more than a thought away.

A knock on the flexiplast dome that was his command tent brought him back to the present. "Come," he said, shifting aside the paperwork in the vain hope that he would not have to return to it.

Katya Chaffee stood in the doorway. Her crisp, rigid stance told him this visit was duty, not pleasure. "A messenger arrived a little while ago claiming to bear orders for you, sir," she reported.

"A messenger?" Archer was surprised. Usually ComStar transmitted orders via their network of hyperpulse generators. He raised an eyebrow. "Seems a little out of the ordinary."

She nodded. "We live in strange times."

That was a gross understatement, Archer thought. What could be stranger than the largest realm in the Inner Sphere cracking open from end to end with rebellion?

"Indeed we do. Send this messenger in," he said. He rose to his feet, his gray-green dress uniform still crisp from his media stint, adding an air of formality to the field camp.

The man who entered was so young, in his early twenties at most, that he made Archer feel suddenly old. The kid was young enough to be his son . . . if he had one.

The messenger snapped a salute, and Archer returned it, albeit in a slower and more relaxed fashion. "I understand you have a message for me," he said.

"Yes, sir. From Prince Victor Steiner-Davion himself." He handed the packet over, and Archer opened it to find a datapad sealed electronically with a verigraph. Verigraphs used DNA for the purpose of security, allowing verification of the recipient as well as the sender.

"Verigraph, eh?" he said, submitting his thumb to verify his identity. An audible click told him that the seal had unlocked. "I'm surprised that the Prince didn't send the message via HPG."

The young man shifted to parade-rest stance, his arms behind his back, legs slightly apart. "Katherine has implemented a number of communication interdictions that have slowed our orders in some areas," he said. "The Prince thought that personal delivery was best."

Archer put the datapad down and gestured to the folding chair in front of his desk. "Risky work, carrying this kind of information, Mister . . ."

The man sat. "Sir, in my business, names can be a liability. You can call me Gramash—Sergeant Anton Gramash."

Archer leaned back in his seat. "That's not your real name, though."

The young man smiled broadly. "Like I said, General, names can pose a risk."

Spies. Until now, Archer had never had any use for such people. Things were changing, though. *He* was changing. A few months ago, he'd been a soldier-turned-businessman. Now he was a rebel general. For a moment, there was silence as Archer pondered the enormity of recent events in his own life and in the galaxy around him. Then he realized with a start that the length of the pause had become awkward and returned his attention to the datapad.

It was thin and dark gray, and it seemed to purr to life as he opened it and set it on the table in front of him. A two-dimensional image appeared on the screen—the familiar and well-loved image of a man who commanded his deepest respect. His former commanding officer and his current leader, Prince Victor Steiner-Davion. There were more lines on Victor's face than the last time Archer had seen him. Like Arthur, the Prince had also lost a sibling to his sister in that same period. He was sure she was the one who'd had Arthur Steiner-Davion killed on Robinson.

The weight of the events that had escalated into civil war showed on the Prince's face. But Archer also saw the same drive and determination from the Clan wars when he had fought under Victor in the Tenth

Lyran Guards. Victor Steiner-Davion himself had pinned the Star League Medal of Honor to Archer's chest on Huntress. And when Archer had decided to stand up to Katherine on Thorin, it was Victor who had sent him supplies and granted official recognition of his command. Yes, the strain showed on the Prince's face, but beneath it, as though etched in granite, was unshakable strength.

"General Christifori," Victor said. "I trust that these orders find you well. My congratulations to you and your command. Your raid on Syrma has forced Katherine to send nearly a battalion of front-line troops to that world to counter the guerrilla operation you established. We're counting on her having to do the same on Alcor as well, thanks to the success of your operations there."

And those had been his orders. Archer and the Avengers were to attack several of the interior Lyran holdings, forcing the Archon to divert front-line troops to restore order. The Prince had allowed him to choose his objectives thus far, and Archer had concentrated on those worlds where innocents, almost always Davion or freedom supporters, were being targeted for oppression by the Archon.

"The fighting on Kathil is proving bloodier than anticipated," Victor went on. "Both sides have been sending in reinforcements, but our forces have successfully freed Bryceland, Sirdar, and Brockway from Katherine's grip."

Below Victor's image, data flowed across a small sub-window on the datapad screen, and Archer saw the names of the worlds where the fighting raged. Algol, An Ting, Alcyone, Demeter—all names he knew, and some of them places he had visited in his time. He would review the details later, but one thing was becoming clear: this thing was turning into a full-fledged war being fought all over the former Federated Commonwealth.

"General, your overall strategic mission remains the same," Victor said. "You will continue efforts to keep troops loyal to Katherine busy chasing you and then forced to secure worlds you've liberated. The only change is in priority . . . and a diplomatic mission of sorts.

"The mercenary unit Snord's Irregulars has lately been restationed on Odessa in the Donegal Province. Our intelligence indicates that Colonel Snord has been refusing Katherine's requests to get involved in the fighting against us. She says her contract prevents her from taking sides in a civil war. We assume that the posting to Odessa was meant to either use Snord as a threat against Morgan Kell's Arc-Royal Defense Cordon or to obstruct your movements in the Lyran interior. With the Arc-Royal Cordon already out of her grasp, she needs reinforcements near there, or she risks appearing soft to her critics. She is apparently assigning Snord's Irregulars and several others directly to the planetary ruler, obviously in an attempt to curry favor with the local nobility."

The Prince paused for a moment, giving Archer a chance to digest his words so far. "The Irregulars have always been steadfastly loyal to the Lyran state, but their contract is coming up for negotiation very soon. I'm sending you and the Avengers to Odessa, where you will contact Colonel Snord and try to persuade her and her unit to side with us . . . or at least not to fight against us."

Victor smiled a bit ruefully. "You and the Avengers have been doing a fine job of creating confusion, so I think you're the man for the job. I know that Odessa is a bit of a haul from Alcor, but the Avengers showing up there, so close to Tharkad, is likely to stir up a hornet's nest in the region. So, we're moving Odessa up from your secondary list of targets to a primary objective. I know this will not be easy for you. The Fisk family rules Odessa with an iron fist, and I understand the Count's son was the man who killed your sister. However, your goal is not to secure the world or defeat the Irregulars, only to see if we can take the unit away from Katherine."

The Prince's voice softened to a more personal tone. "I don't want to delude you, Archer. Intelligence also indicates that there's a good chance the Irregulars have been placed there as bait, in hopes of drawing you into a fight with them. As eccentric as Snord's Irregulars can be, they are a formidable unit. With their contract coming due, however, we have a unique opportunity to take this asset from my sister. Given their traditional support of the Archon, it would send a powerful message if they decided to change sides. I could send a diplomat or negotiator, but my instincts tell me that you, as a pure military man, would stand a better chance of appealing to Rhonda Snord.

"The datapad includes a complete file on the unit, their history, TO&E—everything you need for the mission. I've also arranged for the necessary JumpShips to get you to Odessa with the best possible speed. I've leveraged some of my ComStar influence to establish an informal command circuit, although formally ComStar is simply taking you along as a passenger on various jumps. So, these are your orders. I trust your experience and discretion in carrying them out.

"I would like you to take my courier along with your unit. If you need to get a message to me, use him to avoid any unnecessary delays. He's already started setting up operations and contacts on Odessa."

Archer glanced at the young sergeant, realizing there must be a lot more to him than met the eye.

"General Christifori," the Prince was saying, "you've

been a loyal supporter and have served our cause well. With men like you fighting on my side, we cannot fail to be victorious. I have the utmost faith in your abilities, and I'm grateful to have a commander like you with me in this fight. Good luck, and godspeed."

The image faded. Archer tipped back his chair slightly and stared at Gramash. "It looks like you'll be staying with us, Sergeant."

"Apparently so, General," the young man said, his tone equally casual.

"I'd like you to work with Major Chaffee, my intel officer. Together, you two should make quite a team."

"I've been briefed on her and the rest of your command staff already, thank you, sir," Gramash said, rising and giving him a salute. "And if I may say, sir, it's an honor to serve with you."

Archer also got to his feet and saluted in return. "Welcome to the First Thorin Regiment," he said. "You'd better go get bunked down. If we're going to Odessa, we'd better get started. It's a long way off, and we've got a lot to do before we get there."

3

Stephensville might once have been more than a wide spot in the middle of the road, but it must have been centuries since it could boast even that much distinction. It was on some maps of Alcor—very detailed maps—but Stephensville wasn't much more than a small bar called Hackman's—the kind of place where locals gathered to enjoy a cold beer and good company. It consisted of two rooms, one of them for storage, and a makeshift kitchen that was far from four stars in rating. It was run by Randolph Hackman, a onetime colonel in the Davion Guards and a staunch supporter of Victor Davion.

Archer had discovered the place because it was located in his area of operations during the most recent fighting on Alcor. It was only a few kilometers from the capital city, which was another reason he'd taken a liking to the place.

On this day, however, Katya had arranged to use the bar for a planning meeting—and to celebrate the unit's victory on Alcor. A lance of BattleMechs and a platoon of infantry patrolled the perimeter in the surrounding woods. Though Alcor had been secured, she wasn't taking any chances with the regiment's command staff all gathered in one location. The bar had also been swept for bombs, bugs, chemicals, and anything else that could be detected or scanned.

Hackman had left them plenty of beer, and Archer couldn't resist taking a few moments to savor a cold, refreshing drink with his commanders. Upon entering the place, he'd caught sight of his own image in the foggy mirror behind the bar. With his short-cropped hair and shaved temples, he looked every bit the MechWarrior. But he noticed that his black hair was visibly streaked with silver and his short sideburns had turned almost white in the past few months. Dark circles under his eyes gave them a hollow look, and the lines on his face were graven deeper. He was being changed by the war, physically as well as mentally.

In just a few months, his unit had also changed dramatically from a mere planetary militia to a force to be reckoned with. Only Archer and a handful of others remembered the beginning, however. The Avengers had grown from a hodgepodge militia regiment on Thorin to more than a battalion of 'Mechs and tanks reinforced with infantry muscle.

A lot of their gear had been captured from the Fifteenth Arcturan Guards during the fighting on Thorin. Next, the Avengers had absorbed the Muphrid militia, including a reinforced company known as the Muphrid Rangers. On Syrma, they had captured the entire Syrma Defense Force intact—nearly a battalion of armor, aged aerospace fighters, and BattleMechs. Then, on Milton, the Avengers had taken out the planet's two companies of 'Mechs and armor and freed several hundred Davion supporters from prison in the process. The First Thorin Regiment was now much larger than a traditional regiment. They also had several companies reinforcing their holdings on Thorin and Muphrid, where they also recruited and trained new troopers.

Playing off the bold series of moves Archer had pulled off since the first days of the Thorin rebellion, the media touted him as a modern-day Stonewall Jackson. He and the Avengers had gone from planet to planet, hitting militia forces, taking worlds, and moving on. But he knew the truth behind the media exaggerations. Many of his new recruits were rusty vets or militia wannabes who were only beginning to hone their skills. They were improving all the time, but he was sure even bigger tests of their fortitude were yet to come.

"All right, people," he began, his voice cutting through the lighthearted banter and conversation around him. "We've got new orders. Our next stop is Odessa."

There was a pause, as everyone reacted in surprise. "Odessa," Katya echoed finally. "The same Odessa ruled by Luther Fisk's family? That Odessa?"

"Luther who?" asked John Kraff. "The name is familiar . . ."

"It happened before you joined us, Kraff," Darius Hopkins said. He was the only non-officer in the room, and he spoke in a low tone as if to protect Archer from painful memories. "It was how our unit got formed in the first place. Luther Fisk is the one who killed the general's sister." He glanced quickly at Archer. Many people knew about the origins of the unit, but few spoke about it in Archer's presence.

The silence that followed was uncomfortable, and Kraff blushed slightly. "Sorry, sir," he mumbled.

"It's all right, son. You didn't know," Archer said calmly. "And, yes, Katya, it is *that* Odessa."

Alice Getts cocked her head slightly. "Odessa wasn't on our list of targets, sir. What happened?"

Archer shot a glance at Sergeant Gramash, who stood

just slightly outside the circle of his officers, then back at Getts. "Two words, Major—Snord's Irregulars."

"We're going to fight Snord's Irregulars?" Harry "Hawkeye" Hogan, the lanky blond captain at the far end of the table, asked incredulously. Both he and Katya had recently been given field promotions.

Archer shook his head. "No. They say they cannot take sides in a civil war, but we believe the Archon is trying to pressure them to fight on her side. Their contract with the Lyran Alliance is running out, so our job will be to win them away from Katherine."

"So, we're sending a regiment in to do the work of one diplomat?" Katya asked.

"Well, the defenders of Odessa aren't going to be too happy to see us arrive," Archer explained. "Also, if friendly persuasion fails, we may have to fight the Irregulars, too."

Katya Chaffee pulled up the unit's dossier on her noteputer and scanned it. "They were first formed by Cranston Snord, a freebirth Clan warrior from Wolf's Dragoons, originally operating as a separate unit that fed intelligence back to the Dragoons. In all their time in the Inner Sphere, they have served only the Lyran Commonwealth and then the Alliance.

"The Irregulars are a sharp unit, but they're also some kind of relic hunters. They apparently look for postings that give them an opportunity to search for valuable artifacts and lost treasure. Since 3037, they've been under the command of Rhonda Snord, another former Clan warrior. During the Clan wars, they discovered an ancient Star League naval base in the Dark Nebula and demolished the Jade Falcon forces that tried to take it for their Clan. They're outfitted with recovered Star League-era and captured Clan equipment, and their ranks include a number of former Jade Falcons."

Hopkins rubbed his chin. "Back when I was on active

duty, there wasn't a MechWarrior or groundpounder who didn't know about the Irregulars. They were known to be fine warriors, but they had a reputation for unpredictability. They'd turn tail and take off after some artifact in the middle of a battle if they got a burr in their butts."

John Kraff shook his head. "They don't sound like too much of a threat. I mean, how old is this Rhonda Snord anyway? From what I've heard, they're nothing more than looters and diggers. What does Prince Victor want with them?"

"Don't underestimate them, Captain," Archer cautioned. "The Irregulars fought side by side with the Kell Hounds, Wolf's Dragoons, and other elite regiments in the Third and Fourth Succession Wars, the War of '39, and the Clan invasion. House Marik once sent its best units to smash them and failed, and they've pounded the Draconis Combine on more than one occasion, too.

"Some of us here know what it's like to fight the Clans," he said, scanning the faces around them. Several of his people nodded and seemed to clutch their sweaty beers more tightly at mention of the Clan wars. "Well, Snord's Irregulars took on the Jade Falcons and beat the piss out of them. Rhonda Snord may be a little long in the tooth, but would you say the same about Morgan Kell or Jaime Wolf?"

Archer took a long swallow of his beer, then set it down. "It's not our job to say whether Prince Victor should write off the Irregulars as no threat. All I know is that he wants them in his camp. Our job is to get them there."

"Odessa's no little haul from here," Kraff said, "and I doubt they're going to be glad to see us drop in. Are we going to have enough intel to even have a prayer of pulling this off?"

Archer waved Anton Gramash over to the table.

"Meet Sergeant Gramash. He's already been to Odessa, laying some of the groundwork for us."

"We've got supporters working on our behalf on Odessa," Gramash told Kraff. "But it won't be easy. Count Fisk has begun a general roundup of suspected Davion loyalists now that he's talked the Archon into putting the Irregulars under his control."

Katya's eyes narrowed, and she shook her head suspiciously.

"What is it, Katya?" Archer asked, turning to her.

"It all sounds too pat, too convenient," she said. "Loki and the LAAF know by now that we often turn up on worlds where they're cracking down on Prince Victor's supporters."

"You think it's a trap?" Getts asked.

Archer nodded at Gramash, who crossed his arms and leaned back in his seat. "According to our intel, there's a good chance of that," the young officer said. "Fisk's crackdown coincides with the Irregulars' posting. It might not be pure coincidence."

"Regardless of whether or not it's a trap," Archer said firmly, "our orders are to go to Odessa, and that's that. He's asked me to persuade the Irregulars to sign on with him, and that's what I'll do. If it is a trap, well, we'll just have to keep our eyes open and be ready for whatever happens."

There was a murmur of "yessirs" as he leaned forward and gazed around him at their faces. "The real question is, how soon can we be ready to go?"

"First Company is fully refitted," Harry Hogan said. "We lost two 'Mechs here on Alcor, but made up for it with salvage and captures from the Home Guard."

Archer looked over at Alice Getts, who commanded the unit's armor. "Second Company is ready, too," she said. "We recovered three Savannah Masters and have merged them in as a light striker lance. They aren't much in the way of firepower, but there's nothing harder to hit than those little buggers once they get going. I've got three infantrymen training as drivers and gunners for them right now."

John Kraff smoothed his thick mustache as he spoke next. "The Muphrid Rangers are ready, too. We've repaired our gear and replaced our losses out of the Home Guard stock."

Archer nodded in satisfaction as the commanders reported in, then looked over at the silent form of Captain Thomas Sherwood, who sat with arms crossed and a thoughtful expression on his face. Sherwood had operated as a deep mole during the fighting for Thorin, and Archer had rewarded him with an independent special ops command. Calling themselves the Sherwood Foresters, the unit was a mix of hardware, infantry, armor, and BattleMechs.

"Well, Captain," Archer said. "What's the status of the Foresters?"

"We've still got some training to do with the forces we're leaving behind here on Alcor," Sherwood said. Before leaving one world for the next, the Avengers always trained a unit to harass whatever forces the Archon and the LAAF sent to retake the planet. Part of Sherwood's responsibility was to build those resistance teams. "I'd like at least another week."

Archer shook his head. "If we're going to get to Odessa in time, we've got to leave tomorrow afternoon. Even then, it's going to take us a good two months to get there. Perhaps we could leave you here with a DropShip, and you could catch up to us on commercial JumpShips when you're done."

Sherwood nodded once, slowly. "Yes, that could work. The Foresters will rejoin you as soon as we finish up here."

Archer shifted in his seat slightly and looked at Katya Chaffee. "So, are we good to go, Major?"

"We recovered enough expendables from the Home

Guards to keep us in business for a short operation," Katya said. "We're a little tight on autocannon reloads, but I've been talking to Sergeant Gramash and he thinks we can probably arrange for a resupply once we hit Odessa."

Archer nodded. A part of him was worried about the possibility of stepping into a trap, but he figured that half the battle was knowing the trap was there to begin with.

"Good. Then, our next target is Odessa, but we aren't going in shooting. Our mission is to get Snord's Irregulars out of the clutches of the Archon. If we pull this off, it'll be a kick in the crotch of Lyran morale without having to wound or kill anyone. The Irregulars' two battalions won't tip the balance of power militarily, but having such a well-known and loyal unit change sides at this stage of the conflict may cause others to question Katherine's legitimacy."

"You can count on us, sir," Kraff said.

Archer smiled at the younger man. "Captain Kraff," he said, "I never doubted it for a minute."

4

The audience chamber of the Odessan royal palace was a grand, Romanesque design. Built on a massive hill that dominated the surrounding area, the palace mirrored the authority of the Fisk family, whose residence it was. Columns marked the perimeter and opened up to a sweeping vista. Seated on a raised dais in the middle of the room, the count enjoyed a commanding view of the city of New Bealton below. The only part of the room not open to the view was the area behind the throne, which led to his antechambers.

From his thronelike seat, he watched as his two female visitors entered the room. One was much older, yet she carried herself like a person half her age. Her short red hair showed a streak or two of gray, but the spring in her step was youthful. In decades past, her tanned skin and shapely legs had made her a poster girl for every aspiring mercenary in the Inner Sphere. Though time had taken its toll, her grace and raw sexual appeal had not dimmed. Today, she wore a crisp, gray-green dress uniform with her unit's insignia, a buffalo nickel, gleaming on one shoulder.

"Colonel Snord," said Nicholas Fisk, making his tone deliberately regal. "I trust that your battalions are settled in their new camp?"

His hands rested on the arms of his seat, and he leaned forward as she approached. Up to this point, he had thought only of the power the arrival of her forces would bring him. He hadn't realized that Rhonda Snord might have some personal appeal as well. He surreptitiously smoothed his formal dark gray robes.

Colonel Snord stopped and bowed her head in a formal, if not overly respectful, acknowledgment. "I thank you for your permission to investigate the ruins of old Bealton. My Irregulars have set up a base there and have already begun to survey the site." She turned and gestured to her companion, who wore her blond hair buzz-cut so short it was almost a mohawk. Her shaved temples marked her as a MechWarrior. Her looks were as striking as her CO's, though she was significantly younger.

"May I introduce my deputy commander, Major Natasha Snord?" Colonel Snord said as the younger woman bowed formally.

Fisk smiled slightly and leaned back in his seat. "I must confess, Colonel Snord, that I believe you're wasting your time. Bealton was bombed with two nuclear devices and a chemical attack during the First Succession War. Any artifacts you might find in the ruins are not worth the risks of contact with that contaminated rubble."

"You may be right," Rhonda Snord said politely. "But one of the buildings is said to contain the ruins of a jewelry exchange with a vault that survived the blast. Its contents would be worth a fortune to anyone with enough patience and skill to locate them."

"Well, I for one am glad you are here to protect us here on Odessa," the Count said. "Giving you access to that debris field is a more than a fair price for your services."

Rhonda Snord looked out on the view of New Bealton to one side of her. "No offense, your Grace, but the chances of any real threat coming this way are pretty slim."

Fisk smiled tightly. "Nowhere is safe, Colonel. Now that I've begun to crack down on suspected Davion-sponsored terrorists, Victor Davion is perfectly capable of sending troops here. I trust that your Irregulars can deal with any problem that arises."

The muscles in Rhonda Snord's face tightened. "My dear Count, I have already had this discussion with the Lyran High Command, so if I seem irritated, you'll have to forgive me," she said calmly. "The Irregulars will not take sides in a civil war. Period. It's in our contract, and you know that. So if you've brought us here to fend off Prince Victor's minions, you've wasted everyone's time."

The Count waved one hand dismissively. "Oh, I understand that you have no desire to defend the Lyran Alliance, Colonel—"

Snord cut him off. "Not true, Count Fisk. We've been defending the Alliance since it was the Lyran Commonwealth. We just won't take up arms against fellow Lyrans, that's all."

"I stand corrected," he said, maintaining his smile. "But I—and apparently the Archon—believe that your mere presence here may prevent any would-be invaders from attacking us."

"We have reviewed the information you provided us on Odessa," Colonel Snord said, with a glance at her companion. "Despite the planet's light industrial base, its location makes it an unlikely target. The only thing that would draw anyone's attention is this recent crackdown on dissidents."

"I take your meaning, my dear Colonel," Fisk

purred in reply. "And we both know there are units out there who will take notice. Archer's Avengers, for example. I believe the real question is: if they come, will you fight them?"

Rhonda Snord crossed her arms and shifted her weight into a slightly more defiant posture. "If we're attacked, we'll defend ourselves, your Grace. Otherwise, as I stated before, we will not participate in a civil war." Her green eyes were hard.

"Of course, Colonel," the Count said, his smile widening. "I would never ask you to compromise your principles—or your contract. As I understand it, you have not yet signed a new agreement with the Alliance. Is that correct?"

"We're still negotiating," Snord replied shortly. "I'm sure that after our decades of service to the Lyran leadership, we'll work something out."

The truth was, as the Count knew, that her contract ran out in two months; negotiations had stalled on this very issue. The Lyran Alliance was offering an attractive monetary contract, but it wanted the Irregulars to agree to fight against Victor Steiner-Davion. The talks had not officially broken off, but they had reached an impasse.

Fisk templed his fingers in front of his face and narrowed his eyes slightly. "Well, Colonel, I'm sure we'll get to know each other quite well over the next few months. I appreciate your visit, but as you might imagine, my schedule is busy. If you need anything, please contact my office, and they will be happy to accommodate you." With those words, he swept one hand in the direction of the door. The two mercenary officers bowed their heads slightly, executed an about-face, and walked in unison out the door.

As they did so, a man stepped into the room from behind the curtains that concealed a private doorway. He was short, with curly black hair and a rough-looking

beard that covered much of his pockmarked face. His
dark eyes were large for his face. Unlike Snord, he
did not bow as he approached Fisk. Following him in
was a much younger man who limped heavily and
walked only with the help of a cane.

"I take it you monitored the conversation?" Fisk
asked the black-haired man, whose name was Erwin
Vester.

Vester nodded quickly. "Yes, I did, Count Fisk.
Colonel Snord is quite a character." His voice was
rough.

"She's an arrogant mercenary," Fisk spat back.
"She's under my command, but she speaks to me as
if she were an equal. The gall . . ."

"Her arrogance is well-earned, Count Fisk. Loki has
been monitoring her for years. She is an apt Mech-
Warrior who is not to be trifled with."

"The past means nothing to me," Fisk retorted.
"All I want to know is whether you and your people
can guarantee that she will fight if the Avengers
show up?"

"*When* the Avengers show up," Vester corrected.
"We can have them at each other's throats before
either realizes what's happening."

"I want these Avengers crushed," the Count said.
"There's risk in the Archon's plan to lure them here."

"Our sources estimate their strength at roughly that
of the Irregulars," Vester said. "However, I don't see
how even the likes of Archer Christifori can hope to
survive against the experience of a unit like Snord's
Irregulars."

The man leaning on the cane laughed, a long
chuckle. "Cheap words," he said. "I expected more
from Loki. Only a fool would underestimate
Christifori."

The Count closed his eyes briefly in irritation as his
son, Luther, limped forward. Luther had been posted

with the Fifteenth Arcturan Guards on Thorin at the start of the civil war, and Christifori had pasted them. Luther had been maimed in the fighting and would never pilot a BattleMech again.

"Yes, Luther, we're all aware of your opinion of Christifori and his people."

"Opinion?" Luther returned, almost mockingly. "Despite anything this Loki spy may have told you, Father, this is no bunch of freebooting rabble-rousers." He threw Vester a scornful look. "I've fought them. Christifori is neither an idiot nor a profiteer. Odds mean nothing to him. He has a cause, and that makes him deadlier even than the Irregulars."

Erwin Vester was unmoved. "He's a mortal man of flesh and blood," he said coolly. "He'll take a bullet just like anyone else."

Luther Fisk turned to Vester. His artificial eye, replacing the one he'd lost in the fight with the Avengers, had a mechanical, almost deadly glare to it. "I've been in your shoes before, Vester. As I said, words are cheap. I thought I could take on Christifori, too. And now look at me."

The count's son did not wait to hear what else Vester might have to say. Stabbing the marble floor twice with his cane, he turned and limped away.

Rhonda and Natasha Snord descended the long, white marble staircase that led out from the palace. At the entrance, they passed four heavily armed guards wearing the Duke's white and blue family crest. These kids looked younger and younger every year, Rhonda thought. Maybe she was getting too old for this.

"What do you think, Mother?" Tasha said, shoving her hands into her jacket pockets.

"About Fisk?" Rhonda glanced around to make sure no one was close enough to overhear. "Arrogant. Egotistical. I don't trust him in the least. In other words, he's a politician." She gave a half smile. "And one thing we should never forget is that he's a *good* politician. He was polite, smooth, and polished, and that tells me he's cunning. I may not trust him, but I think I understand him. Men like him don't rise to this level of power without being very clever. Don't let his words fool you, not for a moment."

"He's right about one thing," Tasha said. "We've always fought for the Lyran banner. What are we going to do about our contract?"

Rhonda shrugged. "It's true that we've been loyal to House Steiner and the Lyrans, but the waters are muddy this time. The worst thing a mercenary unit can do is get dragged into a civil war. Your grandfather always taught me that there are no winners in that kind of fight."

"Do we have a choice?" Tasha asked.

Rhonda nodded. "We always have a choice. Maybe I'm wrong about not wanting to get into this war, but I'm not comfortable with this crackdown on the so-called dissidents, either. I've done some research on my own. The Count's son was a spoiled brat who bucked for a military posting in the Fifteenth Arcturan Guards. He personally killed Archer Christifori's sister, which was what brought Christifori out of retirement. From what I've heard, Archer's Avengers left him a four-star cripple."

"Have you ever met this Christifori?"

"No, but I know he's a veteran of the Tenth Lyran Guards and that he fought on Huntress and won himself a Star League Medal of Honor. Anybody who tangles with the Clans and wins is someone deserving of respect." While Rhonda's own experiences with the Clans had become the stuff of mercenary legends, her daughter's only knowledge of them were some border clashes with the Jade Falcons.

"I've got our two battalions deployed so that if the

Avengers do make a move on New Bealton, we can be on top of them right away," Tasha said.

"Good," Rhonda said, checking her wrist chronometer. "I don't particularly want to fight Archer's Avengers, but if we do end up head to head, they'll be sorry they ever tangled with us. As a precaution, I want our security perimeter doubled. Contact that joke of a local defense force commander—what's his name?"

"Captain Malcolm."

Rhonda nodded wearily. "That's him. Tell him I want to run some drills with his people. Let's not take this duty too lightly. Maybe the Avengers will ignore us and maybe they won't. But if even one shot goes off, I want to be ready to squash their testicles like toothpaste."

Tasha looked puzzled. "I thought you wanted to avoid a conflict."

"I've known men like Christifori my whole life," Rhonda said grimly. "He's not just a general—he's a leader. Even the Clans respect him. If anything starts, I'll have to go for the kill hard and fast—because if I don't, he'll go for the kill with me."

5

DropShip **Colonel Crockett**
Nadir Jump Point, Donegal System
District of Donegal
Lyran Alliance
11 April 3063

The Tactical Operations Room aboard the DropShip
Colonel Crockett was a tiny, cramped place even on
the best of days. Today, however, the TOR seemed
even smaller, given the number of people present. Archer Christifori and the members of his command staff
were crowded around the ferroplast table anchored to
the DropShip deck. Piping ran along the ceiling of the
room, and the dim lighting did not brighten the dull
gray paint.

The DropShip *Colonel Crockett* had been part of
the booty they'd captured on Syrma. It had been left
sitting on the spaceport tarmac by a Lyran regiment
when Archer and his unit landed and liberated the
planet. It was a newer ship, Overlord-class, which ap-
pealed enough to Archer that he'd made it his command vessel. However, even he had to admit that the
decision had been premature. The vessel had enjoyed
only slipshod maintenance, and its environmental
problems left the air humid and heavy in the TOR.
The "prize" vessel's engines needed a full, and costly,

overhaul as well. It was a running joke among the Avengers that leaving the *Crockett* behind had been the Lyran High Command's deliberate attempt to cripple their unit.

As the unit arrived in the Donegal system on their way to Odessa, the ship was currently docked to the JumpShip *Warspite*. JumpShips traveled between stars, recharging at the zenith or nadir points of a star's gravity well before "jumping" again as much as thirty light-years to the next system. DropShips did the mule work of transporting personnel and cargo.

To expedite the long trip to Odessa, Prince Victor had arranged for an informal relay of several fully charged and waiting JumpShips to carry the Avenger DropShips more quickly from point to point. The *Warspite* was the last link in that chain. The crew was cordial but not friendly, adding to the tension of the trip. The spacers were used to hazardous duty, but that did not generally include taking a ship to a planet only two jumps from Tharkad, the heart of the Lyran Alliance.

Archer tried not to let it get under his skin. After all, they were deep in "enemy territory." Besides, they only had one more jump to go. He stood at the narrow end of the table and wiped at the sweat already forming on his brow. John Kraff's shuttle had experienced docking problems, and it had taken a few minutes to get everyone settled. The docking rings were yet another item on this tub that needed fixing, Arthur thought irritably.

"We're a single jump away from Odessa," he began, "so I wanted to go over deployment and rules of engagement before we arrived insystem."

Reaching down, he activated the holographic-projector controls built into the table's surface. A three-dimensional image of the planet Odessa flickered to life in the air over the table. The white light it gave off made the faces of his officers glow momentarily, then the whole thing flickered out again in a hiss of static.

Archer shook his head in disgust. Alice Getts rose slightly from her seat and pounded the tabletop with one fist. The holoimage came to life again, then stabilized to show a slowly rotating globe. Here was Odessa, with its two polar icecaps, its dark blue northern and southern seas, and in the middle, a belt of land around the equator. Getts sank back into her seat to a smattering of tongue-in-cheek applause.

"It's good to see that the *Crockett* is living up to her reputation," Archer said.

"It's not a bad ship, sir," Getts joked. "It's just been treated that way."

Archer nodded and grinned at her briefly. "Back to business, people. I know you've all reviewed the LZ location maps and the assumed deployment of the Irregulars. This is just a final session to make sure there are no mistakes or unresolved issues."

"Strangest damn mission I've ever been on," John Kraff said. "Why not just have you go down, sir? After all, the only thing Prince Victor wants is for you to negotiate with the Irregulars."

"We achieve quite a bit by being there in force," Archer answered. "First of all, the Lyran High Command will get reports of our arrival. With Loki agents active on every Lyran world, our showing up so close to Tharkad with two-plus battalions of force *has* to get a rise out of them. Secondly, if our talks with Colonel Snord don't go well, we can't afford to have her roaming around looking for targets of opportunity. We'll be there, and she can take her anger out on us rather than becoming the Archon's tool for mischief somewhere else."

He turned his attention back to the spinning holograph of Odessa. "We'll be landing outside the former city of Bealton, or the ruins of it, I should say. The planetary capital of New Bealton is only two hours away. The Irregulars have set up base in the ruined area, where they've got permission to go relic-hunting."

"You're dropping us just over an hour and a half from there," Getts said, pointing one stubby finger at the holoimage. "That will form a more or less equidistant triangle between their base, our base, and the capital."

Archer glanced at Anton Gramash, who stood a short distance away from the group encircling the table. "That's right, Major. According to Sergeant Gramash, who has briefed you all individually, we'll be facing one company of local militia, based out of New Bealton. The Prince has some supporters on Odessa, but they are few and far between."

Gramash picked up on his cue to speak. "The local militia is mostly a handful of weekend warriors and some veterans. Count Fisk has funded them pretty well, however. They have one lance of heavy 'Mechs that are almost brand-new, and the Count would probably have expanded the militia into a private army if the Archon hadn't placed the Irregulars under his direct command. From the landing zone, you'll be poised to respond either to them or to Snord."

Archer nodded and continued his own briefing. "It's late spring in the region we're dropping into. The weather should be decent, and most of the area has been cultivated for farms. It's mostly open terrain—plains and rolling hills with only a few forests."

"Great ground for BattleMechs, that's for sure," piped up Hawkeye Hogan.

"That it is," Archer concurred. "But we're not here to splash the Archon's people unless they come for us. The rules of engagement are as follows. First, if the local militia makes a showing on the field, we remove them from the picture. These are the Count's people, and he's a major supporter of the Archon. We have to make sure they're neutralized." *Neutralized,* Archer thought. What a sterile way to talk about killing those who would be trying to kill him and his people.

"Snord's Irregulars are a different story, however. We're going to persuade them to side with us, not to fight us. No one fires at them without my express orders. They may make a show in force, but we understand they won't be drawn into a fight that might be construed as being part of a civil war. A clause in their contract prohibits such involvement, and we believe that they will not fight unless we start something."

Kraff chuckled. "That must really be giving old Katherine Steiner the red-ass. Here she's got a major team of butt-kickers on her side, and they won't do her dirty work. We're talking *major* red-ass." There was a general chuckle of agreement.

"Don't kid yourselves," Gramash said. "The Irregulars' contract is coming due in a month or so. And from what I've learned, the Archon has taken a personal interest in making sure the unit remains under her control. For all we know, Colonel Snord may have already accepted an offer too good to refuse and signed on again while we were en route. It's unlikely, but if that's happened, our LZ could be hot as hell an hour after we drop."

Archer tapped at the holographic-projection controls. The image of Odessa faded away, and a map of the landing zone shimmered into view. "We chose this area for several reasons. It has fresh water, it's highly defensible, with several rocky hills we can turn into hot spots, and it offers access to two major roads leading directly into New Bealton."

He pointed at the three-dimensional map that covered the tabletop. Three hills dominated the LZ, while a nearby plain offered their DropShips and aerospace fighters a good area for deployment. "I don't plan on us having to slug it out, but there's no point in acting stupid either," he added.

He crossed his arms and narrowed his eyes slightly. "There's a chance that this is a trap, that we're being lured in. We won't know until we're on the ground, but the most effective part of any trap is surprise, and since we're already tipped off . . ."

". . . the Archon's little surprise is a bust," Kraff finished. There was a murmur of amused agreement in the room.

Katya Chaffee spoke as the laughter faded. "From what Sergeant Gramash tells me, our LZ is also relatively close to the resistance movement's HQ. The Count's crackdown has netted a lot of IBs, which has made Prince Victor's supporters more than willing to assist us."

"General, sir, regarding those innocent bystanders," Hogan said, "do you mean for us to, um, 'assist' in their due process?"

Archer smiled. "You mean rescue them, Hawkeye?"

"In a manner of speaking, sir, yes, sir."

"Well, let's just say it sure would be a waste of time to travel all the way to Odessa and not bother to raise a little hell."

"Mother-frigging right," added Kraff.

"*But*," Archer said, seeing his staff's enthusiasm, "our first order of business is to deal with the Irregulars." He got a low chorus of "yessirs" in response. "Good. Then we understand each other. Drop order is as follows: Captain Kraff and the Rangers will secure the primary LZ. They'll be followed in by Hawkeye's troops. Alice, we're going to shuttle you to another LZ two klicks away. Your mission is to secure Hill 103 so that Darius can set up the comm center and repair stations there. The Rangers and Hogan's boys will fan out and secure Hill 107 and the terrain in between."

He pointed to the holographic display, which showed the landing zones in shimmering red light. The hilltops pulsed red as he spoke. "Once secured, we'll have the high ground and be able to cover the roadways. That should send a ripple of fear through the ruling nobles and hopefully the Lyran High Command."

"Here's to that," John Kraff said enthusiastically.

"If there are no questions, we jump in two hours and have a four-day burn insystem. Combat air patrols will scramble as soon as we emerge. Remember, people, we're only a few jumps from Tharkad. No matter what, we're likely to stir up the proverbial hornet's nest when we arrive."

"Like the man said," Alice Getts said, a smile on her round face, "here's to that—General."

Rhonda Snord walked beside Tasha, who was pushing the wheelchair slowly as the two of them and the man in the chair made their way past the spaceport customs officers and into the city of New Bealton. The afternoon sun was already starting to wane, its orange light casting long shadows on the tarmac. The wheelchair was an antique that Rhonda's father had purchased somewhere, but it was equipped with a power unit.

Cranston Snord leaned forward in his seat and squinted through his glasses at something in the distance. Rhonda followed his gaze to see if she could tell what had caught his attention. The man in the wheelchair had once been a legend for his cunning and ruthlessness—and for using the Irregulars to fill his profitable museum on Clinton. Of course, all that was three wars and five decades ago. Cranston Snord was now partially crippled by age and injuries from decade-old wounds.

"One hell of a rear area you've managed to get yourself posted to," he said, surveying the spaceport. "I doubt this place is even on the Jade Falcon maps. I thought it would be nice to drop by on my way back to Clinton, but I wouldn't want to get stuck here."

Rhonda took hold of one of the chair's handles as a sign that she would take over. "Tasha, why don't you join the rest of the unit? I'd like some time with the colonel." The younger woman nodded her comprehension and bent to kiss her grandfather on the forehead before departing.

"She's a pistol," the old man said approvingly. "From what I saw in the reports, she's been locking horns with some of the Clanners in the unit, right? Either she's headstrong or she's not smart enough to know what she's tangling with."

Rhonda smiled faintly as she began pushing the wheelchair forward. "A little of both," she said.

There was a pause, and then Snord leaned back, tipping his head up and back to look at his daughter. "Tell me, Rhonda, do you think she's ready to command?"

Rhonda's stride slowed as she thought about it for a moment. "Probably not, if I were judging only by her age," she said. "We raised her in the Irregulars, though, and that gives her a level of understanding about military operations that some people wouldn't master in twenty years of fighting. Her only weakness is that she's a hothead. She needs to learn patience and self-control. In time, I'm sure she will."

"Sounds like you when you were her age," he said with a small laugh.

"Did you think I was ready for command then?" Rhonda asked. A part of her didn't want to know the answer, but she was curious just the same.

"Well, I felt a little like you do right now. I didn't want to see you grow up. I kept trying to find reasons not to turn command over to you. But time overcame me," he said, slamming his palm into the padded armrest of the chair. "I waited too damn long. By the time I had enough brains to hand things over to you, I was too feeble to fight anymore."

Rhonda rested her hand briefly on his shoulder. "There's plenty of fight left in you," she said.

Her father shook his head. "Don't kid yourself, girl. It's time you pulled off those rose-colored glasses. I'm old, and this arthritis is enough to keep me from doing much more than watching battles on the nightly news." His voice echoed with the longing for something that could no longer be.

Rhonda looked down at her father and continued to push the chair forward, past a row of shops that were closing up for the evening. "Well, at least you're still around to keep the rest of us on our toes," she said.

"Speaking of that," he said, "what in the name of hell are you doing on Odessa? In *my* time, we took postings that allowed us to fight, not patrol."

"Politics," she said bitterly. "Count Fisk is trying to pressure us into a new contract. I think he's also trying to lure one of Victor's units into coming here. Fisk and Katrina Steiner would like nothing more than to see us embroiled in her little civil war."

Snord's face tightened. "I knew the real Katrina Steiner," he said angrily. "This little hussy is no Katrina. She's a cheap knockoff at best."

"So, what do you think I should do?" Rhonda asked.

He waved a hand and shook his head. "It's your unit, girl. It's been your unit for years. This is a call only you can make."

She opened her mouth to speak, then was surprised

when her father kept talking. "But if I *were* to have an opinion, I'd say that the worst thing you could do is get dragged into a civil war. I put that clause in our contracts for a reason. I saw what happened during the last big civil war in the Free Worlds League. All the mercenary units that got dragged into it lost either their reputations or their lives."

"The Irregulars have worked for the Steiners since the unit was first formed," Rhonda said. "But the unit's face and its structure have been forced to change many times. Maybe now is the time to change again."

Her implication was clear. Though Snord's Irregulars had served House Steiner for fifty years, maybe the moment had come to seek a home with another of the Great Houses of the Inner Sphere.

"Perhaps," Cranston said. "But I think I'm one of those people who's learned to appreciate history better than most people. It's your call, but don't forget the past."

"Speaking of which, I'd love to have you tour the digging site in old Bealton," Rhonda said. "We've narrowed the search to a two-block area, and I've vowed to find that vault no matter how long it takes us."

A beep from her wrist communicator interrupted the thought. "This is Colonel Snord," she said crisply.

"Captain Malcolm here," came back the voice of the local militia leader. "Our satellites have just picked up incoming DropShips. Our scans show that they belong to the First Thorin Regiment. Two Overlord-class vessels, two Union. I'm on the way right now to join my command. Count Fisk has asked that you meet with him to discuss our response. Copy?"

Rhonda looked at the communicator as if its weight had suddenly tripled. "Roger that, Captain. How far out are they?"

"Four days," came the response.

"Very good," she said. "Inform the Count that I'm on my way." She stepped to the side of the wheelchair and looked down at her father. "I'm afraid our tour of the dig site will have to wait."

"So I heard," he said, smiling slightly. "If Christifori's bringing four DropShips, I doubt very much that they're empty. Don't fret, though. If it comes to a shooting match, these Avengers are no match for our Irregulars."

"It's not the fighting that has me worried," she said, moving behind the chair again and turning it around to go back the way they'd just come. "It's the politics."

6

It had been a long descent onto Odessa: four days of travel, capped off by a thirty-minute burn-in. As the DropShip finally settled into its landing pit, the deployment ramp hissed open and the midmorning sunlight poured into Archer's cockpit. He couldn't remember his legs ever feeling so stiff or his butt so sore from sitting in the seat of his 'Mech. He smiled, remembering what Darius Hopkins had said a few nights ago. He'd joked that the aches came with increased rank—the reason he'd stayed an enlisted man. Archer guessed his old friend was right.

He hit the release control for his restraint harness, which snapped off as soon as the maglocks disengaged. Then Archer throttled his splotched-green *Penetrator* forward through the bay door and down the ramp to the ground.

In his long career, he had seen so many worlds, but it was always a thrill to arrive at a place he had never been. His first sight of Odessa showed him a yellow-orange sun, some wispy clouds streaming by, and around him rolling hills dotted with occasional copses of trees and clumps of undergrowth. Rocks, dull and gray, cut upward here and there through the long grasses.

"Specter One is on the green and moving to Hill 107," he said into his neurohelmet microphone. He pivoted the *Penetrator*'s torso to the left and right as he moved, taking in the lay of the land, comparing what he saw to the tactical display on his cockpit's secondary monitor. Satisfied that he had his bearings, Archer throttled the 'Mech's fusion reactor higher and began moving quickly toward the smaller of the two hills a kilometer away.

"This is The Brain to all commands," he heard Katya say in his earpiece. "Primary LZ is secure. All units are on the ground and deploying. No bogies in the air or on the ground yet." There was a pause, and Archer could see on his comm system that she had switched to a more discreet command channel. "General, it looks like your message to the Irregulars had some impact."

He'd been thinking the same thing, but was trying not to make too much of it yet. "Don't get too cocky, Brain," he warned. "For all we know, Rhonda Snord is waiting over that next hillside with both of her battalions, getting ready to melt us to puddles."

Two days into the burn to Odessa, he had sent a personal message to Colonel Snord. It was short and to the point: "The First Thorin Regiment is landing on Odessa not to conduct military raids but to open negotiations with Snord's Irregulars. We will not fire unless fired upon." He had also provided her with several frequencies that the two of them could use to communicate once the Avengers were on the ground. Though he had not received a response, he was starting to think that the absence of activity by the Irregulars was Rhonda Snord's answer.

"They knew our approach vector," Hopkins said.

"If they wanted to get us, they would know where we are. It looks like no one's home."

"That's not exactly bad news, old man," Archer said.

"I never said it was," Hopkins retorted in his crusty voice.

Archer adjusted his *Penetrator*'s course and saw the rest of his command lance forming up along both sides of him. One of Hopkins's favorite sayings came back to him as they did: "You can't lead from the rear."

"Ranger One to all commands," he heard John Kraff say in his earpiece. "I have unidentified movement on my long-range sensor perimeter. Faint readings moving north by northwest at two-three-one zulu. Two medium 'Mechs. Most likely advance units or recon probe." There was a hint of excitement in Kraff's voice. Archer knew he was already charging his weapons as a precautionary move, awaiting any indication that he should fire.

"Brain to all commands," Katya said. "Confirmed enemy BattleMechs on the edge of the LZ, just north of Hill 103 at two-three-one zulu. Transponder signals indicate that these are not the Irregulars but the planetary militia. Repeat, this is the planetary militia."

Archer adjusted his tactical display, zooming out to get a broader picture. The forces of Getts and Hogan were already on Hill 103 and in the valley below. Major Getts had her armor split and moving slowly into position on both hills.

Something didn't make sense, though. The planetary militia was a mere reinforced company. Yes, they had good gear, but the Avengers outnumbered them at least seven to one. It was risky for them even to be near the LZ . . .

. . . unless the Irregulars were joining the fight as well. His heart began to pound at the thought, but he continued his deliberate gait up Hill 107.

"Specter One to all commands. Rules of engagement are in effect. Hold your fire unless fired upon."

"Saber One to Specter One, flash-sitrep," came the voice of Leftenant Francine Culver in her *Lucifer* aerofighter somewhere high overhead. "I have incoming bandits, four fighters. They are making a strafing run."

Hold your fire until they hit their trigger studs, Archer repeated silently, knowing he didn't have to speak the words again. Then it was John Kraff once more. "Enemy has opened fire. Permission to engage!" His voice rang with a mix of excitement, fear, and unbridled joy.

"Fighters are firing," Culver said. "Moving to engage."

Archer preheated his extended-range large lasers, relics from the Clan wars, and rose over the crest of Hill 107 to see, in the distance, a thin and tiny line of BattleMechs attempting to pepper the edges of his own battle line with long-range fire.

"Specter One to all commands," he said. "Engage at will!"

Count Nicholas Fisk stood in the portable command dome, wearing a crisp, pseudomilitary gray uniform with flared-thigh riding pants and tall, polished officer's boots. He crossed his arms and stared at the field holographic projector on its makeshift stand. Rhonda and Tasha Snord flanked him, gazing at the image in disbelief. The flowing green holographic hills and the tiny glowing images of BattleMechs told a clear story, as did the looks on the their faces.

"Your Grace," Rhonda said, her voice edged with anger, "you can't send in the militia this way. Captain Malcolm and his people will be slaughtered." She continued to stare at the holographic scene. The Odessa planetary militia consisted of only a dozen or so 'Mechs, a lance of fighters, and a lance of hovercraft.

They were outnumbered nearly six to one by Archer's Avengers, who also had the advantage of the high ground.

Fisk shrugged slightly. "The odds are long. I grant you that, Colonel. But what choice do I have? It is my duty to defend this planet. If you would agree to give me the help I need, I wouldn't have to sacrifice the militia. Bring in your Irregulars now, and I can pull Captain Malcolm and his people out of the fight to coordinate an assault with you."

Rhonda Snord's face flushed. She and the Count had been in a verbal fencing match for days, and the air had grown especially tense after she received a message from General Christifori. He was supposedly not coming to fight.

"Count Fisk," she said in an uncompromising tone. "My contract—"

"Is an electronic document," he said matter-of-factly. "This, Colonel Snord, is reality. We all have to make choices. You are making a choice right now. You're forcing me to send good men, good Mech-Warriors, to almost certain death. But you can choose to save them instead."

Rhonda gritted her teeth in fury and was about to tear into the Count when Tasha pointed to the air above the display. "Christifori's fighters are arriving," she said. The glowing red fighters swept in on the militia's fighters. One by one, the green holographic fighters of the militia peeled away, most of them tailed by the enemy. In a matter of minutes, the green lights simply did not exist.

Rhonda looked down at the palm communicator lying on the desk and then back at the Count. "I know what you're thinking, Colonel," he said. "You want to call back my unit. Just so you don't waste your energy, I've given Captain Malcolm orders to obey only my commands."

"He'll be massacred if he rushes that regiment with only a company," she said angrily. "You're killing him, him and his command."

"*Au contraire*, Colonel. *You* will have killed him, or your inaction will have." He threw a dour glance at Tasha, standing at her mother's side. "He was doing his duty—that's how the public will see it. And they will view your Irregulars as traitors who refused to save the planet's defenders from the guns of their enemies."

"This is blackmail," Snord said.

"No, my dear Colonel," Fisk returned, finally letting his own anger bleed into his voice. "This is war. You must decide whether you are going to honor the intent of your agreement with the Lyran Alliance or be hamstrung by a few petty words on an insignificant contract."

Rhonda Snord turned to her daughter, whose face wore the same look of anger and frustration that she felt. Fisk had positioned himself perfectly. To the public, he would appear as the great leader doing whatever he could to protect his people. In reality, he had manipulated the Irregulars into a position where they might be forced to capitulate while shaming them to boot.

Rhonda had been right in her estimation of the man. He was cunning, and more.

"Splash Bandit Number Two," Francine Culver's voice said confidently. "Sorry about the two that got through, General."

"No losses here, Saber One," said Alice Getts. "Besides, that pair only made one pass. I doubt they'll be flying those machines again unless someone digs them out of the craters." Her armor units had unleashed a barrage of fire that had engulfed the two fighters attempting to attack the regiment.

"Ground forces are converging on Hill 103," cut in Katya. "I show just over a company in force."

This made no sense, Archer thought, looking at his display almost sadly. He'd been a military man most of his life, but destroying human lives pointlessly was something he had never understood. He wondered if the militia was trying to lure him out, then decided that didn't make sense either.

"Captain Kraff, hold your position on the hilltop," he said. "Send two lances along the left flank to hit them from the side. Major Getts, bring your companies out into the valley and position them along the right flank."

Maybe if he could box them in, they would surrender, Archer thought. Maybe it wouldn't be necessary to carry out a slaughter.

"Bloody damnation, sir, they're coming right up the hill like we're not even here," Kraff said.

"Engage them," Archer said, knowing he must. "Brain, see if you can get their CO on-line."

The hillside around him suddenly came alive with fire. The brilliant blue of PPC fire burst in all directions, as did the wispy trails of hundreds of missiles. Emerald-green pulse laserfire seemed to make the air between the two forces crackle, while lances of solid red laser beams raked the flanks. The Odessa militia was being hit on three sides at once, from the high ground, by superior forces. They didn't stand a chance.

Archer saw a militia *Cestus* come up on a small rocky outcropping, firing its gauss rifle up toward his position. Lasers had eaten away at its dull green armor during its painful advance, then it was hit by an airborne swarm of at least twenty long-range missiles. They exploded at once, shredding armor on the 'Mech's legs and arms as it tried to fall back. A burst of bright azure PPC fire cut into one of its heavily damaged legs. Armor exploded into the air, and the

Cestus reeled under the attack, spinning slightly to one side and then disappearing from Archer's field of view.

Farther in the distance he saw an *Enfield* pause and unleash its large pulse laser and Defiance LB 10-X autocannon at Sergeant Muller's *Lynx* as it came to a landing halfway down the hillside. The stream of shellfire stitched its way along the torso of the larger 'Mech, ripping armor plating apart. Beyond that, a lightweight militia *Javelin* dropped mid-run, plowing up the ground as it died—a victim of Alice Getts's ground armor forces.

"General, you can contact the militia on broadband channel one-five-five-one," Archer heard Katya say as he watched the *Enfield* wither under a barrage of pulse-laser fire.

He engaged his mike. "Militia commander, this is General Christifori. Surrender your forces now!" he called. The *Enfield* turned to face the autocannon fire tearing up the sod around its feet as Hopkins's infantry fired three of their manpack PPCs into its legs, searing off even more armor there. There was no answer from the enemy commander. In mute resignation, Archer started to raise his own targeting reticle to lock on to the *Enfield*.

Just as he was about to fire, three scarlet lances of large-laser fire pierced the *Enfield*'s arm and cockpit. The right arm exploded, leaving myomer fiber hanging like torn muscle tissue. The beams that sliced into the cockpit did worse, digging through the armor and deeply into the interior. The *Enfield* seemed to shiver under the assault and then collapsed before Archer could even squeeze off a shot.

An Odessan *Whitworth* rose up where the *Enfield* had fallen and turned to face Archer, firing a barrage of twenty long-range missiles. He didn't fall back or attempt to dodge the wave of deadly warheads. His hand instinctively engaged the anti-missile gun in the center of the *Penetrator*'s chest.

A stream of small exploding shells roared out at the wall of approaching missiles. Many of the warheads exploded in midair, shredded by the shells. The remaining dozen or so missiles peppered his *Penetrator*, which rocked under the impact but held its ground easily. Archer nudged the joystick and brought his targeting reticle onto the *Whitworth*, but it broke into a run before he could get a clean lock. He managed to fire one of his large lasers, hitting the smaller, faster BattleMech in the right leg and leaving it with a deadly limp.

Dull gray smoke billowed from the leg as the MechWarrior desperately attempted to escape his attackers. And then four other Avengers targeted the hapless 'Mech. From the explosion that engulfed the BattleMech, there was no hope that it could survive. The *Whitworth* toppled forward like a drunken marine. A puff of a white smoke blew from the cockpit, and Archer saw a streak in the air as the MechWarrior punched out. The parasail opened some fifty meters above the battle zone. The MechWarrior had survived, but his ride didn't. Oily black smoke and red flames obscured the location of the *Whitworth* and its new crater.

This was not the kind of combat Archer liked. This was slaughter, plain and simple.

"General," said Alice Getts, "I can get my hovercraft in their rear, sir. We can cut off their escape."

Archer glanced at the tactical display and saw that his force was enveloping the enemy. All he had to do was give the word, and this would be over in a matter of minutes.

"They're retreating, sir," Katya said. "What's left of them is bugging out."

"Permission to pursue and destroy, sir?" Kraff

asked, his voice crackling with the thrill Archer recognized from combat—that mix of excitement and the rush of victory. He stared at the display and walked his *Penetrator* farther down the hillside, hoping to catch a glimpse of the fleeing militia.

"Hold your ground, Avengers," he said. "I think whatever's left of them has gotten the point."

"They're breaking," Tasha Snord said, pointing to the holographic display. The handful of green images, all that remained of the militia, were attempting to retreat. The First Thorin Regiment had them nearly surrounded, but Captain Malcolm had managed to find the one hole still open to his rear—his only hope of getting any of his people out. Of the company of twelve BattleMechs that had started the assault, only four were left to try.

"I can't believe you're doing this to them," Rhonda snapped at Count Fisk.

"Me?" the Count said with fake innocence. "Colonel Snord, I assure you that it's you who killed those men by refusing to fulfill your duty to the Alliance."

"You're responsible for the deaths of innocent people," she said through clenched teeth.

"They are patriots dying to protect this world and the Archon," he replied coldly, giving her a defiant stare. "If you would only do your duty, there might be a way to—"

"It's over," Tasha said coldly, still looking at the holographic display. "Only two of the 'Mechs made it out. It doesn't look like the First Thorin is pursuing."

Rhonda's eyes narrowed. "Christifori doesn't *have* to pursue. He knows they're not a real threat to him. He knew all along." She turned again to face Nicholas Fisk, riding her fury like a wild animal. "You wasted them." How could this poor excuse for a ruler send people to their deaths just to score political points?

He drew a long breath and let out a sigh, completely unfazed. "Colonel Snord, when word of what you allowed to happen gets out, it will leave a serious stain on your unit's reputation. I doubt anyone will be interested in hiring the Irregulars after this. The Lyran Alliance has always been your home, and I'm sure I can explain to my fellow citizens what happened here—if you choose to sign the contract we've offered you. The time has come, Colonel, for you to decide what is worth fighting for."

Then, with regal precision, he turned on his heel and exited the field tent, leaving Rhonda and Tasha alone. Rhonda ran both hands through her short hair as she stared at the display in despair.

"Is he for real?" Tasha said indignantly. "He's trying to say this is our fault. He can't seriously think anyone will believe him."

Rhonda shook her head. "They will because he'll alter records, manipulate the media, and in the process, drag us through the mud."

"We can't let that happen," Tasha said.

"If we side with Victor, we get pulled into a civil war. If we side with Katherine, we're just as compromised. Count Fisk will never admit that the militia went to their deaths under his orders."

"So what do we do?"

"I'm not totally sure, Tasha," Rhonda admitted. "But one thing is certain. Nobody is going to destroy the reputation of this unit or the people under my command. Not so long as I have anything to say about it."

Archer adjusted his cooling vest as he walked to the edge of the crater where a militia *Hatchetman* had fallen in the short but furious fight. The cool air felt refreshing on his bare legs as he stood looking down at the mangled BattleMech on the hillside below. A team of Avenger technicians were climbing over the war machine, seeing if it could be made operable, salvaged, or simply gutted for parts. Many of the techs were covered with black grime, residue of the missile blasts that had torn the arm off the 'Mech. A pair of medtechs were on the ground, tending to the fallen MechWarrior.

Archer knew this battle had not been necessary. Someone had thrown this company of militia at his regiment, ordered them to attack against his high-ground position. They'd never had a chance of either success or survival.

Katya came up and stood looking down at the 'Mech for a bit as well. "We saw two of them flee the field," she said, "apparently heading toward New Bealton."

Archer shook his head. "This whole thing was pointless."

Katya glanced behind her at the figure that was approaching them. "I agree, and here comes Sergeant Gramash. Maybe he can tell us something."

Gramash walked up and gave Archer a quick nod of acknowledgment. "General, there are no indications that Snord's Irregulars were involved in this," he said. "Everything points to Count Fisk as the source of the militia's orders. But it looks like the media is trying to place the blame for this 'disaster' on the Irregulars."

Archer's brow furrowed. "That doesn't make sense."

"It does if Fisk is trying to pressure them into a new contract," Katya put in.

Archer rubbed his forehead. "Politicians. The one constant in the universe. Sergeant, have you had any luck in linking up with your local contacts?"

Gramash shook his head. "I've got meetings set up in the next two days, sir. All eyes are on us right now, and I didn't want to tip off anyone attempting to monitor our communications."

"So, what do we do now?" Katya asked.

Archer looked from her to Gramash. "We send a message to Colonel Snord to parlay . . . and see if we can sway her to our side. With Fisk playing so dirty, she just might be more disposed to see things our way."

"What if she doesn't?" Katya asked

Archer's eyes narrowed. "Well, Katya, let's hope we never have to figure that one out."

═══ 7 ═══

Hill 103, Odessa
District of Donegal
Lyran Alliance
16 April 3063

Archer stood facing the image of Colonel Rhonda Snord that floated over the portable holoprojector unit in his command tent. She was older than he was and with an obvious strength about her.

"Colonel Snord, I appreciate the fact that your Irregulars did not participate in the attack on my forces," he said.

She crossed her arms. "If my Irregulars had been attacking, General, there wouldn't be any of you left on Odessa. But let's cut to the chase, shall we?"

He smiled slightly, liking the fact that she didn't mince words. "I suggest we meet face to face. A formal parlay. It will give us a chance to put our cards on the table. To be blunt, I know your contract is coming up for renewal. Prince Victor would respectfully like an opportunity to secure your services."

Snord didn't even blink. "Given recent events, I think there's some merit in such a meeting. But, General, I have to be equally blunt. I have no desire to involve this unit in an action that pits the FedCom against itself. Your arrival on Odessa has put my unit in a predicament with our current employer, and my unit's reputation is taking a beating along with it."

Archer nodded. A mercenary unit's reputation was everything. There were the formal ratings from the Mercenary Review and Bonding Commission, but the public perception counted for just as much. Both could impact the merc unit's bottom line—the rates it could demand from an employer. From what he had seen the night before on the holocasts, Count Fisk was blaming the battle's failure on Snord's unwillingness to fight.

"I look forward to hearing your position on the recent fighting," he said.

"Very well," she said, uncrossing her arms. "I suggest we meet tonight, say at 2100 hours? There's a place between our two positions, Moseby's Crossroads. We can meet there."

Archer looked over at Katya, who was already pulling up the map, and at Sergeant Gramash, who was pointing to the location. "I'll be bringing one of our intelligence people and one of my advisors," Archer said, deciding on the spur of the moment to take Gramash.

"And I'll have one of my battalion commanders," Snord replied. "The location is isolated—no buildings. We should be able to talk freely without fear of being monitored."

"Good," Archer said. "I look forward to it."

Rhonda Snord clicked her heels in the Lyran fashion and gave him a curt bow. Archer responded with a brief salute. *Honor given and received.*

The holoprojector clicked off and the image disappeared. He stared into the now-empty space for a moment, and then Katya Chaffee was standing in it.

"Colonel Snord is right," she said, putting her noteputer down. "The location for this meeting is out in the middle of nowhere."

"And?" he asked.

"If anything goes wrong, you'll be a long way from help. Why not take a lance of 'Mechs along as an escort? They could stay nearby . . . just in case." There was a hint of worry in her voice.

"I was planning to have Hopkins drive if that will make you feel better," Archer said. "Besides, this is a formal parlay. There's no way Snord would try anything. The MRBC would be all over the Irregulars if she violated the sanctity of the parlay."

"Of course," Katya said, lowering her gaze slightly. "I just want to make sure we've got all of our bases covered."

Archer smiled. "I appreciate that, Katya. And just to make certain, I'm giving you command of the regiment until I return."

Rhonda Snord turned toward the officers gathered to see her off. "I shouldn't be more than a couple of hours," she said. "In my absence, Major Snord will be acting commander of the unit. I want full patrols out to the edge of the Avengers' patrol corridors. Let them know that despite what the Count's got the media saying, we're not holed up or hiding."

One of the taller MechWarriors, a former Jade Falcon named Norris, stepped forward. The Irregulars were organized like a standard Inner Sphere military unit, but Norris still liked to call himself "Star Captain," and Rhonda let him.

"Colonel Snord," he said, "you are not truly considering changing alliances, *quineg*?"

She shook her head. "Norris, you'll find that it's not uncommon for a CO to keep all options open during mercenary contract negotiations. I'm not committing us to anything yet. But I do want to hear what he has to say."

It was obvious from the set of Norris's jaw that he

was confused by the whole business. The former Clan warriors in the ranks of the Irregulars often struggled with life as mercenaries. This one performed well on the battlefield, but he often chafed at the complexities of regimental management and administration.

"Major Sneede will be with me," Rhonda said, nodding to the older man standing at her side. Shorty Sneede had been with the Irregulars since her father's time. Though well past the age of retirement, he still held command rank, while taking a back seat during field duty. To Rhonda, he was a link to her father, a part of the original company that had composed Snord's Irregulars when she was a young girl.

She turned back to the others. "Stay on full alert," she said, meeting the eyes of each of her officers. "We've got a full regiment of potential hostiles out there, so keep frosty, people."

Lieutenant Shake stepped forward. "Sir, why not deploy a company for security, just to patrol the perimeter? At the first sign of trouble, we could be right on top of it."

Rhonda waved her hand dismissively. "Marcos, I appreciate your concern, but Shorty and I will be in BattleMechs. What could possibly go wrong?"

The Rotunda-class armored car made its way slowly down the road as the sun set behind a bank of clouds, casting a purplish light over the landscape. Archer was in the passenger seat next to Hopkins, while Anton Gramash sat hunched in the back, next to the loading racks for the short-range missile launcher.

"We should have taken a larger vehicle," the young officer grumbled.

At the wheel, Hopkins chuckled. "What's the matter, boyo? Not enough room for those legs of yours?"

"It's not that," Gramash said, shifting position

slightly. "It's the fact that I'm going to be back here for half an hour."

"Reminds me of that time on New Avalon," Hopkins said, casting a sideways glance at Archer. "You and that wire-haired cadet in that transport you liberated. What was his name?"

Archer chewed on his lower lip in thought. "Raymond Grace," he said finally, smiling. "And don't forget Andrea. I never thought we'd shake those MPs."

Hopkins was recalling the time he and Archer's sister had come to Archer's graduation ceremony at the NAIS. Those were the happy days of Archer's youth—wild, impetuous, free. Before he had fought in so many wars, and long before he ever dreamed that he'd lose his sister to the power-hungry schemes of someone like Katherine Steiner-Davion.

"Whatever became of him?" Hopkins asked.

"He got posted to the Davion Guards, but I lost track of him after that."

Hopkins nodded. "So many kids. I've lost track of a lot of them, too. Never you, though."

Gramash spoke up from his cubbyhole in the back seat. "Is it true that you trained General Christifori, Sergeant Major?"

"That's right," Hopkins said proudly. "He learned all of his good moves from me."

"It wasn't just the good moves, old man," Archer said. "I learned some pretty wicked stuff from you as well."

Hopkins laughed. "All part of being a soldier."

Archer glanced at his wrist chronometer. "We're making good time. Looks like we're even running a little ahead of schedule." As the Rotunda approached some trees near the road, Archer pointed to them. "Pull over for a minute," he said.

"You see something?" Hopkins asked, cutting the

armored car's speed and allowing it to coast to a stop alongside the trees.

"You could say that," Archer said, undoing his seat harness. "I see a place to take a quick leak before the meeting."

Darius shook his head. "You *are* getting old. What is it, the weight of those stars on your shoulder pressing on your bladder?"

"Very funny, Sergeant Major," Archer said, popping open the door and letting the cool evening air rush in. The sun was now only a sliver of light on the horizon as he got out of the car and headed for the trees. The sun set late in the day on Odessa.

"Keep the engine running," he said over his shoulder.

He was still thinking of that long-ago night Hopkins had mentioned. Archer had been no more than a kid, a young officer fresh out of NAIS and drunk on beer and adrenaline. He smiled to himself, thinking of the good old days before he'd lost his political innocence when he caught something in the distance beyond the trees. At first, he thought his eyes were playing tricks on him. He fastened his fly and squinted into the darkness. There was movement out there, but in the twilight, it was hard to make out what or how distant.

"Darius," he called out, still staring at the place where he'd seen something. "You picking up anything on the sensors?" He waited for a response, still searching for the source of the movement.

"I'm getting a lot of static here," Hopkins called back. "Comm system's acting like it's jammed."

Jammed? That made no sense. Archer felt his heart begin to race and his senses go into overdrive. As he turned back toward the Rotunda, he felt a slight vibration in the ground beneath his feet. He was a soldier, his instincts trained to catch these kinds of things.

Something was wrong out here. Dead wrong.

8

Moseby's Crossroads, Odessa
District of Donegal
Lyran Alliance
16 April 3063

Rhonda Snord piloted her *Highlander* cautiously down the road, followed by Shorty Sneede in his smaller *Lancelot*. Her 'Mech was painted dull green and bore two insignia. One was the image of a buffalo nickel, a coin dating back to long before the Star League on ancient Terra. The other was a yellow lightning bolt topped off with the letters TCB on the *Highlander*'s right torso. The letters stood for "Taking Care of Business," the motto of an ancient Terran rock and roller whose memorabilia she collected.

"How you doing back there, Shorty?" she said into her neurohelmet mike.

"Just like always," came back the major's crusty voice. "Covering your backside."

Doing a quick mental check of the cockpit controls, she saw a faint light on the secondary display. Her long-range sensors had picked up something, however faint. A signal at maximum range, off to the east. She punched in a tighter scan and saw that it was a personal distress beacon set for the transponder codes used by the First Thorin Regiment. Just as she was about to get a better lock on its position, the signal disappeared.

"Shorty—" she started to say, still adjusting her sensors.

"I saw it too," he called back. "We're a few minutes from the crossroads. Do you think Christifori sent out patrols this far forward?"

Rhonda slowed her BattleMech to a walk. "Not likely. Not with us coming to a meeting in the area. Damn peculiar."

"I painted it as an emergency beacon, Rhonda. We need to check it out." Protocol demanded that an emergency signal be answered, no matter whom it was from.

"Looks like we're going to be a few minutes late," she said, switching to the channel she used with the unit's base. "Jailhouse Rocker One to Junk Yard. Jailhouse Rocker One to Junk Yard. We've picked up a distress beacon at coordinates five-five-niner-three-zulu and are moving to investigate." Then she turned her *Highlander* in the direction of the signal and began to move off the main road.

Nothing came back over the radio. No static. No response. "Shorty, you give it a shot," she said. "My comm system must be on the fritz." But something told her it wasn't.

Sneede repeated Rhonda's message to the Irregulars' command post but picked up the same dead air. The sudden loss of signal made her slow the *Highlander*'s pace even more. Something didn't feel right.

"Check your long-range sensors," she said cautiously. "I don't like the feel of this."

Then her long-range display lit up again. This time, the emergency signal was fainter, as if it had moved farther away. "That's odd as all hell," she said.

"Colonel," Shorty said, more formal now, "I can't say for sure that we're being deliberately jammed, but something is blocking our communications, and whatever that beacon is, it's leading us farther off course."

"Bait?"

"Sure seems like it to this old dog."

All Rhonda's inner antennae went on alert. "Pretty ballsy of Christifori, if it is some sort of ambush. Let's turn and start running north. If it is a trap, we can punch through their perimeter and hopefully get closer to our base and out of this communications dead zone."

"Gotcha. That, or we can fall back, signal the Junk Yard, and get a larger force up here."

She considered that for a moment. "No," she said finally. "We have to take Christifori at his word, but be careful. Begin a full run on my command."

"Give the word, Colonel."

"Three, two, one," she said, slamming her throttle control all the way forward. "Rock and roll!"

Her *Highlander* made it nearly 350 meters before three bursts of particle projection cannon fire flashed through the twilight like bolts of lightning. The azure flash-blasts slammed into her 'Mech with such force that it felt like she'd run into a stone wall. Arcs of energy danced around her cockpit exterior as the charged particles ripped away at her armor. Her body strained against the restraints until they dug into her flesh. She fought the rush of blood to her head.

Streaks of flame raced across her field of vision, a wave of at least forty long-range missiles sweeping past her into the night. They had not been intended for her, but for Shorty Sneede. She heard a rumble of impacts off to one side as she checked her sensors, finally spotting the source of the attack.

Six BattleMechs were closing in from every angle. Somehow they had masked their approach, probably by being shut down and hidden under holotarps equipped with some emission-deadeners. It was an old trick. All you had to do was power up quickly, and you could take someone at fairly close range. Fast-starting a fusion reactor took some finesse, though.

Fine, she thought. You surprised me. Time for you to get a taste of this . . .

One of the 'Mechs, a *Vulcan*, landed off to her side and began to bring its weapons to bear.

"Stick close, Shorty," she called as she moved to face it. In a single fluid gesture, she swept her targeting reticle onto the smaller 'Mech while also bringing her gauss rifle onto the same target interlock circuit—her thumb trigger. The light on the reticle changed to green as the *Vulcan* MechWarrior, realizing he was within deadly range, opened fire with almost everything he had. Unflinching, Rhonda depressed the trigger as the tone of weapons lock sounded in her ear.

The *Vulcan*'s machine gun and medium pulse laser missed by a wide margin. The flamer, even from its extreme range, did manage to splash some fire across her *Highlander*'s legs and feet. The large pulse laser played emerald bursts of laser light across her right torso, digging away some of her armor.

But the *Vulcan* did not remain in the fight long. Rhonda's silvery gauss slug had done its job. The hypersonic slug had slammed into the right thigh of the *Vulcan* with such force that the smaller 'Mech spun as if dancing a jig. As it came back around, she could see that the leg armor was all but gone and that what was left of the leg was mere mangled debris, torn myomer muscle, and leaking coolant. The *Vulcan* dropped from her field of vision as she moved to the side, worried about how Shorty was faring.

A *Black Knight* came up to flank her just as she saw the fallen form of Shorty's *Lancelot*. Rhonda bit her lip. In the dim evening light, the 'Mech was still glowing hot where weapons fire had heated its internal structure. A small pool of fire seemed to belch from its torso, spilling onto the ground and lighting the grass on fire. The *Lancelot* wasn't moving.

The *Black Knight* was.

It swept its PPC toward her as she felt her 'Mech quake from a wave of short-range missiles fired by another enemy. She played the joystick with consummate skill, landing the targeting sight squarely on the moving *Black Knight*. It stopped on a small rise and fired even as she did.

Her missiles had just cleared their tubes when the bright blue flash from a PPC tore at her at close range. The shot dug into her center torso, where she had already been hit, eating away her remaining armor.

Rhonda's missiles poured into the humanoid-shaped *Knight* and lit up the twilight with a series of orange blasts. Her short-range missiles plowed into its neck, just below the cockpit, gouging the armor so deep that the gash in the 'Mech's throat glowed red and yellow from the heat of the blast. The heat in her own cockpit rose slightly, and she felt the fluid in her cooling vest begin to shift in an attempt to bleed off the excess heat.

A shot hit her hard from the rear, and she fought a wave of vertigo as she used her neurofeedback to keep the *Highlander* on its feet. The sensors told her a grim story. Two of the enemy 'Mechs were down, but the others were closing in on her from all sides.

She juked to the right just in time to avoid a blast from the *Black Knight*'s pair of large lasers. Their bright crimson beams stabbed into the darkness, narrowly missing her. Her nerves were tingling with adrenaline as she jogged her *Highlander* back to the left and swung her targeting and tracking reticle onto the *Black Knight*.

Her plan was simple: get past the *Knight* and out into the open to signal for reinforcements. She wasn't happy about leaving Shorty—injured or dead—behind, but she was badly outgunned and outnumbered. She jabbed her primary trigger and felt the jolt as her gauss rifle fired again.

She couldn't see the slug go down-range, but she saw where it hit, striking the PPC housing on the *Knight*'s right arm and sending armor plating flying in every direction as it drilled a running gouge along the length of the armor. The kinetic impact of the blast knocked the arm to the side, and for a moment, she hoped it would rip off—but the tough myomer muscles that powered the 'Mech's movements held.

Time to take out that PPC, she thought. She activated her jump jets, and with a roar like a tornado, her *Highlander*'s giant form took to the air. The heat in her cockpit was no longer just an irritant but a grim liability. She tasted salty sweat on her upper lip as she ran her tongue over it. Her whole body leaned to the side as if to compensate for the *Black Knight*'s rough landing only meters away.

At point-blank range, she saw the "A²" emblazoned on the enemy 'Mech and cursed. *Christifori!* Up to now, she'd barely had time to think who might be attacking her because she'd been so focused on just trying to stay alive. The sight of the insignia infuriated her. He had set her up for an ambush under the guise of a parlay. Angrily, she jabbed the leg controls of her *Highlander* and sent a sweeping kick into the leg of the *Black Knight*. She was ready for the impact. The *Avenger* BattleMech was not.

She felt the armor on her *Highlander*'s foot crumple as it dug deeply into the *Knight*'s shin. She couldn't use her weapons—not at this range. She gritted her teeth and switched the joystick to control her next attack—a punch. Using every drop of her skill, training, and experience, she drew the *Highlander*'s huge metal fist back, then drove it forward again into the viewport of the *Black Knight*.

Already damaged from her previous attack, the enemy 'Mech's cockpit no longer had enough armor to withstand the force of her punch. Her giant fist tore through the front of it, through the command console and ejection seat, and deeply into the 'Mech's battle-computer. There had been a MechWarrior in that seat. Now there was only a red smear on the fist of her *Highlander*.

The *Black Knight* had begun to teeter to the right when she felt her *Highlander* take another shot to the rear, this time from a PPC, its excess energy arcing a white-blue ribbon over her shoulder. Her ears rang for a moment, and she tasted bile in her throat as she pulled back on her controls, attempting to compensate. *Gyro hit.* She fought to steady the *Highlander*'s balance even as neurofeedback seared her brain cells.

She stepped the 'Mech forward and prepared to break into a run when suddenly her comm system came to life. The jamming had lifted.

"Jailhouse Rocker One to Junk Yard," she said, even as a wave of missiles slammed into her 'Mech's legs as she struggled to get away from the ambush scene. "We are under attack. It's the Avengers. Shorty's down. I've got four enemies here. Full alert. Send reinforcements."

Rhonda struggled to talk and pilot at the same time as several green bursts of pulse-laserfire soared over her shoulders. Two hit her left arm, knocking it forward as she ran and throwing her balance even more out of whack.

Leaning over in her command seat, she juked hard to the right and jammed the throttle full forward. Her hope was to sweep across the enemy's field of fire, making her much harder to hit. She picked up a *Kintaro* attempting to cross her path several hundred meters down-range. It fired its long-range missiles at her, but she could tell instantly that they were going to miss. She brought all twenty of her own LRMs to bear, and fired back a millisecond after she heard weapons lock in her ear.

Her 'Mech shook from another powerful hit, and she heard a grinding noise from under her seat as the impact of the shots tore into the bowels of her BattleMech. The heat in her cockpit instantly seemed to double—the fusion reactor's shielding had been damaged. This time the cockpit temperature did not begin to drop but continued to feel like a deadly sauna. She swung again to the left, leaving the *Kintaro* bathed in at least fifteen missile hits.

"Colonel," she heard someone say in her earpiece, then recognized the voice of her comm officer, Jack Strickland. "We can't get a fix on you. We need your twenty, over."

Rhonda had just opened her mouth to reply when her 'Mech was struck twice. One shot, a PPC, tore her already damaged arm off at the shoulder actuator, sending it flying out of her field of view. The sudden loss of the arm pitched the 'Mech's center of gravity. She attempted to compensate just as another shot dug into her right torso from the rear.

That one, from a pack of short-range missiles, devoured the gyro housing and sent a ripple of energy into her neurohelmet. She screamed but did not hear it. Her vision seemed to tunnel, the edges becoming more blurred. Sounds were lost, and a ringing filled her ears. There was a rumble. Had her 'Mech fallen? Her lips were wet—salty. Not sweat this time, but something thicker. She tried to focus and saw a pool of blood filling her field of vision.

As the surrounding enemy 'Mechs pumped several parting shots into her BattleMech, Rhonda Snord passed out.

9

Near Moseby's Crossroads, Odessa
District of Donegal
Lyran Alliance
16 April 306

"We've got BattleMechs out there," Archer yelled as loud as he could into his neurohelmet mike. "Get moving!"

Darius Hopkins had the sleek Rotunda armored car squealing into motion even as Archer began running toward it. A hissing noise filled the air, followed by an explosion as a salvo of long-range missiles streaked into the car about twenty meters in front of him. There was a terrific blast that felt like a large hand swatting Archer into the air. His hearing deadened instantly, and his head rang like a bell from the force of the explosion. He was tossed like a doll into the air and then back into the brush, gasping for air. His lungs ached.

As Archer fought back the dizziness and confusion, he heard the sickening grinding of metal as the Rotunda attempted to move away. His nose was blocked, and he blew out through his nostrils, feeling something wet and slick—blood—splatter his face. Sitting up slowly, he saw the squat form of the armored car in the distance, swerving desperately. It was engulfed in flames, and he could make out the shapes of three BattleMechs in the light of the laser and autocannon fire they were pumping into the tiny car.

Hopkins was putting up a good fight, though an ultimately futile one. He fired the Rotunda's two-pack of missiles at one of the 'Mechs, and they hit but with barely enough power to scuff the paint. The BattleMechs closed in—an ambush, pure and simple.

Archer rose slightly, dizzy, the sounds around him still sounding muffled in the cool night air. Without thinking, he started to run toward the fighting. It was a clumsy half-fall at first, then he picked up speed and began to gain ground.

The tiny Rotunda, seeing its way blocked, turned one hundred-eighty degrees, its tires screeching as it tried to put distance between itself and its attackers. The vehicle was facing Archer, and for a moment, he thought that Hopkins might spot him and that somehow the two of them might escape. He waved his arms, thinking they were going to make it.

When the death blow came, he saw it as if in slow motion. One of the BattleMechs, a *Hunchback*, unleashed its deadly autocannon against the retreating Rotunda. Some of the shells missed, hitting just behind and off to one side of the vehicle. Then the *Hunchback* pilot found his mark. Most of his rounds slammed into the still-burning aft of the vehicle, then climbed their way to the roof, eating away at the car as they went. As Archer watched in horror, the Rotunda seemed to contort and twist as if it were melting before his eyes in a bonfire.

Then it exploded.

For the second time, he was thrown through the air, though not so hard as previously. The Rotunda's tiny LTV fusion reactor breached at the same time the short-range missile ammo erupted. Archer ended up lying on the ground with the wind knocked out of him, momentarily paralyzed and bathed in the heat from the dying vehicle nearby. He couldn't focus, and as much as he wanted to move, his body almost refused to respond.

With a supreme effort, he half-rolled onto his right side just as the *Hunchback* loomed over him in the light from the fire. Clearly visible on its torso was the buffalo-nickel—the unmistakable insignia of Snord's Irregulars. Archer hadn't had time to think about who'd attacked him and the others until this instant. Now his anger swelled as he recognized the mercenary logo, then turned quickly toward the Rotunda.

The entire front of the car was in flames, some of it mangled beyond recognition. Archer told himself he had to get up, that he had to try and save Hopkins and Gramash. He was trying to use one arm to lever his weight off the ground when he saw in horror the gigantic, armor-plated foot of the *Hunchback* lift almost four meters in the air over the Rotunda. Powered by pure malice, the foot smashed down through the hood of the already decimated vehicle. Despite Archer's damaged hearing, the sound seemed to reach into his soul—the mournful tearing of metal, grinding of armor, and snapping of circuits and plastic. A wave of smoke drifted over him, heavy with an oily, almost sweet smell.

The final act of destruction seemed to sap his remaining strength. Collapsed on the ground, he lay there as the Irregular BattleMech turned and left. It walked slowly, as if the pilot were scanning the area for other signs of life.

Archer finally managed to move, half-dragging, half-crawling his body to a position behind a large tree. He knew the heat from the fire would obscure his infrared signature and that the tree would block the enemy's visual or motion detection. Once there, he collapsed back onto the ground. Somehow, fate had decreed that he would live. Now, he had to make his men's deaths count for something, and the only way to do that was to warn the rest of his command of this cowardly betrayal.

"Report," the commander ordered over his helmet mike.

"Bravo Lance reports the mission successful," the *Hunchback* pilot replied. "There's no way anyone could have survived."

"Did you verify the bodies?" the commander asked.

"Not possible, sir. But for what it's worth, I squashed the remains of the car like a bug with my 'Mech's foot. Whatever wasn't burned is now a paste."

"Excellent," the commander said. "Alpha Lance reports success as well. Fall back to rally point two-zero-eight sierra."

"Will we be departing?" the MechWarrior asked.

"Negative, Captain. We need you here as insurance. The Count will be bringing in the rest of your regiment when the time is right. I'll be sure to forward a summary report to my commanders. You may even gain the attention of the Archon-Princess herself."

"Thank you, sir," the MechWarrior said.

"No—thank *you* for your service to the Alliance. You've already done much to restore the reputation of the Wolverton's Highlanders. I'm sure that Colonels Blackstone and Feehan will be pleased. But for now, security is the key. Remember our briefing. No one outside your company is to know what you did or even that you were here."

"On my honor, sir."

"Indeed," replied Erwin Vester. "You've earned your pay tonight."

Archer Christifori staggered like a drunken man over to the burning car. He looked in the front window and saw that most of the driver's cockpit had been destroyed in the final attack. There was a sickening red stain covering the inside of the cracked windshield. Peering closer, he saw a vague shape that might once have been Darius Hopkins. He was unquestionably dead. Even if Archer could have gotten close enough, it was pointless trying to check for a pulse.

He peered behind Hopkins and saw the battered form of Anton Gramash, still sitting in a tiny pocket of the back seat that had not caught on fire. The heat and the chemical-laced smoke were obstacles to getting at the young officer, but only for a few moments.

Wincing, Archer reached past the flames and found a pulse in his neck—weak, but still there. His training told him not to move an injured man, but in this case, no help would be coming. Archer adjusted Gramash's head and shoulders, then pulled. Surprisingly, the body slid out of the Rotunda with little resistance. Archer barely noticed the burns on his own hands from the flames he had been unable to avoid.

He pulled Gramash's limp and bloodied form away from what had become the tomb of Darius Hopkins. Gramash was bleeding from dozens of cuts and scrapes, but most looked superficial. He was breathing, though his breath was coming ragged and uneven. Archer knew he needed help right away. There was a good chance the young man had suffered internal injuries. But there was nothing he could do for him here, not without gear.

He was about to activate his wrist communicator, but it wasn't there—probably knocked off during the attack. He went back to where the explosion had first thrown him and found the device lying by the road, glimmering in the reflected flames.

He activated it and sighed in relief when it worked. "Specter One to all commands," he said. "We've been ambushed. Full alert. The Irregulars attacked us. I need a medical team here now. There's at least a lance in this area, so send in flankers and protection." His hearing was not yet recovered, and it was hard for him to tell just how loud he might be yelling. He paused and faintly heard the duty officer's voice respond.

"Security confirmation code, sir," the young voice said.

Archer wiped his face, and a smear of sticky, semi-dried blood came off on his hand. Smart kid, he thought. "Christifori Alpha Bravo Sierra."

There was a second long pause. "Yes, sir, General, sir. We have troops on the way. The major's here, sir."

Archer turned toward the fire in the distance and felt his shoulders sag as he thought of Darius Hopkins dying this way.

"General, are you okay?"

Archer immediately recognized the voice as Katya's. He had to tear his attention away from the burning wreck before he could speak. "Got the wind knocked out of me. Gramash is badly injured."

"What about Darius?"

Archer looked again at the fiery remains of the Rotunda, the only source of light around him now. He couldn't find the words to answer her right away. "You'd better get our troops out on full alert, Katya," was all he could say. His emotions were too overwhelming for him to even speak about the death of Darius Hopkins. "Rhonda Snord and her people pulled a fast one here. They'd be stupid not to try and exploit it."

His long pause and refusal to answer her question must have told Katya what she needed to know. "I understand," she said gently. "Help is on its way."

Archer stared at the fire and the bloody smear on the Rotunda's front windshield—all that remained of his oldest friend. The civil war had cost him his sister and now the man who'd been like a father. He shuffled back to where Gramash lay and dropped like a bag of sand next to the unconscious man. He landed on his knees, ignoring the pain.

Someone was going to pay for this, Archer vowed. He didn't say the words out loud. He didn't have to.

10

The Junk Yard, Bealton ruins
Odessa
District of Donegal
Lyran Alliance
17 April 3063

Three centuries ago, the city of Bealton had been
the thriving capital of Odessa. Then came the First
Succession War, when the Draconis Combine dropped
a pair of nuclear bombs on the city, turning it into a
wasteland of radioactive and toxic rubble. To make
sure the city would never be rebuilt, they had followed
up with several chemically based, biotoxic bombs as
well—salting the proverbial earth.

New Bealton had been built only a few hours away,
and the ruins did not attract many visitors until the
Irregulars set up their command post here. Rhonda
gave priority to finding the ancient vault reputed to
hold a fortune in jewelry because it could potentially
earn them even more money than their mercenary
contract.

That had been before the betrayal and the ambush.

Now the command post was a swirling hub of preparation and planning, the Irregulars' portable, plasteel
living domes abuzz with activity. Using field gantries,
techs were loading up the unit's BattleMechs and per-

forming last-minute maintenance. Gone was the face of the archeological dig.

The base, which consisted of seven domes strung together, was nicknamed the Junk Yard, but the name was deceiving. It boasted an assortment of sophisticated sensor gear, radar controls, communications monitoring stations, and so on. One dome was for tactical planning. Another was the field hospital, where the Irregulars' three medtechs had been working feverishly to save the life of their commanding officer.

Tasha winced at the sight of her mother lying in the field-hospital cylinder. The recovery team had found Rhonda two hours after her last transmission, and the only way they could pry her from her 'Mech's cockpit was to cut her out. Rhonda Snord was in a coma with grave internal injuries from broken ribs and punctured lungs. She was still better off than Shorty, though. He had burned to death in his cockpit. Though Rhonda Snord had fought on hundreds of battlefields, she'd never been hurt this bad.

From what the medtechs reported, Rhonda was in critical condition, and the only thing keeping her alive now were the machines. Monitors and IV feeds built into the field medical cylinder provided constant readings and adjusted feedback as needed. She might be like this for days or even weeks—maybe forever. The damage from the neurofeedback had been considerable. Two of the leads in her neurohelmet had melted from the surge, burning her skin. Unable to take her eyes off her mother's fallen form, Tasha was shocked to think that here was one of the finest mercenaries in the Inner Sphere . . . lying near death.

She didn't even notice that someone else had come up behind her until he laid a hand on her shoulder. Almost jumping out of her skin, she turned to see that it was Count Fisk, and felt her cheeks burn with anger and frustration.

"I came as soon as I could, Major," he said, speaking in a low and respectful voice that enraged Tasha with its hypocrisy. "I heard that she is in critical condition."

"Yes," Tasha said, tenderly stroking the side of the medical life support cylinder that held her mother.

"I find it hard to believe that Archer Christifori would pull such a stunt. Have your people verified who the attackers were?"

She closed her eyes momentarily. "Yes. We recovered the cockpit battleroms. Both of them showed that the attacking 'Mechs were members of the First Thorin Regiment."

Battleroms were heavily shielded recording chips in a 'Mech's computer system that recorded all sensor and movement data. Tasha had ordered them reviewed the minute the recovery teams were on-site. She didn't want to believe that Archer Christifori had tried to murder her mother, but the data didn't lie. She could hardly believe it, but the truth could not be denied: it was all a setup.

Thus far, she had expected only the Count and Captain Norris to be pleased about the sudden turn of events. She knew that Fisk was covering his satisfaction with fake sympathy, but somehow his words were comforting anyway. Norris had been more direct, more "Clanlike" in expressing himself. The loss of Shorty Sneede put him in command of Second Battalion—roughly half of the Irregulars.

The Count's long gray cape trailed behind him as he moved about the dome as if it were his own private fiefdom. "Christifori has been a thorn in the Archon's hide for a while now. However, this time he overplayed his hand. Don't you agree, Major?"

She said nothing for a moment. "This can't go unpunished," she said finally. "I'm going to bring my battalions to ready status. I've already begun formulating an assault that should break the spine of these so-called Avengers. When we're done with them, they'll think twice about ever tangling with Snord's Irregulars again." Tasha noticed that Fisk could barely conceal his delight at her words.

"The problem is that the colonel left me in charge thinking it was just for a few hours," she went on. "She never intended for me to command the entire unit in a major operation."

The Count shook his head. "Don't worry yourself with such thoughts," he said. "The colonel left you in charge—that's all you need to know. *I* think you're more than equipped for the job." He laid one hand on the life-support cylinder that held the unconscious Rhonda Snord. "I've ordered some doctors to attend her. She'll get the best care possible. You have my word."

Tasha's face hardened. "And you have my word, Count Fisk. Archer's Avengers will be scattered to the four winds by the time I'm done with them."

General Archer Kendrick Christifori stood with his arms at his sides, his fists clenched, his expression stony. His uniform was still stained with blood from the attack, and he had only allowed the medtechs to stitch the larger of the cuts on his chest and to bandage the small burns on his hands. His uniform shirt was in tatters from where they'd had to cut it away to get at the wounds. Archer didn't care about that. He had looked worse in his time, but rarely had he felt this bad.

Rhonda Snord's treachery made her lower in his eyes than any enemy he'd ever met. He had battled on dozens of worlds in his military career, including a voyage all the way to Huntress to wipe out Clan

Smoke Jaguar. His enemies had always fought with ferocity, but also with honor. That was something he understood. But this . . . assassination had hit him hard.

The death of his sister had brought him out of retirement and back into uniform to fight against Katherine Steiner-Davion. Those wounds had yet to heal, but somehow this was different. The attack that had killed Darius Hopkins had been intended to take Archer's life as well. If he hadn't stopped to take a leak, he'd probably be drugged and unconscious just like Gramash right now—if not dead like Darius.

Katya entered the tight confines of the command post and stopped, keeping her distance. Always able to read him so well, she apparently sensed that he needed space right now.

"What's the status of our patrols?" he asked her.

"We've had some reports of shots traded with the Irregulars," she said. "Pickets and patrols on both sides have sniped back and forth. Those from our side have been reprimanded. Oddly enough, the Irregulars haven't pressed an all-out assault. I thought they would hit us hard, counting on the fact that you were incapacitated."

"The word is 'dead,' Katya," Archer returned in a dour voice. "Incapacitated is what Sergeant Gramash is. Rhonda Snord wanted me eliminated. She had no way of knowing I wouldn't be in that car." He felt like an exposed nerve.

"Pull up a map of everything between our current position and those ruins where the Irregulars are based," he said.

Katya activated the portable holographic display, and a three-dimensional image of the terrain flickered into existence. In the opposite corner of the display were the ruins of the old city of Bealton. It was flanked on two sides by a wide river probably too deep for a BattleMech to navigate. As Katya's fingers danced over the controls of the display, small blue lights showing where his forces were deployed came to life. The lights ringed Hills 103 and 107 and high-lighted a patrol between here and the city.

He studied the map for a few moments. "We have only an incomplete picture of the disbursement and supply conditions of the Irregulars," he said, and Katya nodded confirmation. "Did Gramash activate his network of contacts here on Odessa? Maybe that would get us more intel on the Irregulars' situation—maybe identify a possible weak spot?"

Katya looked frustrated. "If he did, he didn't tell me how to contact any of them or even who they are."

"Damn!" Archer slapped the table so hard that the holographic map actually flickered off and then on again. "And now he's in a medically induced coma with all of the contact codes locked in his skull?"

"Yes, sir," Katya said, unblinking.

Archer told himself to calm down. Now was not the time to make rash decisions, not when he was in the grip of emotion and not thinking clearly. He had learned that much by now—when he was angry, he made mistakes. "They probably think we're going to overreact and rush out to engage them. We outnum-ber them. Fighting on ground of their choosing might be just what Snord is hoping for."

"Orders, sir?"

"We're going to have to think this whole thing through carefully. I've been ambushed once already. I have no intentions of going through that again."

"Perhaps we should contact Colonel Snord," Katya said. "Maybe we could talk to them, try to find why they did this."

"You can contact her, all right. Send a message to her base. I want a full report of what happened here sent to the Mercenary Review and Bonding Commission. You can tell her that much. Let her know that her little betrayal is going to cripple her unit's status in the Inner Sphere. But other than that, say nothing. She may think I'm dead, and that suits me fine—maybe we can use it to throw her off balance when the time is right."

Katy Chaffee stood in front of the holographic projector, with Alice Getts and John Kraff on either side of her. The reduced image of Major Tasha Snord flickered in front of them.

"Major, as I originally requested, please put through your commanding officer," Katya said.

"As if you are unaware of her current condition, Major Chaffee," spat back the younger Snord. Katya was impressed that Tasha knew her on sight, a sign of some intel-gathering on her part as well. Of course, people didn't become hot-shot mercs like the Irregulars by being sloppy. Yet, that only made her wonder all the more why they would carry out an ambush for no apparent reason. There were some puzzle pieces that simply didn't add up . . . yet.

"Well, then, let me advise you of the reason for this communication. General Christifori wanted you to know that we've sent a message to the MRBC regarding your actions."

Snord's eyes narrowed venomously. "After what you've done, I'm not surprised that you'd spread such a lie," she said. "Fine. Let the lies come. Lie all you want. Everyone will know the truth soon enough. I, too, have sent a message—this one to Prince Victor to let him know about your commander's treacherous actions. So, if you want to jerk my chain, Major, I'm more than happy to jerk yours as well. At least we have the truth and some measure of honor on our side."

"What are you talking about?" snapped Kraff.

"You know very well what I'm talking about," Tasha retorted. "If I were you, Major Chaffee, I'd be asking myself if I was really prepared to deal with the repercussions. Trust me. The Irregulars take an assassination attempt on their CO personally—*very* personally."

"What are you talking about, Major?" Katya said, totally bewildered.

"Don't insult my intelligence," Snord said. "I'll see you all pay for what you've done." Snord's small image reached out to her transmission control and then flickered out of existence.

Getts looked over at Katya. "What was all that about?"

Katya shook her head slowly. "I don't know, but I intend to find out."

11

Hill 103, First Thorin Regiment Command Post
Odessa
District of Donegal
Lyran Alliance
18 April 3063

Rain pattered against the portable command dome, but Archer barely noticed. The skies had been gray and rainy all day. Besides, he didn't give a damn about the weather, anymore than he worried that his nose was running because of the increased humidity and the slight drop in temperature. At Katya's prodding, he had at least changed clothes, shedding his blood-soaked and torn gear for clean fatigues.

The only thing he cared about right now was getting back at the Irregulars, and making them pay dearly for what they had done.

He had called his commanders in to discuss the plan he'd come up with. The consensus was that the Irregulars had, for whatever reason, decided to take Katherine's side in the civil war—despite the famous clause in their contracts. Perhaps they believed that the deaths of Archer Christifori and Darius Hopkins would so demoralize the Avengers that they would lash out wildly and become vulnerable to further ambushes. Believing Archer dead, the Irregulars may have thought the First Thorin Regiment would crumble and might even sue for peace.

Fat damn chance.

A couple of things had gone wrong. One: he'd survived the ambush. Two: the regiment hadn't gone out recklessly seeking revenge. Putting aside his grief and rage, Archer had pulled them back rather than rushing to attack. He would go after the Irregulars, all right, but it would be in a controlled sweep aimed at inflicting maximum damage rather than in a mad rush for revenge.

It had not been an easy decision. Archer's orders from Prince Victor had been to keep the Irregulars from becoming a fighting force for the Archon-Princess. In a manner of speaking, he could still do that, but not in the way he'd first planned. Now that the Irregulars had chosen sides, he would take them out of the fight by destroying them completely.

Archer continued to study the holographic battle, thinking through the three-pronged battle plan he'd devised. The primary assault would be led by Hawkeye Hogan, who would lead a battalion of 'Mechs against the mercenary base in the old Bealton ruins. While Hogan moved in carefully, Alice Getts and the armor and infantry of First Battalion would anchor themselves on Hills 103 and 107. They were best-suited for defensive actions in case Snord pressed her attack. Hogan's unit was the key, however. By sending out such a large contingent Archer would force the Irregulars to throw almost everything they had against it.

He turned to young John Kraff, whose unit would also have a key role to play. Archer would hold Kraff's company of Rangers in reserve, ready to react if the Irregulars resorted to a sweeping flanking maneuver or another similar tactic for which they were known.

"I'm going to shift you out to the southwest, along our left flank," he told the young captain. "You'll move forward, but you'll be virtually isolated from us." He pointed to the map, and a series of lights appeared to show what would be the Muphrid Rangers position, far off to the left near the Gavin Highway.

"Don't get me wrong, sir," Kraff said, "but if they show up with any force larger than us, we'll be awfully far from any support."

He was right, of course. The Rangers could be wiped out before Archer could scramble even a lance of support. He wished Thomas Sherwood's company were here to augment Kraff's unit. The Sherwood Foresters were better suited for this kind of special operation, but they were still en route from Alcor.

"I'm counting on the fact that our main-body assault will tie up the bulk of the Irregulars," Archer said. "If you do encounter the enemy in force, you'll do whatever you can to pin them down until I can divert troops there."

"And if I don't encounter the enemy in force, sir?"

Archer activated the controls on the display, and the icons of the Rangers began to move along the highway toward the capital of Bealton. "You'll be traveling parallel to the main body of our assault. If we rout the Irregulars, you'll sweep in to cut them off from Bealton. If they employ a controlled fallback, then you'll be hitting Bealton about the time they try to swing in and use it as a defensive base."

Kraff leaned over the map. "What can you tell me about that road, sir?"

"We know from our fly-overs that it's paved, four lanes, and should be a fast route. It dead-ends near Bealton, however, and what you get from that point on is roadway that hasn't been maintained for centuries."

"Why the left flank, sir? Will someone else be covering the right?"

Archer gestured toward the display. "The terrain on that side consists of swamps and bogs that the locals say are impassable at this time of year. So, with the river behind the Irregulars, they really have only two ways to come at us. One is along your route; the other is straight on. Either way, we'll be ready for them."

"The Rangers won't let you down, General," Kraff said, snapping a fast salute.

Archer saluted back. "I know you'll do your best, Captain—that's why I'm giving you the assignment. It's an important one. Now, go and get your people ready."

Kraff saluted again, then turned and left the command dome.

Archer stood looking at the map for a few moments longer, contemplating the tiny points of light that represented the lives of his troops. His shoulders sagged, and he let out a long sigh. He was sending good men and women into another battle, and some would not be returning. He'd been a soldier long enough to know that was simply the nature of war. But was it worth it? Was the cause enough to justify the price some would have to pay?

Archer rubbed his eyes and felt a wave of weariness wash over him. It had been a while since he'd slept, and it would be even longer before he allowed himself the luxury. Right now, he had to be a leader, not a man who'd lost a good friend. He had to let his troops see him so that they could draw strength and courage from their commander. There would be plenty of time later for sleep.

He opened his eyes again and saw Katya Chaffee standing in the doorway. She walked in, holding a mug of coffee in one hand. "I thought you might be able to use this."

He reached out and accepted the steaming cup in both his hands, breathing in deep the inviting scent. "Thanks, Katya," he said, then took a grateful sip of the hot drink.

"How are you holding up?" she asked, her eyes full of concern.

"I'll be fine," he said, a non-answer.

"We recovered Darius's remains after we picked you and Gramash up," she said. "I checked his records and found no mention of family."

"No. He had none. His sister was all he had left, and she died a few years back."

"Should we hold a service for him?"

Archer considered for a moment. "We should do something. He liked bagpipe music. Maybe we could find a piper when this is all over."

Katya took a deep breath, looking like she had something to say but wasn't sure whether it was a good idea. "I hate to bring this up," she blurted finally, "but there is the matter of Darius's command. He had two platoons of infantry under him. We need to appoint someone to lead them."

"How are they doing?"

"They're pretty broken up about it. If it's possible, he was almost as close to them as he was to you. He trained them when they were just militia and has led them ever since."

Archer looked away for a moment, hiding his pain. "Who do you think should take his place?"

"Alice Getts says that Adrian Glyndon is the most logical candidate. She had some field experience during the Clan wars, and she's tough as an artillery round."

"She's a sergeant now, right?"

Katya nodded.

"Well, effective immediately she's promoted to the rank of sergeant major. Draw up the necessary paperwork, will you, Katya?"

"Very good, sir," she said.

"Any word on Gramash?"

Katya frowned slightly. "The doctors say they have to keep him out until they can be sure his spinal damage is on the mend."

Archer finished off the last of his coffee and set the cup down on the edge of the display table. "I hate going into this kind of operation blind," he said. "And I hate having to kill good MechWarriors." His voice rose angrily as if it had drawn energy from the caffeine he'd just consumed. "Mostly, though, I hate having somebody trick me."

"Archer," she said soothingly, coming over to his side. "There's something odd about all this. When I contacted Tasha Snord to let her know we were reporting their actions to the Mercenary Review and Bonding Commission, she implied that *we* were in the wrong somehow. She talked as if we had attacked *them*. And why should Tasha Snord have taken the call instead of the colonel? Damn peculiar."

Archer shrugged. "It's the typical merc reaction, don't you think? Trying to paint us as the bad guys."

"I'm not as informed on the Irregulars as Gramash is, but I do know that none of this is their style. Rhonda Snord is known to be unpredictable, but she's never been accused of being dishonorable. Ambushing you like a cowardly assassin doesn't fit her modus operandi at all."

Archer felt mildly irritated by her words. "Katya, I was there. I saw the BattleMechs. And you saw the battlerom we pulled from the Rotunda. Those were Irregular 'Mechs that took us out."

Katya laid one hand lightly on his shoulder. "I know

what we saw—what you saw. But my job is intelligence. I'm just telling you, as an officer and as a good friend, that what we saw may *not* be what we think it is. Right now, all I've got is a gut feeling, but that's real too."

Archer looked at her for a moment. Katya had helped him through the first terrible days after Andrea was killed. And she'd been one of a handful of people who'd helped pull the Avengers together. She and he were more than just friends, but he'd never tried to make it more for fear it was inappropriate behavior for a commander toward a subordinate. A part of him wanted to pull her close, to hold her, but this was obviously not the time or the place.

If anyone else had walked up and told him that she had a "gut feeling" about something as important as the ambush, he would have ignored it. But not Katya.

"So, what are you saying—that we should call off the attack?" he asked. "I trust you with my life, Katya, but I need some kind of hard evidence."

She nodded, obviously frustrated. "I know. I still don't have anything solid. Not yet at least."

"Damn," Archer scrubbed at his forehead as if that would wash away the weariness. "Katya, you're more to me than an officer in this unit. You know that, even if I've never said it out loud before. But without solid proof, I can't . . ."

"I understand," she said, dropping her eyes.

Archer cupped her chin in one hand and lifted her face toward him. "No, you don't. I'm going to ask a lot of you now. With Gramash down, we're blind. You're going to have to set up your own intel net here on Odessa. Find me that evidence, and you have my word I'll put an end to the fighting." Then he released her.

She gave him a quick salute. "I won't let you down."

"I never thought you would," he said, saluting in return. He smiled suddenly, a weary smile but the first he'd shown since the ambush on Moseby Road.

"For now, I think we'd better get a move on, Major. We both have a lot of work ahead of us."

=== 12 ===

South of Bealton, Odessa
District of Donegal
Lyran Alliance
18 April 3063

"**S**ensors show at least two companies, possibly three, moving on our position, Major," Norris reported from the cockpit of his *Masakari*. No, he reminded himself, not a *Masakari*—his 'Mech was a *Warhawk*. A smile stole over his lips at the thought of facing the Avengers in battle at last.

"Copy," said Tasha Snord. "It looks like our plan is working—we've pulled them out for a fight. Captain H'Chu, hold the line in your current position. Norris, wait for my word to engage your element."

"I hear you, Major," Deb H'Chu said in her gravelly voice over the command frequency.

Norris settled back in his seat and tightened the restraints around his cooling vest. He swept the controls with a glance, deciding he was satisfied with what the long-range sensors were telling him. Archer's Avengers were closing.

But it was so un-Clanlike. He shook his head. It was hard enough understanding the other members of his own unit, let alone Inner Sphere trash-warriors like this First Thorin Regiment. As a Jade Falcon, Norris had fought Snord's Irregulars in the Dark Nebula, where he had been captured and taken *isorla*. Rhonda Snord, true to her Clan origins, had allowed him to eventually earn his way back into the ranks of the warrior caste. Now, the death of Shorty Sneede gave something he'd desired for a long time—command of a full battalion of the Irregulars. Yet, it was all coming to him without a Trial of Position. He would never grow used to the strangeness of these Inner Sphere folk. . . .

Even inside the insulated cockpit of his *Warhawk*, he could hear a rumble in the distance. The uninitiated might have mistaken it for the arrival of a spring thunderstorm, but Norris knew it was not nature, but the thunder of war. He wrapped his hands around the joystick and throttle control for his Clan war machine. Captain H'Chu was engaging the enemy. Good. Soon Norris would have retribution for the dishonorable attack against Colonel Snord.

His sensors told him that the vanguard of the First Thorin Regiment was now starting to hit the wall of BattleMechs under Major Snord and Captain H'Chu. He watched the long-range sensor sweep and almost laughed aloud with pleasure. Combat was what he lived for, what he had been genetically bred and trained to do from the moment he had emerged from his iron womb.

"Awaiting your command, Major Snord," he said with a hint of impatience.

"Stand by," she replied.

Nearly half a minute passed. Norris stared at the long-range sensors, which showed that the Avengers were fielding a full battalion of 'Mechs, outnumbering the Irregulars that stood in their path. Despite that, Major Snord was holding them at bay. She was adequate enough, he thought—for a freebirth.

Suddenly his earpiece activated. "Scavenger One,

you are clear for your penetration," he heard Tasha Snord say. "Good luck."

"Luck has nothing to do with what I will do to them," he said in a low voice. He switched to his unit frequency. "Scavengers, form up on me. You know the plan. Let us teach these scum the price of betraying honor."

Then he throttled his *Warhawk* into a full run straight into the heart of the fray.

Captain Harry "Hawkeye" Hogan slowed his *Battle Hawk* to a walking pace as he turned perpendicular to the approaching wave of Irregular 'Mechs. The *Hawk* was lightweight, but in his hands the small BattleMech fought in ways its engineers had only dreamed of. He pivoted the 'Mech's torso and activated his anti-missile system as a salvo of six short-range missiles began to bear in on him. A relentless stream of shells spewed out from his 'Mech's head, eating up all but one of the missiles. The last errant projectile hit his right leg, but did little more than scar its dull green paint.

"Specter Ten to Assault Force Alpha," he said into his neurohelmet mike. "Command Company, take the right flank. My company, hold the center. Charlie Company, take the far left flank." As he spoke, a sleek gray *Excalibur* stepped out from a clump of trees it had been using for cover and started to bear down on him.

"Not this time, big boy," he said, triggering his jump jets. The *Battle Hawk*'s cockpit suddenly felt like a hot summer day on a sunny beach as the *Hawk* rose from the grassy hillside in a roar of plasma flame. He angled it to the right, making himself a much harder target for the larger 'Mech. Then he landed hard, the knees of the *Battle Hawk* seeming to moan under the strain. As he hit the ground, he saw the sod near his right foot peel back as an enemy gauss rifle slug dug deep into the ground.

"Crudstunk!" he cursed, pivoting at the torso to fire. He yanked the joystick until the targeting reticle drifted onto the center of the massive *Excalibur*, then triggered the primary firing stud. The air came alive with emerald pulse-laser bursts, which danced over the torso of the *Excalibur*, searing off armor plating as if the machine were being flayed alive. Another of his 'Mechs, a much heavier *War Dog* piloted by Captain Damon Huntt, fired its gauss rifle, hitting the *Excalibur* in the left leg.

The 'Mech seemed to sag slightly under the impact as its pilot fought to maintain balance. Then he turned and fired his own gauss rifle at the larger *War Dog*, the shot smashing squarely into the *Dog*'s chest, tipping it backward as armor plating ripped and shredded.

Hogan fired his tiny Streak SRMs at the *Excalibur*, and this time both warheads plowed into the enemy's left arm. Gray smoke hung over the *Excalibur* as it continued to fire at Damon Huntt's *War Dog*.

Suddenly, off to his right, Hogan saw at least two lances—no, make that three—of enemy 'Mechs race past him at a full run. He was stunned to see them, not just because of their speed, but because they weren't stopping to help their comrades. Instead, they were racing straight through the middle of the firefight and heading toward Hill 103.

Hogan understood immediately what was happening, and that there was nothing he could do to stop them—not while he had this *Excalibur* to deal with. He switched to the local battlefield command channel. "Specter Ten to Charlie Five. Grab your lance and break off on a heading of one-one-two. Pursue those Irregulars that just ran past us. They're heading for our rear."

He then switched to the regiment's command channel. "Specter Ten to Specter One, priority code blue."

"You're on discreet, Hawkeye. This is Christifori, go," the general replied.

"Trouble heading your way, sir. A full company of BattleMechs, all weight classes. A strike force of Irregulars has punched through our lines and are bearing down on you as we speak."

Again, he targeted his pulse lasers and fired, two of the shots missing as the *Excalibur* pilot began to move away and focus on Huntt's *War Dog*. His one good shot dotted the 'Mech's side, leaving a series of damaged armor plates and smoking holes in its wake.

"Thanks for the heads up, Specter Ten. Hold his friends in place, and we'll keep you posted."

Archer headed for the doorway of the portable command bubble, tightening the harness of his cooling vest as he went. He'd held back his command lance for use as floating reinforcements where needed. Now, he was going to get a chance to fight again. In a way, he longed to be back in the cockpit. There, he was master of his domain, in control of and responsible for his own actions. Everything had seemed to get so much more complicated now that he was a general. . . .

Katya hurried up behind him. "Those 'Mechs are heading in this direction like a bat out of hell," she said.

He began to walk toward his *Penetrator*, which stood waiting nearby. "You think they're heading for the DropShips?"

"Not with just one company," she said, keeping up with him as they reached his 'Mech.

He reached out for the first of the handholds he would use to climb up to the *Penetrator*'s cockpit. "They're on their way here, aren't they?" he said, his eyes fixed on his temporary command post sitting on a ledge of Hill 103.

"Best guess," she confirmed.

"Send word for Getts to put some armor in place. Have her artillery get ranged for the approaches to our command post. I'll take the regimental command lance out and see if we can slow them down."

He looked at her hard and long. "And you take care of yourself, you hear?" He had already lost one person close to him in this operation; he did not want to lose another.

"You too, General," she said, giving him a quick salute before turning to lope back to the ferroplast command dome.

Within minutes, Archer was settled into his cockpit, with the hatch sealed behind him. He slid his neuro-helmet on and plugged it in, then his fingers flew over the preheat sequence.

"Enter security code phrase," the battlecomputer's disembodied voice demanded.

"It is history that teaches us to hope," he said firmly, letting himself be inspired by the words of Robert E. Lee. Now *there* was a general, he thought.

"Startup sequence authorized," the voice confirmed. Archer took the joystick, switched to his right-arm controls, and moved the laser arm of the *Penetrator* in a specific gesture.

"Identity confirmed," the voice said. Immediately, a throbbing began in the machine under him, and the lights on his command console flickered to life. Every BattleMech was equipped with a security system to prevent an enemy from stealing it. Some of these operated on simple voice commands; others required a sophisticated sequence of movements. Archer employed both, even though the latter was considered somewhat obsolete.

He checked his long-range sensors and could find

no enemy activity, but he did see Alice Getts's armored tanks lurching into action. He double-checked his cockpit controls and confirmed that the *Penetrator* was more than ready for a battle.

"Specter One to the Brain," he said into his neurohelmet mike.

"That rogue Irregular company is bearing in from the north," Katya said. "They're five klicks out and closing rapidly. The bulk of the Irregulars are still hitting our vanguard. Both sides are taking losses. Charlie's people who were in pursuit have turned back to hold the front."

He noted her tone, especially at the mention of losses. Things weren't quite going as planned, a tendency that was becoming typical of the unit's operations on Odessa. "Contact Getts. See if she can scramble two of her lances to assist Hawkeye."

"Yes, sir," Katya said. "You got that incoming company covered?"

"Roger that. I'll take care of them," he said, switching channels. "Command lance, this is Specter One. Form up on me and prepare to engage."

Norris could see the hill looming in the distance. It wasn't steep, but it was large. Off to one side was a smaller hill. Both were stony, covered with sparse grass and the occasional clump of trees and scrub brush fighting to stayed rooted in the rocky soil. On those hills was the command post of the First Thorin Regiment—his target.

The plan Tasha Snord had come up with was typically Inner Sphere but still offered some degree of honor. While Archer's Avengers were tied down in battle, Norris would punch a fast company through their lines to hit their command and control center.

This was not revenge, he told himself. Neg, this was

retribution. He considered the distinction small but important.

"Norris to Striker Lance," he said, coming up on a small rise that gave him an even better view of the rocky hill. "Target in sight. Remember our orders. We hit the command and communications post and then pull back as quickly as possible."

He switched off and started his *Warhawk*'s run toward the base of the hill. To one side, he saw Sergeant Balston's lance form up. One of its 'Mechs, an older-model *Mongoose*, was hissing smoke from a heat sink damaged when they punched through the Avengers 'Mechs.

Just a little farther, and Christifori and his people would learn the true price of honor. His long-range sensors came alive with faint but possible targets.

"Artillery!" Archer barked as the company of Irregulars charged straight at him from the bottom of the hill. "Fire at will!"

Several salvos of Arrow missiles streaked over his head from behind, arcing down toward the valley as Alice Getts swung her ground armor into play. A fearsome Von Luckner stopped some one hundred meters to his left. It unleashed a wave of LRMs as the Arrow warheads exploded on the incoming Irregulars. Dust and smoke briefly obscured his vision.

Glancing at his short-range sensors, he saw what was happening. Formed up in a V-shape, the Irregulars were charging at his command post. They were not stopping to engage his forces, but were boring down on their objective with deadly determination.

Damnation! he cursed silently. With his joystick, he swept the possible targets and settled on a *Crab* near the center of the "V." He locked on with his extended-range lasers and fired.

The *Crab* reeled as Archer's refitted Clan weapons

struck its right side and arm. Globules of melted armor plating splashed into the air as the enemy MechWarrior fought to maintain control. The hillside was killing some of the enemy's speed now, and the Avenger ground armor had leapt into the fight with full fury.

This wasn't like fighting the local militia; these MechWarriors were skilled, and it showed. "Brain, this is Specter One," Archer said. "Evacuate the command post. I think we've got company coming." He knew that there were several dozen supporting technicians and logistics staff at risk in the post.

"Sir?"

"You heard me, Major," he said as the *Crab* attempted to return his fire. One of its large lasers missed cleanly, but the other one hit his left leg, exploding several armor plates as it sliced a nasty gash up and across the thigh of his *Penetrator*.

He prepared to fire his medium pulse lasers but never got the chance. The nearby Von Luckner let go with its primary weapon, a deadly autocannon. The stream of shells ripped into the *Crab*'s already damaged right torso, devouring the remaining armor and punching deep inside. The *Crab* seemed to shudder, and stopped dead. As it began to fall, its MechWarrior managed to squeeze off a last shot from one of his large lasers at the Von Luckner. The bright red lance of light struck the tank's frontal armor, leaving a nasty smoking trail. As the *Crab* dropped, a *Masakari* bounded over it, lumbering up the hillside.

Archer recognized the *Masakari* immediately as a Clan 'Mech the Clanners knew as a *Warhawk*. The sight of the Clan war machine sent a chill down his spine. After the devastation he'd seen on Huntress, it was an enemy he'd hoped never to have to face again. He'd known that the Irregulars had several former Jade Falcon MechWarriors in their ranks, but for some reason hadn't expected to face such a deadly instrument of war.

A ripple of white-blue flashes of energy ran down the hillside from another Avenger 'Mech. Archer thought at first that the PPC fire was aimed at the approaching *Masakari* and was a miss. Then, he saw it strike the flank of an enemy *Stealth*, wrapping the smaller 'Mech in searing arcs of electrical discharge.

Meanwhile, the *Masakari* and several other 'Mechs were charging straight at Archer, and he locked on with his medium pulse lasers. The *Masakari* pilot apparently had the same idea. A wave of red energy from its large pulse lasers erupted in the air between them, and the *Penetrator*'s torso was pummeled before Archer could fire. While another wave of Arrow missiles rained down on the advancing Irregulars, Archer's *Penetrator* sagged under the deadly barrage of laserfire. He took a step back in an effort to keep his balance as one of the extended-range PPCs lanced out at him, narrowly missing his left side.

His sensors told him that a lance of the Irregulars had already been downed, and the *Crab* had gotten back on its feet and was attempting to withdraw. The remaining eight BattleMechs, however, continued to press forward. He had to fight his joystick, but he finally managed to drop his targeting reticle on the *Masakari* as it continued to close on him. He heard the tone of weapons lock in his ears, and he let go with three of his medium pulse lasers without waiting for confirmation. Two found their mark in the 'Mech's legs. The temperature rose slightly in his cockpit as Archer fought to keep weapons lock. It was about to get a lot hotter. He triggered the third target interlock, letting go with his other three medium pulse lasers.

The heat in his cockpit rose again as if he'd just opened a giant oven door. He fired his pulse lasers again, and they stitched another line of holes in the

ferro-fibrous armor of the *Masakari*'s right arm and
legs. Its movements seemed sluggish, as if it were
straining against the damage he had unleashed.

But the 'Mech didn't stop.

Instead, it brought both of its ER PPCs into play
against Archer. One hit him in the right torso; the
other stabbed into his chest. The *Penetrator* was designed to handle this kind of punishment, but not to
take that much damage in one burst. As it stumbled
back and to the right, he tried to compensate for the
impact and the sudden loss of tons of armor plating.
It was impossible to do both at the same time, and
the *Penetrator* fell backward, grinding into the rocky
ground.

Archer fought to keep his eyes open and to remain conscious.

As Norris's *Warhawk* and two other BattleMechs
paused near the fallen *Penetrator*, he finally spotted
the portable field command and communications center.

"Target in sight," he called. "Fire!" He let go with
his large lasers, shrugging off the wave of heat that
rose in his cockpit.

The *Jackal* and the *Spartan* with him fired as well.
Missiles, PPCs, and laser bursts slashed into the
Avengers' command and control center, sending the
portable domes up in smoke. Fires erupted in the
chaos of the target zone, and several sympathetic explosions also cooked off. A light breeze came up,
clearing the smoke, and Norris saw not a sign of movement in the debris field.

"Mission completed. Withdraw at flank speed," he
commanded. Between him and the blackened hole
that had been the C&C center was the downed *Penetrator*, struggling to rise to its feet.

So, the *Penetrator* pilot still wanted to fight. Norris
almost chuckled as the 'Mech rolled onto its side and

managed to get a foot and a knee planted. This was the kind of foe he admired, one who did not shirk from a fight. It was tempting to stand here and slug it out, but he had learned a few things since becoming part of Snord's Irregulars. He had learned the importance of knowing when to trust honor and when to trust orders.

He leveled one of his PPCs at the semistanding *Penetrator* and made sure it was charged. Then he unleashed a devastating barrage of charged particles. Even at this range, the charged particles seemed to explode on contact with the armor. The *Penetrator* heaved over, its arm taking most of the damage. Norris could see the enemy pilot fighting the pull of gravity, but then the huge machine simply toppled down onto the ground of Hill 103 once more.

Norris turned and started down the hillside, activating an open channel so the fallen MechWarrior could hear him.

"You fight well, freebirth," he said. "But you battle Snord's Irregulars. We are superior. You are fodder."

"Oh, really?" Archer muttered, his second attempt to rise finally succeeding. He glanced at the smoking remains of the command post and winced at the thought that he might have lost some of his key personnel—perhaps even Katya.

"Brain, this is Specter One," he called to her. "Report."

There was a painfully long pause before Katya Chaffee's voice came over the line. "We're here and alive," she said, her commline crackling with static. "Two wounded, but the rest of us got clear with most of the gear. No central coordination for a while, though."

"No problem. I'll run the war from my cockpit," Archer said.

His long-range sensors painted a story that was not all bad, despite the loss of his command post. The Irregulars' strike at the heart of his unit had cost them almost an entire company of BattleMechs. Four were still attempting to break away, and two of those were probably doomed. He was bitterly angry that the *Masakari* was one of those likely to escape. Archer didn't like to lose.

His own losses were slightly less: nine 'Mechs. But this was not just about hardware or lives. This was about victory. After the *Masakari* pilot's parting shot over the commline, Archer's thirst for revenge was even greater than before, if that were possible.

The time had come for some tricks of his own.

He switched to the Muphrid Rangers command channel. "Specter One to Ranger One," he said.

"Ranger One here, General," John Kraff replied.

"Execute your primary plan," Archer said.

"Bloody damn straight, General."

Archer could not help but chuckle. "A simple 'yes, sir' would suffice, Captain."

"In twenty minutes, General, you'll be saying it my way," Kraff returned.

Archer nodded to himself. If Kraff moved fast enough, he might very well be right.

13

Nicholas Francis Fisk nodded in acknowledgment as Erwin Vester entered his private antechamber. The room was stark white, with almost no decoration, but it was better suited than his audience room for a meeting with a Loki agent.

Count Fisk didn't care much about the man one way or the other. He was just an operative. The organization itself was powerful and ruthless, however, and only a fool wouldn't fear them. He didn't intend for anyone to know that, however.

He was a Count. Vester was a tool. The man was like a gun. Aimed properly, a gun would serve its purpose, but if mishandled, it could kill the person wielding it.

"I've been monitoring the communications channels," Vester said, "and it sounds like our plan is working."

"You mean *my* plan, don't you?" Fisk asked.

"*Our* plan, your Highness," Vester said, doing a poor job of feigning respect. "*Your* plan, my management."

Fisk smiled humorlessly. "So, the Irregulars and the Avengers are beating each other senseless."

"The battle continues, but it looks like Tasha Snord sent in a company of troops, and they smashed the Avengers' command and control capability. That may be enough to even the numerical odds between the two forces."

"Excellent," the Count said approvingly. "And what about the Wolverton's Highlanders?"

"I have their advance unit concealed in a facility some distance from here. Colonel Feehan was somewhat apprehensive about the mission, but he realizes that it's probably his only chance to redeem the unit's reputation." The Highlanders were a lightweight to medium BattleMech mercenary regiment that had also been assigned to Count Fisk's control. Vester had suggested using them to trigger the conflict between the Irregulars and the First Thorin Regiment, and had covertly smuggled their heaviest firepower onto Odessa.

"Keep them under wraps, Vester," Fisk ordered. "At least for now. We can ill-afford to have them spotted."

"I am well aware of that, Count," Vester replied curtly. "Colonel Blackstone, Feehan's new boss, is suspicious about our plans for the unit, but I've managed to feed him enough misinformation to keep him satisfied for the moment. I'm curious, though. What will your response be if the Irregulars lose their fight with Christifori?"

Fisk waved the question away as if it were trivial. In some respects, it was. He had carefully considered the game he was playing from all the angles.

"If the Irregulars lose, I could toss the Wolverton's Highlanders at Christifori's regiment," he said. "I've held them in reserve, waiting at a pirate point that would get them to Odessa in less than seventy-two hours. In that scenario, they would be on a mission to relieve the Irregulars, a daring last-minute rescue."

Vester nodded. "And with the Irregulars' contract about to expire, you'd think they would accept any terms rather than be left alone against a superior force."

The Count chuckled. "Either the Irregulars end up fighting for the Archon-Princess, or they end up destroyed. Either way, Victor won't get any use out of them. And, in the endgame, Archer's Avengers will be destroyed. From where I sit, my dear Loki-lackey, this is a win-win scenario for the Alliance and for me."

A pulse throbbed in Vester's temple at the use of the word "lackey." "You would be well advised, my lord, to be careful of downplaying Loki's role—or the extent of our influence."

"I was merely pointing out that you are a Loki operative," Fisk said, backpedaling slightly.

"Indeed," Vester said contemptuously. "This operative has killed over twenty people in his career. Including some who have claimed noble privilege."

"Is that a threat?" Fisk asked, rising slightly from his chair.

"No, simply a statement of fact." The two men glared at each other for an instant, and then Vester changed the subject again. "There is the matter of the local militia, my lord," he said. "Captain Malcolm has been waiting to meet with you for several hours."

Fisk shook his head pityingly. "Malcolm always did manage to overlook the obvious. He keeps wanting to know why the Irregulars didn't reinforce him and what actions I plan to take against them. Pity he never understood my thinking on this matter."

"Indeed, sir."

"Tell him he can begin rebuilding his unit with some replacement 'Mechs I have stored in a warehouse. Assure our dear captain that I understand his unit's great sacrifice in this struggle and that I will make up to him the damage done him by the Irregulars. Perhaps I shall give him a medal."

"Whatever you deem appropriate, Count," Vester said dismissively. "That is your issue to deal with, not mine."

Fisk was seriously annoyed by the spy's tone, but decided to overlook it for now. "Thank you, Mister Vester," he said loftily. "Now then—we have work to do."

Tasha Snord halted her *Spartan* and leveled its extended-range PPC at a nearby Avenger *Stalker*. The burst of energy created by the weapon spiked the heat in her cockpit, but it also left a huge blister of destruction on the *Stalker*'s olive green armor paint. The armless BattleMech reeled to one side under the assault, but then shook off the damage and pressed on.

Her long-range sensors were starting to paint a picture she did not relish. The two sides had sent the bulk of their forces barreling into each other, but apart from Norris's breakthrough, the Avengers and the Irregulars had been trading blows like tired boxers for the past hour. Attrition was beginning to take its toll on her troops. Though the Avengers had given up some ground, they were proving to be as tenacious as her own MechWarriors.

A pair of Streak SRMs came twisting through the air at her, and she was forced to engage her McArthur anti-missile system. A vibrating swarm of small anti-missile rounds splayed out at the incoming missiles, devouring them in midair. She checked her ammo levels, which showed that she had used up all but two ammo charges in the time since the battle started. Her own Streak SRMs were down to less than ten reloads.

A shorter, broader *Masakari* whose transponder painted it as a friendly BattleMech came up alongside

her. It was covered with scars and burn marks, and
slick green coolant spilled from one of the gashes in
its torso, which trailed wispy white smoke as the coolant hit boiling-hot armor. It was Captain Norris.

"Good to have you back, Norris," she said as he
unleashed his PPCs at the *Stalker*. He missed the
'Mech's right leg as it continued to blast an Irregular
Nightsky. The *Nightsky* quaked under the wave of missile and laser fire, shedding armor with each violent
vibration. Its pilot finally activated his jump jets and
fled from the much larger *Stalker*.

"Thank you, Major," Norris said as both he and
Tasha fired at other targets. "But the Avengers should
be falling back now that they've lost their command
post."

"Well, they're not," she said, firing at a *Hussar* that
darted past her. Three of her short-range missiles
found their mark on the lightning-fast BattleMech.

"Perhaps you are not pressing them hard enough,"
Norris prodded, firing his PPCs again. By now, ripples
of heat were rising off his armor plating, telling Tasha
just how hot he was running.

"Our people are pushing damn hard, Norris. Perhaps the damage you did to the Avenger base was
not sufficient," she snapped. Norris was implying that
somehow she and the other Irregulars were letting
him down.

"Perhaps we should pull back to Hill 403. We could
regroup there, then carry out a thrust at these Avengers that would rout them once and for all," he said.

Tasha pulled up the tactical map display and
scanned it quickly as she let her *Spartan* bleed off the
excess heat her firing had built up. For Norris, a former Clanner, to consider tactical withdrawal as an option made her decide that she didn't *completely* dislike
him after all. Their past arguments were the stuff of
regimental legend, but now he was proving his worth.

Hill 403 was several kilometers back toward old Bealton. Like most of the hills in the region, it was a mostly barren piece of rock, but it just might be enough to stem the Avengers' push.

"Good call," she said, switching to the unit's broadband channel. "Irregulars, we're pulling back in an orderly fashion to Hill 403. First Battalion, hold the left and center. Second Battalion, you have the right flank. I want a slow fallback with cover fire."

Her words set off a ripple of confirmations and cheers on the comm channel.

"They're falling back, General," Archer heard an excited voice say over the commline as he let go with another blast from his extended-range large lasers, missing an enemy *Thug* by mere meters.

"I can see that, Corporal Williams," he said calmly as his 'Mech vented off the heat it had built up.

"Looks like we have them on the run," Damon Huntt added as he brought his *War Dog* up. He fired his gauss rifle, which found its mark on the *Thug* that Archer had missed. The hypersonic slug buried itself in the mashed armor plating on the *Thug*'s left shin. Not deterred, the Irregular 'Mech fired its pair of PPCs at an Avenger SRM carrier, sending armor spraying in every direction.

"I'm not counting them out of the game yet," Archer said. He saw an Irregular *Hussar* break off from the battle and retreat to the rear at a full run. Smoke billowed from a hole in its torso, leaving a misty streamer in its wake.

"Specter One to the Brain," he said, hoping that Katya was all right.

"Brain is on-line again, sir," she answered. Apparently, she had used the past half-hour to get a makeshift command post operational.

"It looks like the Irregulars are dropping back. Any

feed on where they're going? Are they in a full rout, or are they just regrouping?"

"I got a feed from Saber Lance," she said, referring to the lance of aerospace fighters the Avengers had in play over the battlefield. "This is more for show. It looks like Colonel Snord has her people dropping back to Hill 403."

"Any word from the Rangers?" Archer asked with a hint of concern. He had issued the command for Kraff's company to sweep into the fight several long minutes ago. They should have hit the flank of the Irregulars by now, but all he'd gotten from them so far was silence. It was enough to worry him.

"Your orders, sir—SOP. He's not to communicate until he engages," she reminded him.

Archer winced slightly. It *had* been his idea for the communications blackout, a fact that had somehow slipped his mind in the press of battle. Did everything have to be a double-edged sword, he wondered?

"Alert me as soon as you get the engagement code from him," he said, moving his *Penetrator* forward several meters toward the *Thug*. He was counting on his Clan replacement lasers to give him the edge he needed.

Captain John Kraff angled his *Axman* to the east, and once again extended his long-range sensors to their maximum sweep. The plan had been for him to come down on the exposed flank of Snord's Irregulars and cut off their retreat. So much for the damn flapping plan, he thought. He was here, but where in bloody hell was the enemy?

"Is anybody getting anything on sensors?" he asked his company.

There was a slight pause before anyone replied. "I'm picking up something faint to the west, at the base of Hill 403," said Leftenant James "Jimbo" Traki, who was leading Stealth Lance.

Kraff signaled his company. "Jimbo says he's got a signal—I say it's better than sitting here with our thumbs jammed up our asses. Let's go check it out. And Jimbo?"

"Sir?"

"If it ain't the Irregulars, you're buying the first three rounds."

"Second the motion, sir," put in Corporal Mbenga.

Kraff swept his *Axman* to the west and throttled his pace up slightly. He checked his sensors and saw the targets, now painted clearly on his secondary display. Three J-27 Ordnance Transports, used to carry missiles and other weapons to the battlefield. He could also make out the signatures of some repair equipment.

He was starting to realize that he was coming up on a field repair facility where the Irregulars would fall back for emergency repairs and reloads. So far, there was no sign of any BattleMechs. Kraff knew that if First Battalion was doing its job, it was only a matter of time before enemy units arrived.

"All right, Jimbo, you're the one sporting the Guardian ECM. Kick that box on and jam their ability to signal the Irregulars. The rest of you, move along the goddamn flanks and cut them off from the hill. Hold your fire if you can. Let's see if we can convince them that machine guns are no match for a company of BattleMechs."

He saw Traki's *Scarabus* jog to the front of the formation, and his secondary monitor showed a slight hiss of static, indicating that the Guardian electronic countermeasures were working. Kraff broke into a full run toward the source of the signals. In mere seconds, he saw the small base nestled on the far side of Hill 403.

He activated his comm system. "Irregular Base, this is Captain Kraff of the Muphrid Rangers. Surrender now, or we'll turn those transports of yours into some nasty craters—and you along with them."

There was a long silence. All along the shallow green hillside, he saw his company sweep in to surround the repair base. A hiss filled his ears, followed by a downhearted voice. "This is Corporal Fletcher. You got us. Hold your fire."

Kraff didn't miss a beat, switching channels to his company. "Pull your shots, boys and girls. Looks like we caught them with their pants down. Kristofer, you take that *Fireball* of yours and lead those transports out of there. Take them back the way we came."

"Yes, sir," Kristofer replied.

Traki came back on the line. "Problems, sir?"

"Let's just say that if this is their fallback point, we could be hip-deep in bad any minute." Kraff paused and adjusted his long-range sensors. Still no sign of the Irregular 'Mechs. He rubbed his chin inside his battered neurohelmet and stared at the screen as if it were lying to him. "Jimbo, keep that Guardian online. It's too damn quiet."

Then the voice of Sergeant Muller sounded in his earpiece. "Ranger Four here, sir. I'm picking up some faint signals on the far side of the hill. Numerous fusion-reactor signatures. They seem to be moving this way."

"All right, boys and girls. Time to earn our pay. Rangers, start up that hill. We'll form up on the crest and see what we can see."

Kraff started his *Axman* up the long slope and heard the BattleMech creak under the stress of keeping up with his throttle setting. He put his large autocannon on the first target interlock circuit. On number two, he rigged the large pulse laser mounted on the *Axman*'s left arm. The trio of medium pulse lasers went to the third TIC. His sensors started to show shadowy images on the far side of the rocky hill. Whoever they were, they were closing fast.

His *Axman* and the rest of the Muphrid Rangers reached the top of the hill and looked down the other side. For a moment, his mouth dropped open. Running up the hill, charging straight at his 'Mechs, was the bulk of the Irregulars. They were turning and firing behind them at the advancing forces of the First Thorin Regiment, which were just emerging from a line of scrub brush and trees at the base of the hill.

For the longest moment of his life, Snord's Irregulars didn't see him.

Then that moment came to an end.

The six short-range missiles that homed in on his *Axman* blasted armor from the 'Mech's chest and legs. The impact jostled him against his restraints and jolted Kraff back into reality.

"Rangers!" he yelled into his mike, sweeping his targeting reticle down Hill 403 at an Irregular *Bombardier*. "Have at them!" And as he locked on to the advancing 'Mech, he and the rest of his company charged down Hill 403 directly into the path of the retreating mercenaries.

Major Tasha Snord stopped at the sight of the charging line of 'Mechs rushing down from her rear.

"Damn it all to hell!" she cursed, and then opened a comm channel. "Irregulars, we have enemies on Hill 403—one company." She surveyed the long-range sensors and saw that the only gaps in the First Thorin's lines were to the north and south of the hill, where the two attacking forces had not yet connected.

It was only one company, but it was apparently a fresh one. More important, it was likely that their small resupply and repair base had already been overrun. Damn, damn, damn! she thought. The odds were still somewhat even, but they had been fighting for a long time. Ammo supplies were running low, and they were still some distance from old Bealton—now the only place the Irregulars had to fall back to.

"How did they get back there?" Captain H'Chu asked.

"It doesn't matter," Tasha said. "Christifori outsmarted us. I don't plan on sticking around to see what other little surprises he has in store." She locked her *Spartan*'s ER PPC on an *Axman* and fired. The heat in her cockpit no longer mattered to her—she was already bathed in sweat. The shot found its mark, ripping armor off the left thigh of the running BattleMech. Tasha only wished she hadn't lost two of the medium pulse lasers in her 'Mech's right arm.

Her mother had taught her many things, one of them being that there was a time to fight and a time to cut your losses. "Irregulars, this is Snord," she said into her mike. "Cut to the south in a full run. Break off your engagements and retreat. Fall back to Bealton, flank speed."

"Neg," came the voice of Norris on discreet. "You cannot be serious. We have never fled the battlefield in this manner."

Tasha pivoted her *Spartan* and started to the south. "We're doing it now," she said, the words catching in her throat. "Christifori stabbed us in the back with that company. Staying and fighting would only get us dead. There'll be another time, Norris."

"Bah!" he spat back. Despite his protests, she saw his *Masakari* turn to the south as well, twisting its torso as it ran and firing off a series of shots to hold the First Thorin at bay. All around her, Snord's Irregulars formed up, lance by lance. Each provided cover fire to the others, peppering the enemy that was drifting farther and farther to their rear.

The whole way back to the ruins, her thoughts were of having to explain to her mother one day why she had run from the fight. Tasha knew it was run or lose everything, but that didn't make it any easier.

"Hold up here?" Kraff sputtered in amazement. "Are you sure, sir?"

Archer watched the last of the Irregulars disappear from his line of sight. "Don't question my orders, Captain, or you'll be scrubbing latrines on the *Crockett*."

Kraff's voice sounded dejected. "Yes, sir."

"And Captain?"

"General?"

"That was one brilliant piece of soldiering you pulled off," Archer said warmly. "The only reason they're running away now is that you and the Rangers caught them off-guard."

"Truth be told, sir, they surprised the hell out of me, too," Kraff said with a chuckle.

Truth be told, Archer was as reluctant to quit the fight as Kraff. But the reality was that his regiment had suffered some heavy damage and losses. Even with a fresh Avenger company added to the mix, the Irregulars were still better shots and pilots than his people. Besides, with the salvage from the fallen Irregulars, the Avengers could rebuild to a greater strength than the Irregulars could.

He held the field of battle, but victory still seemed far from his grasp. The risks of pursuing were too great—no matter how much he longed for vengeance.

Archer switched to the command frequency. "We're going to set up a new command post here," he said. "Brain, organize the supplies and logistics. Priority on repair gear and medical. I want full security perimeters around this hill and the surrounding countryside." He paused for a moment, drawing a long, deep breath. "And to all of you, a job well done."

"What do we do then, sir?" asked Katya.

Archer didn't hesitate in his reply. "We box them in, close them up, and force them to concede—or die."

Book Two
The Winter of Our Discontent

Strategy is the art of making use of time and space. I am less concerned about the latter than the former. Space we can recover, lost time never.

—Napoleon Bonaparte

In the long run, luck is given only to the efficient.

—Helmut von Moltke

14

Old Bealton, Odessa
District of Donegal
Lyran Alliance
19 April 3063

Archer Christifori climbed up through the brush and the tangle of thick roots and vines to the top of a low rise. He wanted to have a look at the Irregulars in hopes of spotting a possible weakness in their defenses.

He crouched near a twisted cedar and gazed down on the ruins of old Bealton, where his opponents had dug in. Centuries ago, it had been a city. Now, mounds of ferrocrete, brick, and twisted metal, many of them over four stories high, stood where buildings had once been. Some of the piles leaned over the streets, seemingly in defiance of gravity.

The "streets" were, in reality, nothing more than gullies and ravines between the piles of rubble. In many cases, these were blind alleys or so narrow that even infantry would have a slow, painstaking time of it. The ground was gray and pink, mixed with chunks of black ferrocrete and the sick color of rust bleeding down the bricks from the rain. As the wind danced over the piles, dust clouds kicked up like tiny tornadoes, eventually spinning themselves out.

Panting slightly, Katya climbed up next to Archer as he scanned the hillside with his enhanced binoculars. The electronic imaging system brought the mounds into much crisper view, though what he saw was not particularly reassuring. Thickets of trip-vines, some nearly five meters high, covered much of the ruins. Trees had also tried to grow in some spots, but those that succeeded were stunted and did little more than block his line of sight.

Near the center of the city, the mounds seemed to get taller. The ravine-streets rose slightly in that area, twisting and turning through the rubble. There were some flat areas, but as Archer zoomed in on them, he saw that they were unstable-looking piles of rock and gravel. He saw signs of some wider avenues that cut through the once proud city, but the ruins towering over them made them deadly fire corridors.

"Hell of a place for a fight," Katya said.

"And that's an understatement." Archer lowered his binoculars to look at her briefly. "A combat environment with all the fun and games of urban warfare. Tight fields of fire, combat at nearly point-blank ranges, limited mobility. Best yet, no maps of the terrain, no way to navigate the place once we get in there, and an enemy that is most likely entrenched and familiar with the ground."

Archer adjusted his binoculars to zoom back out so he could take in the surrounding area, and was heartened at least slightly by what he saw. Behind the city was a river, the Potomac. A drop-off kept him from seeing much of the waterway, but if Gramash's intel was accurate, the waterway was too wide, too swift, and too deep for any 'Mech to cross it. Furthermore, the drop-off of nearly thirty meters from the city to the river would create an impressive barrier for even the nimblest of BattleMechs. The river blocked nearly a third of the city, boxing it in.

Katya aimed her own binoculars down at the ruins. "I see some infantry off to the west. Looks like an observation post of some kind," she said.

Archer didn't bother to look. At a strategic level, a small outpost of infantry didn't matter. He had a tougher nut to crack.

"There are some avenues that cut to the center of that mess. They must have been highways at one time," she said, pointing to the far right and left sides of the city. "We could use those as ways in."

"We're going to have to. Most of the side streets look more like debris than street."

"You know that Colonel Snord will have those major streets covered, don't you?" she asked.

Of course he did. Hell, if it were him, he'd have ambushes set up that would scare the living hell out of the enemy. That did not change the situation.

"Yes, I know, Katya. I also know that we're going to have to try anyway. The Irregulars have used up a lot of their expendables. Thanks to Kraff, we've recovered about nine tons of missile reloads—it's not much, but it's a good start, and every ton we got is a ton the Irregulars don't have. Added to that, repair facilities inside all that crap have to be less than perfect. They can't be resupplied, either."

"Remember, though," she said cautiously, "we're on a world that could be described as hostile. Our supplies are limited as well. We came prepared for a week or so of action—maybe more if we start conserving now. After that, we start facing supply problems as well."

"We're good in the short term, though."

"Just don't push it too much. If Gramash were conscious, he could probably get us supplies through his local contacts. I've tried to make some connections myself, but the best I've managed are some basic spare parts. He was the only one who had the contacts to keep us supplied for a longer term."

"What do our medics say?"

"They're the ones keeping him in a coma," Katya said.

"What?"

"It's part of the healing technique. According to them, it's necessary for his recovery."

Archer bit his lower lip in frustration. He could order them to revive Gramash, but doing so might put the man's life at risk. One life against the survival of the entire regiment—it seemed an easy enough choice. But he remembered the ambush, the bloodied corpse of Darius Hopkins. Darius had been a soldier's soldier. One of his favorite maxims was never to sacrifice good warriors, and Archer would honor him in that.

"Seeing this terrain up close, I don't think there's enough room down there for Snord to land three DropShips to evacuate personnel either," she said.

The Irregular DropShips were at the New Bealton spaceport. Archer thought there were a couple of places where a single DropShip might be able to touch down if the pilot was both lucky and drunk at the time, but he didn't think Snord was going to evacuate any of her force. She needed everyone she had to fight his regiment.

Archer scuttled around on the hard ground to find a more comfortable sitting position. "What's your estimate of the Irregulars' losses?"

Katya pulled out a noteputer from a thigh pocket of her fatigues and tapped at the tiny gray buttons to retrieve the information. "From what we've seen, they're down by more than two companies of BattleMechs and armor. We've recovered the 'Mechs and captured the MechWarriors as well. Our techs think we can get a company's worth of the gear operational."

"If I had a company's worth of MechWarriors to

pilot them, that would be great," Archer replied drily. "Assuming normal refit ratios and rates, that puts them at just under one battalion strong right now."

"That's about the size of it," Katya said. "But we didn't see their support gear in the fight. The Irregulars have some of those Padilla artillery tanks, and we never saw them either. That means they still have them tucked away somewhere out there." She gestured vaguely toward Bealton.

"And we lost a little more than that," Archer said grimly. "A full battalion's worth of our troops was knocked out of the game, at least for the short term."

"But our personnel losses were light, and we've been lucky with most of the repairs. About a company and two additional lances should be operational by tomorrow morning, including MechWarriors, drivers, and gunners. The rest of the repairs will take more time."

Archer shook his head. "We've got them bottled up in these ruins," he said. "But for us to successfully punch through their defenses, we need a numerical advantage of three or four to one."

"Military theory 101," Katya said.

"Yeah, but I don't have those numbers, and I'm not likely to get them," he snapped. "If we had Gramash, he could probably help us pick up a handful of MechWarriors. Not enough to make a serious difference, but it would help."

"What are you going to do?" she asked cautiously. Archer wasn't hiding his frustration over the fact that active intelligence on Odessa was impossible as long as Gramash was unconscious.

He surveyed the ruins of Bealton again. Things had been going wrong ever since they'd beaten back the local militia. Not only had he lost Darius Hopkins, but his intelligence man for Odessa was out of commission. Worst of all, he wasn't accomplishing his mission.

Instead of winning over Snord's Irregulars for Prince Victor, he was in a minor war with them. Though the Avengers held the field at the end of the last battle, their losses made him feel victory was slipping through his fingers like a handful of sand.

"We'll maintain the perimeter we already have in place," he said finally. "I want two lances of BattleMechs designated as a floating defense in case the Irregulars attempt to break out. We'll use the regimental command lance and one other."

"Strictly defensive?" she asked. She didn't say what she was thinking, but he knew anyway: it wasn't exactly his style.

Archer frowned. "You know me better than that, Katya. We're going to probe this rat's maze a little, see what they've got, keep them on their toes. We'll start with those two major entrances into the city. Not fast actions—that's the kind of stuff that gets you ambushed. We'll go at it slow: assault 'Mechs leading the way with full artillery support. I wish we could do a little more with our fighters, but a combat environment like that won't allow it."

"We fight them block by block then?"

"If we have to. I'd like to think that Colonel Snord would capitulate, but that's not likely to happen at this point."

Archer winced slightly at the thought of what the fighting was going to be like. He'd been in urban combat before. It lacked the elegance of fighting out in the open, where mobility played more of a role. He'd considered trying to starve Snord out, but rejected the idea. He'd be handing her the initiative by forcing the Irregulars to strike out first. That wasn't his style, either.

"No, we have to go after them," he said, half to himself, "before they come for us."

*   *   *

The huge mound of debris was open on one side, creating a cavern nearly four stories tall. At one time, it must have been a parking garage. The upper levels had held during the bombing, but the lower levels had crumbled, either from time or from the damage that had destroyed most of Bealton three centuries ago. All that interested Tasha at this point was that the place would provide some cover for her techs to repair the damage the First Thorin had inflicted on her command.

She had fielded two battalions of mostly Battle-Mechs against them, and the fight had taken a considerable toll. The biggest problem was that she'd had to yield the field of battle, which meant being unable to recover or salvage any of the BattleMechs she or the First Thorin had lost. Instead, Archer's techs, meanwhile, were cannibalizing her 'Mechs for parts, ammo, or outright repair. The best she could do was order the repair of the machines that had survived to fall back to Bealton.

She watched as a team of techs worked on the burned and torn chest of her BattleMech in the old parking garage. With the help of a makeshift gantry, they were crawling over it to cut off damaged armor plates and to hoist new ones into place. Ammo loaders were also scrambling all around the cave, coordinating the reloads. While still in her cockpit, all she knew of her 'Mech's damage was the digital readouts showing her battle computer's assessment. Now, from the rubble-strewn street, she could see the raw destruction that had been inflicted.

Captain Norris strolled over. His shaved head was slick with sweat, and he ran a hand over it, wiping away the excess moisture as he came toward her. His face and neck muscles were tight, as if he were fighting back anger . . . or possibly even constipated. The last thought almost made Tasha laugh, but she knew that wouldn't help improve her generally unpleasant dealings with Norris.

"Major," he said curtly, as if he despised her rank, "we have numerous problems to discuss."

"Go on, Captain," she said, crossing her arms, mentally preparing for the worst.

"I have checked with the techs, and we are low on ammunition—primarily missile and gauss rifle rounds. At present, we have only enough to last a few hours of fighting."

She had asked him to investigate the supply issue, wishing to hell she hadn't lost those transports. As a major on garrison duty, she'd never previously had to deal with supplies. Now that she was in command of the whole unit, the problem rested squarely on her shoulders. "We'll have to issue orders to conserve ammo and concentrate on the energy weapons."

"There is more," Norris said, not acknowledging her words. "Our fresh-water supply is down to eight days, and rations are limited to seven days."

Tasha frowned at that news. Fresh water in the ruined city was almost nonexistent. Even after three centuries, pockets of lingering radioactivity still made purification difficult. Also, all chemicals present in the onetime metropolis had been seeping into the ground water for centuries, making it deadly. The river water might sustain purification, but getting down to it was tricky. The unit's 'Mech purification systems would provide some potable water, but eventually they would fail as well. When it came to food, however, she didn't know what they'd do.

"Damn," she said, without meaning to.

"We cannot remain here for long, Major," Norton said. "As soon as repairs are completed, I suggest we attempt a full-scale breakout. If we can reach New Bealton, we can resupply there. If nothing else, at least we will be in open country where we can maneuver rather than be penned up like cattle." He waved his hand around the canyon of debris.

"I'm aware of that, Captain," she said stiffly. "But anything we know, Archer Christifori knows, too. Our infantry scouts have surveyed the city perimeter, and they've spotted his BattleMechs and tanks out there. They have the two major exit routes covered. Besides, we haven't located the bulk of his force yet, so we still don't know exactly what we'd find if we did punch through."

"We must leave," Norris said flatly. "To remain here will put us in a siege situation. We cannot afford that."

Tasha did her best to suppress her irritation at his arrogant tone. "I understand that, Captain. But if we try and punch out right this minute, with only a fraction of our repairs done, we wouldn't stand a chance of getting through. Bealton may be ugly and inhospitable, but it's easy to defend, and we have the avenues of attack rigged with ambushes. If we wait for Christifori to come for us, we can bloody his nose enough to let us get out."

"Bah," Norris spat. "Defensive combat is dishonorable. We should strike out now, with everything we have."

"This has nothing to do with honor," Tasha replied. "It has everything to do with survival and sound military thinking."

His face went beet-red, and his gaze bordered on hatred. "Survival is nothing without honor," he said as if quoting. "Your leadership has gotten us trapped here like a warble-rat in its den. Perhaps your grasp of the situation is clouded by what happened to your mother."

"Are you implying that I'm not fit to command, Norris?" Tasha demanded, her control slipping. She could tell that he was pleased to have gotten a rise out of her.

"I have been a member of this unit for years now," he said. "I have come to appreciate the warrior in your mother, but you are untried. Perhaps you should turn over command to someone who is more suited to it."

There it was, his motive, his desire. "Like you?"

He shrugged. "Not necessarily me. But there are those in the unit who agree with my approach to combat."

Tasha spun on him again, eyes ablaze. "No, Norris. My mother didn't expect to be ambushed and left unconscious, but she did leave me in command. I won't disobey her for you or for anyone around you. This isn't the Clans, Norris. You can't try to take command from me by fighting in a Circle of Equals. We do this my way."

Norris seemed unmoved by her anger. As before, he looked smug at having upset her. "Very well, Major. I was merely offering you an option."

She glared at him with contempt. "I know what you were trying to do. I also know that you never pulled this kind of crap with my mother. If you had, you'd have been out of here a long time ago—or dead. Mark my words, Norris, I am in command. Follow my orders and direction or you'll wish to hell you'd been knocked out of commission and not my mother."

She turned her back and walked away, but Tasha was sure the matter was not closed. She had not heard the last of Norris.

15

Archer looked at Joey-Lynn Fraser and smiled. Just six months ago, she had been the leader of a street gang on Thorin, but had rallied to his cause when he rebelled against the Fifteenth Arcturan Guards. Her gang, the White Tigers, had gone from being hoodlums to freedom fighters. With excess salvage recovered from the defeated Guards, he had formed a company around her—the White Tiger Company of his Second Battalion.

Even before her gang days, Joey-Lynn had spent four years in the military, where she'd trained to pilot a 'Mech. Now she was Captain Fraser, military commander and MechWarrior. The Avengers had picked up a number of recruits—former Federated Commonwealth vets and a number of militia members—to fill out the ranks of her company.

The White Tigers, like John Kraff's Muphrid Rangers, tended to fight independent of other units. Archer had decided to let them maintain some of their streetwise edge and to build on the bond they felt with one another. They were devoted to the cause of removing

Katherine from power, and that was enough for him. Another commander might have tried to crush their wilder spirit or bend it to his will, but Archer reluctantly admired it.

The morning sun was just burning off the lingering mists as he gestured toward the ruins in the distance. "From here, you can see the point where we want you to try and punch through, Joey," he said, gesturing to a gap in the rubble. "We've detected an open area about four hundred meters in. It must have been a plaza or a park at one time. If you can deploy in the debris on the near side of that space, we'll be able to mass the rest of our forces and concentrate our firepower on the Irregulars."

She nodded and lit up a small cigar, a habit she had taken up lately. It wasn't exactly the stuff of recruitment posters, but Archer found it amusing. Joey was a tough customer, and she played it to the hilt. "What kind of support can you give us, sir?" she asked.

"Well, I have Saber Lance on standby until you move out. They can provide some bombing capability, but, in an urban environment against mobile tactical targets, it won't be much help. You've got a *Raven* in your company, right?"

"Yes, sir—Private Staryn."

"And isn't Sergeant Armisted's *Bushwacker* mounted with TAG?"

"Yes, sir. Armisted's in Charlie Company. They removed his machine guns and mounted his 'Mech with target acquisition gear two months ago."

"Well, you've got three 'Mechs totally out of commission, so we'll transfer him into your command for this operation. With those two BattleMechs mounting TAG, we can use our pair of *Catapults* as indirect fire. The TAG 'Mechs can paint the targets, and the *Catapults* can drop in the Arrow missile support."

"When does this party take place, General?" she asked.

"Two days from now, tops. That should give you enough time to look over the tactical field as well as coordinate all the different elements of the op."

Joey-Lynn took a long drag on her stubby cigar and let the gray smoke trickle out of her nostrils. "What do we do once we get a toehold in that mess, sir?"

"I'll send in reinforcements. If we're lucky, it'll force the Irregulars to pull their defensive ring into the center of the city to conserve firepower. That will let us push on other sectors and move in closer ourselves. The Rangers will run a feint on their part of the line at the same time you strike. That should force the Irregulars to split their defense and give you a better chance of success."

Joey looked into the distance and studied the ruins, where a thin fog still lingered along the base of the rubble mounds. "Hell of a place to fight a war."

Archer nodded, and held her gaze when she turned back to him. "The one thing I learned in all my years as a soldier is that there *is* no good place to fight a war."

Joey Fraser saluted, responding to the gravity of his words, then left to rejoin her company and get to work.

The path down which the White Tigers were advancing was a valley in a rock-filled hell. There were still pockets of morning mist clinging to the knees of their BattleMechs as Joey-Lynn Fraser moved forward. It was tight quarters. Only two 'Mechs could walk abreast at a time as they progressed, which strung her company out in a long column, and that made her nervous.

The temptation had been to rush in at a full run, sprinting to the objective to seize and hold it. But the threat of mines and the number of possible ambush sites held her back. Rushing in blindly might leave her surrounded, trapped, and beaten before any of them fired a single shot. Taking it slow was more prudent. It wasn't what she wanted, but what was best.

Joey's *Gallowglas* was in the second rank of the column, walking alongside Grant Watkin's *Clift*. She continually swept every centimeter of the terrain with her sensors, but the tons of alloys and metal debris in the rubble made sensor readings erratic, even at short range. With each footfall, her nerves wound even tighter.

"You got anything up there, Smokey?" she asked Leftenant Thal, piloting the *Caesar* nearly forty meters ahead of her.

"Noth—whoa. Looks like I've got a reactor reading up ahead, just around that mound of red stonework on the right. Warbook is running now—it's a *Shogun*."

"Hold up," Joey ordered the whole column. "If we can paint him, he sure as hell can paint us. Saber Lance, how about a low-level pass of the area, a little strafing run?" She hoped her aerospace elements would damage the enemy a little and maybe give her a better view of what was ahead.

"This is Saber One. We'll be there in two," said Francine Culver.

"As soon as the fighters start their run, we move forward," Joey said. "The lead 'Mechs will round the corner up there and engage that *Shogun* at the intersection. I'll break to the left at that same cross-street with you, Grant. Von Kliff, I want you and Fang Lance to move directly forward seventy-five meters and hold. Three-way split at the intersection—got it?"

There followed murmurs of acknowledgment and confirmation. She settled back in her seat and hit the auto-tightening controls for the safety straps holding her in. Her short-range sensors picked up the approach of Saber Lance's aerospace fighters sweeping in from the north over the ruined city. A word popped into her mind, and she uttered it almost realizing she was speaking into her mike: "Showtime . . ."

The fighters came in low, led by the sixty-five-ton *Lucifer*. Its Holly long-range missile racks puffed out streaks of white-gray smoke as a wave of twenty missiles leapt out in front of it, followed by a barrage from its large and medium lasers. Then came a *Chippewa*, which banked in tight through the decaying buildings, unleashing its own salvos of LRMs and lasers at the *Shogun* hidden behind the building up ahead.

Joey never got a chance to order her troops into action. The sight of the sweeping fighters spurred them into an impulsive rush to their assigned target areas. Just as Smokey Thal's *Caesar* rounded the corner, she saw a wave of fire belch out from the unseen enemy. The air was alive with emerald bursts of light and stabbing crimson lances of energy.

Then came the voice of Saber One. "Culver here. Crudstunk, Captain! There's a lance of 'Mechs down there. Pull your boys and girls back!"

Joey's short-range sensors suddenly came alive with dots of red light, indicating enemy 'Mechs. They had been hidden in the debris, powered down or running in low-power mode. Now they were out and engaging the only targets in their line of sight—Thal's *Caesar* and Corporal Manstein's *Vindicator*. A bright blue burst of light from a PPC filled the air, and she saw the *Vindicator* stagger under the assault.

"Smokey and Jimmy, pull back!" she commanded. She and the rest of the unit did not have targets yet, and in this terrain, they were not likely to. The *Caesar* was closest to the rubble of the building and managed to stagger back out of the field of fire. The building itself was a seven-storey pile of debris still blackened from the bomb that had destroyed it centuries before. As Smokey turned, she could see that much of his frontal armor resembled the building; blackened holes gaped everywhere on his torso and arms. A nasty gash sliced through his armor near the front cockpit area, where a missile or autocannon round had done its dirty work. The *Caesar* staggered and began walking back toward the rest of the White Tigers.

Manstein's *Vindicator* was not nearly as lucky. She watched as it fell into the street, under a withering barrage of laserfire. The *Vindicator* discharged its tiny LRM five-pack, but that was a gnat's bite compared with the fire it faced. Jimmy managed to roll the BattleMech on its side even as another missile barrage ripped and shredded its armor.

The *Vindicator* got up on one knee and had begun to stand when it took a direct hit to its head from a charged-particle blast. The 'Mech's head seemed to cave in under the impact as the last of its armor was blasted free, raining down in puddles onto the rubble of the street. There was no hope for Jimmy, no chance for him to punch out. The PPC burst had carbonized him instantly.

Joey had lost two BattleMechs to the Irregulars two days before, but both MechWarriors had survived. This time someone under her command had died. She took a step forward, ready to charge up to where Smokey's *Caesar* was staggering back toward her column. All she wanted was to rush in and destroy the ones who had done this.

She stopped mid-step. She would gain nothing from running around that corner except the fate Jimmy's smoldering *Vindicator* had met. She finally got a visual on the lance of Irregulars as they stepped out into the intersection, their weapons leveled at her column. The *Shogun* showed some damage, mostly to its arm. A towering *Guillotine* stepped forward next to it. For a moment, time stopped. She saw another 'Mech round the corner and dash behind the two larger enemy BattleMechs, jockeying for a better firing position.

This was not a fight she was going to win. For the first time since the ambush began, she could see that. That intersection was the only path to her objective, and it was firmly in the hands of a force that could give as good as it got. It also had the advantage of crossfire. She pounded her fist against her cockpit console.

Then the *Guillotine* fired, its suite of medium lasers well-suited for urban combat. The shots bathed the legs of Smokey's *Caesar,* ripping away armor plating in every direction. The *Caesar* staggered forward like a drunk, moving along a mound of rubble to stay out of the line of fire.

Joey and Grant Watkey fired at the *Guillotine* at the same time. Watkey's shot found its mark first, a PPC blast from his *Clint* ripping into the center torso to savage the armor plating. Joey's large and medium lasers followed a millisecond later, digging deep into the same part of the *Guillotine*'s armored chest. The holes belched smoke, hinting at further damage within, but the 'Mech seemed barely affected by the assault. It slowly turned and locked on to Watkey's *Clint.*

Joey thought of something. "Staryn, lock that TAG onto the building next to those 'Mechs on the right. Call for immediate fire for effect."

"Sir?"

"Do it!" Joey commanded as the *Guillotine* unleashed its short-range missiles and medium lasers at Watkey's *Clint.* Two missed their mark, throwing rocks and debris in every direction as they plowed into the rubble next to the *Clint.* The rest hit Watkey in the right torso and arm. The laserfire that followed seemed to pepper every centimeter of his limbs. As the salvo ended, she saw that he had taken damage on almost every part of his 'Mech: it was charred and scarred, with twisted armor plating and numerous deep holes.

Smokey torso-twisted his *Caesar* and fired his gauss rifle, it slug a silvery blur as it slammed into the *Shogun*'s hip. The round ripped into the front of the hip and blasted out the back side, tearing away at the armor plating with devastating effect. The impact tore the *Shogun*'s aim down and to the left, raising a massive cloud of dust when it hit.

Joey heard the roar of incoming Arrow missiles, a deeper sound than long-range missiles, followed by a series of explosions that made the ground under her feet quake violently. More dust and debris rose in the air, billowing toward her column like the breath of a dragon. It covered their 'Mechs with a fine layer of dust as she scanned ahead. The *Shogun* was still showing on her sensors, though it had moved behind the rubble to the left of the intersection. The *Guillotine*, however, was not visible on her sensors.

The fog of dust settled, and she saw the ruins up ahead. The Arrow salvo had slammed into the building, which had collapsed in the street, burying Jimmy's *Vindicator* under tons of concrete and debris. The *Guillotine* was still somewhat visible, lying two-thirds buried on its side. There was a rumble as its ammunition cooked off from the damage of the fall, shaking loose more rocks and debris. Flames licked from a hole in the rocks, which also belched black smoke.

"Specter One, this is White Tiger One," Joey said, staring at the scene of fire and death as Smokey attempted to limp what was left of his *Caesar* back to the column. Suddenly, a fast-moving *Sentinel* crossed the intersection, a stream of autocannon rounds blazing from its KWI Ultra autocannon into the legs of the already-damaged *Caesar*. Smokey tried to turn and return fire, but the *Sentinel* had already sprinted out of his line of sight.

The *Caesar* quaked under the assault, and Joey-Lynn saw a small blast hit its right knee. The armor peeled back, and a thin trail of black smoke rose from the fried actuator. Smokey attempted to take a step, but the knee refused to move. The *Caesar* toppled forward, landing a mere ten meters from Joey's own BattleMech.

She winced at the sight, and heard General Christifori say, "Go ahead, White Tiger One."

She didn't respond immediately, calling first to the fallen *Caesar*. "You okay down there, Smokey?"

"You are kidding, aren't you, skipper?" he said, his breath ragged in her earpiece. He was alive enough to be sarcastic, at least. Joey switched channels to respond to her commanding officer.

"Sir, the Irregulars hold an intersection up here. I've lost two 'Mechs, one permanently. I can't get enough firepower up there to do the kind of damage I need to."

There was a long pause. "You're closer to it than I am, White Tiger One. What do you want to do?"

What she wanted to do was to kill the Irregulars. They had taken the life of one of her men—another victim of the Archon's tyranny. She wanted to charge forward with her entire column and see just how much harm they could do.

Staring at the road, though, she saw the enormous quantity of rubble that had rained into the street. Now only a single BattleMech at a time could pass—and even then, it would be slow going. To continue forward would give her a chance for revenge, but the price would be many more lives. And in the end, there was a damn good chance the Irregulars had a similar ambush rigged at the next intersection—and the one after that.

"Sir, we're penned in up here," she said finally. "I suggest we fall back. Trying to move forward, at least right now, is going to cost you this entire company and not very likely to win your objective."

Again, the long pause. "Understood, White Tiger One," Christifori said. "Get yourself back home."

Archer rubbed his brow as he leaned forward and breathed in the steam still rising from the cup of coffee in front of him. Katya came over and put one hand on his shoulder. "If Joey-Lynn says it's no good, I believe her," she said.

He raised his head and looked at her. "Yeah, I'm sure Joey's right. I was just hoping we could punch through. It was worth a shot."

"We had to try."

He nodded sadly. "And now we're about to start fighting a true siege. We don't have the firepower to punch in, and chances are they don't have what it takes to punch out."

"Stalemate?" Katya asked.

"Worse. A battle of attrition. Both sides will wear each other down to nothing."

"We're better off supply-wise and logistically than the Irregulars," she pointed out.

"I've seen this kind of thing before. We stand a good chance of winning, but we'll only grind ourselves up in the process," Archer said. "There usually isn't any winner in this kind of fight—only two losers."

"Then it comes down to leadership," she said. "I know you won't let us down. You've held us together from day one, and you'll keep right on doing it. We all have faith in you, Archer."

Katya believed what she'd said, but Archer knew what the whole unit was wondering and that no one wanted to say aloud. How many more of them would have to die to hold the unit together?

16

"**H**ere's what I think, Major," Captain Deb H'Chu said, commenting on Tasha's plan for getting them out of Bealton. "It's a long shot, but I think that if we concentrate in a single thrust, we might—I stress *might*—be able to punch through the First Thorin's lines. If we do, we can make a break for New Bealton." Her words echoed slightly in the semi-open parking garage that was serving as a makeshift 'Mech repair bay and barracks for the Irregulars.

"I don't know," Tasha said. Since the Avengers' recent thrust, the fighting had turned into a game of cat and mouse in a series of sniping attacks, long patrols without sleep, and stalemate. The strain showed on all their faces.

Norris leaned back against a crumbling stone pillar. "The plan does have some merit," he said. "It's a narrow corridor that will slow us down and reduce our capability to spread out enough to concentrate our firepower, but no one would expect us to use it as an escape route. The problem is we'll be bottled up and facing potential disaster if the Avengers counter with enough force to stop us."

"There's the question of the noncombatants as well," added Marcos Shake. "We can't take them all with us. I suggest we leave behind a token force to negotiate their safe passage or surrender under the terms and conditions of the Ares Conventions."

Tasha felt as if an additional hundred kilos had just been loaded on her shoulders. For a mercenary unit like the Irregulars, the loss of logistical support was nonviable. All of them, from techs to MechWarriors, were feeling the pressure from the loss of supplies and gear in the earlier battle. Trying to operate with further losses would leave the unit crippled, even in the short term. And, for Tasha personally, that would mean having to surrender her mother to the enemy as one of the wounded. That was an option she was not willing to consider.

"Unacceptable," she replied. "We have to get them out with us or it's a no-go."

Norris slammed one beefy fist into the other. "We should not drag civilians into this, Major. This is a fight between true warriors. Civilians have no place on the battlefield."

"We don't have a choice," she snapped. "Leaving them behind would mean we'd never have a chance to rebuild and take on the First Thorin again."

Norris growled slightly, then drew a long deep breath. "Very well. But there will be a point where you will have to commit us forward or pull us back. If we do this in the manner you suggest and fail, it will cost us our offensive capability. Our forces will be too weak to break out. In other words, Major, this move will cost us more than we want to pay if it does not succeed."

Tasha stared at him, angry but knowing he was right. "Well, then, Norris, I guess we'll just have to make this work."

*   *   *

Major Alice Getts slowed her Von Luckner to a stop at the edge of the clearing that marked the perimeter of the First Thorin's patrol line. About a hundred and fifty meters across the clearing, the ruins began. Why the general had her patrolling this sector was hard for her to understand. She and Icepick One, newly promoted Sergeant Major Adrian Glyndon, had checked the area several times. If the Irregulars were going to try a push, this would be one of the last places they would use. The rubble was almost impassable, traversing the area would require crossing an open clearing, and her company was situated in a wooded area under heavy cover. If the Irregulars chose to try something in this sector, they were foolish, crazy, or both.

But if that was the case, why was the hair standing up on the back of her neck?

"Icepick One, this is Sledgehammer One. Are you picking up anything on your sensors?" Her voice was wary. Something didn't seem right.

"We're getting nothing on the sensors. But"—there was a pause—"I'm picking up some dust in the distance."

"Dust, huh? Where?"

"Section three-oh-three-bravo," Glyndon said. "Probably just one of their routine patrols."

Getts said nothing and leaned back in her seat to think. The tank cockpit was dank and dark, the air heavy with the sticky-sweet aroma of decades' worth of sweat. Yet, she fought in this machine as if it were a part of her body. After the many battles she'd seen in her time, she'd developed a feel for the battlefield that was almost a sixth sense. She trusted her instincts—and right now they were telling her there was a problem.

"We ain't seen dust clouds before. And anything that can kick up that much dust is bigger than just one or two 'Mechs," she muttered to herself. "Icepick, get your people on-line. I think the crap's about to hit the fan."

She switched over to the command channel. "Specter One, I've got signs of movement at section three-zero-three-bravo. All I've got is a gut feeling about it, but they may try to come through here."

Archer Christifori's voice came back cool and calm in her earpiece. "Understood, Sledgehammer," he said. "Hold tight. Help is on the way."

The first wave of Irregular BattleMechs arrived in a way that both startled and awed Alice Getts. All were jump-capable, and the whole group of them rose simultaneously from their concealed positions, kicking up a wave of dust as they cleared the debris and closed on her position.

An eighty-five-ton *Gunslinger* slammed into the ground with such force that her tank quaked with its landing. Nearby, a dull gray *Wyvern* came down, too, its knees flexing hard under the impact of its jump. The 'Mechs fanned out as they landed in front of her company, who stared at them in sheer respect and amazement. In the distance, many more BattleMechs were coming, rumbling through the mounds of debris.

She knew she was outnumbered, but her unit had to hold them so they couldn't get through to the rest of the Avengers.

"Fire!" she barked to her company.

A wave of missiles, lasers, PPC fire, and artillery shells lashed out at the advancing Irregulars, and Alice switched back to the command channel.

"General," she said quickly. "Turns out my gut was right. You'd better hurry."

Archer pivoted his *Penetrator* at the waist and heard the deep tone of target lock as his targeting reticle danced over the icons of numerous opposing Bat-tleMechs. Through the haze of dust and smoke, he opened up with both of his Clan-built ER large lasers at a *Gunslinger* about to fire on a Burke, one of Ar-cher's tanks. It was the third 'Mech he'd attacked in the same number of minutes, and he was fighting the heat buildup.

Both of his shots found their mark—one on the *Gunslinger*'s right chest, the other scarring the dull gray replacement armor from elbow actuator to the shoulder. The *Gunslinger* shook off the attack and fired its pair of gauss rifles at the Burke, mangling the tank's armor.

Then the *Gunslinger* turned toward Archer, who juked right, not waiting for the attack. The *Gunslinger* began to fall back, drifting away from the edge of the woods, where Getts and her people were still fighting. In the middle of the clearing, a Savannah Master was a charred memory while a fallen enemy *Mongoose* was still belching flames from its ruptured fusion reactor. A pair of Galleon tanks had been tossed onto their sides like so many children's toys, their armor twisted from the damage they'd taken before the final explo-sions crippled them. Other Irregular BattleMechs, in-cluding the deadly *Masakari,* were pulling back from the fight into the cover of the ruined city.

The aborted breakout by the Irregulars had taken a toll on Getts's Sledgehammer Company. Archer and his regimental command lance arrived on the scene within a few minutes after her call, but his armor and infantry were already viciously battered.

The Irregulars had pulled off a stunning assault. They had used their jump-capable 'Mechs to sweep past the Avengers, forcing them to split their line and face attacks from both directions. The remaining ground-bound 'Mechs and armor came more slowly but had less opposing firepower to deal with. As the last 'Mech pulled out of his line of sight and back into the city, Archer admired the courage and sheer audacity of the move.

It had almost worked.

The jumping 'Mechs' second leap had brought them directly into the midst of his command lance. It was close-quarters fighting, and the Irregular 'Mechs were already running hot after two long jumps. Subaltern Wally George in his *Watchman* took one out in less than a minute, while Andy Stickland in his *Hercules* destroyed one and crippled another. Archer scored damage on at least four more.

When the Irregulars' jumping 'Mechs realized they weren't going to succeed, they fell back in good order. By the time Archer arrived, the Irregular ground forces were carrying out an orderly withdrawal as well. His lance of aerospace fighters had arrived just in time to help Alice Getts push them back.

"You may own the bottle, Snord," he murmured, staring at the ruins, "but I own the cork."

"Sir?" asked Getts, still on the command frequency.

"Nothing," Archer said quickly. "Good work here, Major."

"Heck of a cost, sir."

"Hell of a one, Getts," he said, thinking of Darius Hopkins. Confident that the Irregulars weren't going anywhere for awhile, he turned his *Penetrator* and started for the field command post. The battle was over, and it was time for the Avengers to lick their wounds and figure out what to do next.

Katya Chaffee stared at the scratched 2D image produced by the battlerom recovered from the Rotunda armored scout car that had been Darius Hopkins's final command. Battleroms were designed to record tactical damage even if the 'Mech or vehicle was destroyed.

It had been a long day, and with the preliminary battle damage assessment done, she could return to her primary duty of regimental intel. The lower window projected a feed of the short-range sensors; it showed a *Hunchback* and a distant *Catapult,* an older-model 'Mech. The large upper window displayed the frontal, "gun-camera" recording from the driver's viewpoint. On her fifth pass through the data, she had killed the audio as well as the data feeds on the vehicle's status. As the Odessan darkness descended around her, she stared intently at the screen, shivering slightly in the chill night air.

Something had been bothering her ever since the first ambush, and her doubts had been fueled by how outraged and angry Tasha Snord had been in Katya's one communication with her. It simply didn't add up. She advanced the footage, watched the *Hunchback* appear in the dimmed lights of the armored car, and paused the image again. There it was, just as it had been a dozen times before, boldly painted with the insignia of the Irregulars. About to crush the Rotunda and take the life of a dear friend.

Then it dawned on her. It wasn't something about the *Hunchback* that bothered her; it was the BattleMech itself. She pulled up the TO&E for the Irregulars, and she began to run her eyes quickly down the lists. She had barely begun when she heard the sound of someone entering the portable shelter. She turned and saw Archer standing near the entrance, his arms crossed, his face looking completely drained of energy.

"I just saw the BDA, Katya," he said. "We lost half a company of ground armor, and some of our 'Mechs will need repair. Four dead and six wounded. You've seen the numbers, too. You should get some rest in case Rhonda Snord decides to give us another little nudge tomorrow."

"She won't," Katya said. "I double-checked the

damage we did to them. They tried a full breakout and were forced to pull back. It cost us both, but in the long run they can't afford to take those kinds of losses. They'll need a day or two just to repair what we've done to them."

He nodded slowly, and Katya figured he'd probably reached the same conclusion. "So what are you up to?" he asked.

"I've found something," she said, unable to suppress her excitement. "I was going over the battlerom from the ambush. Something about it has been nagging at me for a while, and I finally spotted it."

"Spotted what?"

"The *Hunchback* that destroyed the Rotunda," she said, careful not to mention Darius by name. "I just ran through the dump on the Irregulars that Sergeant Gramash provided us. I can't believe I didn't spot it before."

"What?"

"The Irregulars don't *have* a *Hunchback* in their TO&E," she said.

Archer took two steps toward her and turned her noteputer around so he could see it. "You're saying that we haven't encountered a single *Hunchback* in any of the clashes with the Irregulars so far?"

"I haven't checked that yet, but I will. It will probably take me a day or so to do a quick interview with everyone and to check sensor-log dumps."

Archer slid the noteputer back to her. "Maybe the *Hunchback* was a last-minute replacement for a damaged 'Mech. That would explain why it's not on the TO&E."

"But if no one else has seen one since—"

Archer shrugged. "So, they haven't deployed it yet—or else someone besides the Irregulars staged the ambush." He uttered the words slowly, as though simultaneously digesting their implications.

"If that's the case, sir, we've been drawn into a battle we shouldn't be fighting."

"I'm not ready to jump to conclusions," he cautioned. "Let's just say you've raised some serious doubts that bear serious investigation." His expression was somber. "You're going to be interviewing everyone anyway, right?"

"Yes, sir," she said formally.

"While you're at it, do a full check against the Irregulars' TO&E."

"Of course," she said.

Archer's eyes narrowed. "Let me ask you a question. What kind of BattleMech does Rhonda Snord pilot?"

"A *Highlander*," Katya said quickly. "That 'Mech has been on the cover of every mercenary magazine dozens of times."

"That's right. Everyone knows she's a *Highlander* pilot. But something struck me when you mentioned the *Hunchback*. You say no one's seen one, but no one's reported fighting a *Highlander*, either. Even our people who've had their rides shot out from under them didn't spot her."

He caught Katya's eyes, and she was glad to see the energy coming into his expression.

"Rhonda Snord has a reputation for leading from the front, but no one's seen her. So, wouldn't you say that raises another question, Katya," Archer asked. "Where is she?"

17

Count Nicholas Fisk stood in the royal gardens, savoring its beauty and the freshness of the afternoon around him. The gardens ringed his hillside palace, which was hidden behind a high white wall that kept it sealed off from the eyes of the ordinary citizens of New Bealton. It was his refuge, a place of serenity where he and his family could enjoy the pleasant shade of the neatly trimmed, brilliant green trees and the fragrant beauty of flowers imported from all across the Inner Sphere.

Two men walked toward him on the cobblestone path. One of them, his son Luther, moved with a pronounced limp. The limp was a legacy of the boy's time on Thorin, when he'd been a member of the Lyran military and had tangled with Archer Christifori's rebels. In an excess of zeal, Luther had killed Christifori's sister, but it had been a sloppy piece of work. The local authorities tried to punish his son, but Fisk had used his political clout on Tharkad to rescue him.

In addition to his maimed leg, Luther had been blinded in one eye during his troubles on Thorin. An artificial implant had repaired his eyesight, but nothing short of Elective Myomer Implants could repair the damaged bones and muscles of his leg. Nicholas Fisk had refused, however, to deal with the filthy Capellan doctors who could perform the surgery.

The other man was Erwin Vester, the Loki agent assigned to him as part of the price for the two mercenary units under his command. He understood the reason Katrina Steiner-Davion had sent Vester as a liaison; it was a good way to keep an eye on her investment. But it was quite unnecessary.

Nicholas Fisk was loyal to a fault, and thus far, he had achieved great success. Soon the Archon would see that Vester was no longer needed and would send the damn spy somewhere else. At least, he fervently hoped so. Erwin Vester was one of the few people the Count had met in years who wasn't intimidated by him.

Vester bowed his head slightly in greeting, while Luther hobbled on past to stand slightly behind his father. "My lord," Vester began formally, "I have completed my analysis, per our discussion."

Fisk rocked back on the heels of his polished black boots and crossed his arms. "So, tell me, Vester. How is our little war going?"

Vester stood at parade rest, holding his noteputer behind his back. "It looks like the Irregulars are penned up in the ruins of old Bealton. They made a breakout attempt three days ago, but Christifori pushed them back."

"What is their combat strength?" the Count asked.

"From what Tasha Snord told me, they are operating with just over a battalion of effective forces."

Fisk smiled. "I imagine this last gambit took some of the wind out of her sails."

Vester nodded. "Apparently Colonel Snord is still out of the picture as well."

The Count smiled broadly. "Yes. Three more days, and then she's hung out to dry—unemployed and under siege. Her daughter contacted me to ask for supplies, spare parts, and reinforcements. Alas, I'm afraid we had none to spare."

"Did she agree to sign a new contract?" Luther asked.

The Count turned to his son. "Not yet. But soon she will have no choice. Their supplies are running low, and they're trapped like rats. If the Irregulars don't sign, they'll be left here as free agents, under siege. It's in their best interest to renew their contract, rebuild, and then assist in the struggle against Victor Davion."

"What if she doesn't sign?" Luther persisted, risking his father's anger.

The Count didn't wish to reprimand him in front of a stranger. The boy was spoiled . . . his mother's fault.

"Wolverton's Highlanders are standing by only a few days away. If the Irregulars refuse to sign, I will call in the Highlanders to relieve them by attacking the First Thorin Regiment—after they've suffered enough losses to make them humble, of course. Their reputation will be so tainted by having a third-rate mercenary unit save their butts that they'll be forced to take whatever crumbs we throw them."

"Colonel Blackstone will not be entirely happy with how we've been using his new unit," Vester said.

"You have dealt with him, I take it?" the Count asked.

Vester smiled thinly. "Loki's reach is extensive, Count Fisk. I guarantee that Blackstone won't interfere. In the meantime, we have also completed repainting and repairing the 'Mechs of the company of Highlanders we used for the ambush."

"You talk like it will be easy to walk through the Avengers," Luther said, "but I know Archer Christifori." He drew himself up as if to show his deformities as a grim reminder. "Don't underestimate him."

The Count turned again to Vester, who now had his noteputer out and was working away on it. "We have been monitoring the First Thorin," he said. "We believe that one of their companies is still on Alcor—or at least is not here. We've lost our operative on that world, so we haven't been able to confirm whether they've left.

"The regiment's other companies have suffered nearly thirty-five percent casualties and equipment losses since coming here. Furthermore, we have no evidence that local Davion supporters are providing them with supplies. The Irregulars are taking a beating, but they're also wearing down the Avengers at the same time."

The Count nodded. "Yes, but I hear from my own sources that Christifori's *Penetrator* is still in service."

The Count could see the sting of humiliation on Vester's face. He had been in charge of the mission to assassinate Christifori, and the Count didn't intend to let him forget it.

Luther was shaking his head. "Statistics and intelligence reports don't tell the whole story. I've dealt with this regiment before."

"I know," Fisk said soothingly. "I'm counting on that. All of those years of military training are finally going to reap their dividends. So, what do you think, Luther? Should we let the Irregulars pummel themselves into oblivion or should I send word now for the Highlanders to come and finish this?"

Luther didn't answer right away, and the Count assumed it was because he had never before asked his son for advice. The ring of dull gray metal that surrounded the young man's artificial left eye was expressionless, but his good eye burned with hatred of Archer Christifori. "If you wait, the Irregulars may be too weakened to assist the Highlanders, and the Highlanders can't defeat the Avengers alone. If you send the message now, they should be here just about the time the Irregulars' contract expires."

The Count smiled at Vester. "You see, Erwin, my son gives me good advice. I was planning to let the Irregulars suffer. But he's right. The time has come to put all our pieces on the chessboard. I want you to link up with the Highlanders already on Odessa and prepare them for the rest of the unit's arrival." He turned to his son one more time. "And Luther, for what Christifori has done to you, I'd like you to serve as my liaison with the Wolverton's Highlanders when they get here."

Luther stood taller as he propped himself up on his cane. "Do you mean that?"

"Of course. Not everyone who serves does so from the cockpit of a BattleMech," the Count said, narrowing his eyes. "And when the time comes to crush the people who crippled you, you will know what to do."

"The code phrase," Anton Gramash said in a dry, almost gasping voice, "is Stonewall. Their countersign should be Little Sorrel." He drew in a long, weary breath. Days of breathing through a tube had left his vocal cords ragged and raw. "I had them stockpiling parts and munitions. Tell them what you need and where you want it." Another deep breath. "These people are skittish, but they're on our payroll and they can help us."

Then he dropped his head back onto the pillow.

Katya nodded and stood up next to his bed in the field hospital dome. Gramash had awakened on his own an hour before, and she and Archer had pressed the medics to allow them a visit. It was crucial that they get the necessary frequencies and code words to contact the local Davionists working for Gramash. It was the only way they could hope to replenish much-needed supplies of food and other expendables.

"We appreciate the information," Archer said, putting his hand on the wounded man's shoulder. "You've been through a lot."

Gramash opened his eyes a little wider, this time with slightly more energy. "Can't understand the ambush. It doesn't fit Colonel Snord's style."

Archer glanced over at Katya, then back at Gramash. "Katya says the same thing. She thinks it's possible that the ambush was staged by a third party to get us into a fight with the Irregulars. Right now, it's just a theory, though. We don't have anything more than speculation and questions about an elusive 'Mech. Furthermore, we haven't seen hide or hair of Rhonda Snord since this whole thing started."

It had taken Katya a while to sift through the data and to interview the members of the regiment. The *Hunchback* that had killed Darius Hopkins and injured Gramash had not been seen since the night at Moseby's Crossing. Nor had anyone seen a trace of Rhonda Snord's *Highlander*.

Mention of this new development seemed to light a tiny spark in Gramash. "Can you get me the data?" he asked, looking at Katya.

She nodded reluctantly. "The medtechs say you need the rest."

"Screw them." Gramash drew another long breath. "I'll need a comm unit in here."

Katya looked over at Archer, who nodded his consent.

"I'll have the unit brought in and the data fed to you," she said.

"I set up a good network on this world," Gramash said, using his bandaged hands to slide his body toward the head of the bed so he could sit more upright. "Someone has to know or have seen something."

"You've already been a big help with the names of the people who can help us resupply," Katya said. "Meanwhile, you've got to concentrate on getting well."

"That's an order," Archer said. "You take as much time as you need, and try not to let Major Chaffee work you too hard."

One of the medtechs came over and began checking Gramash's vital signs, which Katya and Archer took as a hint that it was time for them to go. Katya was glad Gramash had finally come out of the coma.

And not a minute too soon.

18

The first thing Tasha Snord saw as she brought her *Spartan* around the base of a pile of rubble was a pair of Avenger BattleMechs about two hundred meters off. One, a *Battle Hawk*, was standing on top of the remains of a building. The other, a dust-covered *Crab*, was lower in the street, using the debris for cover.

At her side, Mistreli's *Black Knight* moved in to provide cover. This latest clash had begun when two small patrols had bumped into each other. Now, both sides were tossing in supporting troops. Such was life during a siege. What bothered her more was that she was getting used to it.

She locked on to the *Battle Hawk*'s gray-and-brown-striped form with her extended-range PPC, firing the instant she heard the tone of target lock. Her *Spartan* seemed to hum as its capacitors discharged a searing blue-white bolt of energy, and the heat spike in her cockpit was worse than usual. That was because the Irregulars' supplies were so low that she had not been able to replace the two heat sinks she'd lost yesterday. The time to complain about it had long since past, and Tasha had simply accepted it. Both shots found their mark in the *Battle Hawk*'s bulky form, rocking it backward and sending chunks of ferro-fibrous armor raining down onto the *Crab* below.

While his lancemate reeled under the assault, the *Crab* pilot fired his large arm lasers in rapid succession, their beams lancing into Mistreli's *Black Knight*. Like Norris, Mistreli was one of a handful of former Jade Falcons in the ranks of the Irregulars. He too had been captured and made a bondsman during the Clan wars, then later been given the chance to regain his warrior status. Though he was an outstanding fighter, even his finely honed edge was failing under the stress of constant battle.

Tasha glanced over and saw that the lasers had done some serious damage to the *Black Knight*'s right leg. Its armor was already damaged from yesterday's clash with the Avengers, and the hurried field repairs had not been enough to repair all of the holes.

"You okay over there, Mistreli?" she asked, side-stepping slightly in an attempt to draw off some of the fire.

Before he could answer, Tasha saw a *Bushwacker* appear off to one side of the *Crab*. This one had been equipped with target acquisition gear, allowing it to draw in indirect fire. It had reared its ugly head several times already today. Each time it locked on to one of Tasha's people, Arrow missiles rained down death from an unseen artillery source. Caught off guard by its sudden reappearance, she wasn't ready when the *Battle Hawk* fired two of its Defiance medium pulse lasers.

Tasha jerked her *Spartan* back a half-step in reaction, and the lasers seared just past her cockpit into Mistreli's *Black Knight* inside. Its right leg, already mauled, lost even more of its precariously thin armor.

She locked her own medium pulse lasers onto the *Bushwacker*, and the humming sounded in her ears.

"I just lost my knee actuator," Mistreli said, sounding angry and frustrated even over the commline.

Tasha fired a trio of laser bursts at the *Bushwacker*, and they ripped into its chest, twisting the armored plating. The *Crab* was advancing, obviously preparing for another shot. Mistreli tried to get out of the way, but his locked-up knee joint left him stranded dead in his tracks.

"Fire at the *Bushwacker*," Tasha told him, ignoring the rising heat in her own cockpit. "Norris, get up here now," she barked.

The *Black Knight* leveled its PPC and one of its large lasers, then fired. One shot, the laser, was a clean miss, stabbing off into the distance. The other flash of energy hit the *Bushwacker*'s thick, stocky legs, but didn't do much but blacken the paint and armor there. Tasha bit her lip. She didn't have the firepower to take the *Bushwacker* out, not with these odds. Which meant that at any minute . . .

A roar of explosions erupted off to her side as a salvo of Arrow missiles arced over the debris and poured into Mistreli's already crippled *Black Knight*. The 'Mech fell back under the savage force of the attack, and sick black smoke billowed from its right hip and torso.

"Damn it, Mistreli," she said. "You'd better be all right in there!"

"Alive," came a coughing voice through a wave of hissing static.

"Good time to leave," she said, firing at the *Bushwacker* with the only one of her pulse lasers that was fully charged and ready to fire. This time, her shot hit the 'Mech's right arm, which flailed backward.

Off to her side, she saw Norris's *Masakari* appear, drawing the *Crab*'s fire while simultaneously devouring leg armor with a furious blast from his PPCs. She joined in the fray, again firing at the *Bushwacker*. It wasn't long before the Avengers finally pulled back, out of her line of sight.

Tasha glanced down and saw Mistreli climb out of his cockpit hatch, still wearing his neurohelmet and coolant vest. He took off the helmet and tossed it down onto his fallen BattleMech. His lips were moving, and though she couldn't hear the words, she knew they were the kind of curses only a former Clansman could come up with.

"What happened here?" Norris asked, acknowledging her finally.

"They met our reconnaissance in force with their own," she said angrily. "That damn *Bushwacker* showed up again and brought in the indirect fire."

"Bah!" growled Norris. "This constant sniping gets us nowhere. We've had six of these encounters, and each time nothing is gained."

Tasha gritted her teeth. "Stow it, Norris."

"I will not," he spat back. "You had us retreat here like Ironhold dingos, and now these Avengers toy with us as if we were a gang of merchants and not warriors. Your tactics have driven us to ruin."

"I said, stow it," she snapped.

"Neg. You have shown yourself incapable of leading this unit. If we were still Clan, I would face you down and remove you from command with my bare hands. You are not worthy of the surname you carry." His words were venomous. They had been squabbling for days, and he had finally lost it.

So had she.

"I've had it with your damn attitude, Norris," she snarled. "I didn't ask for this command, but I've managed to keep the unit together and functional. Yes, we're penned in, but we're wearing the Avengers down, and I think we'll be able to punch through soon.

We'll rebuild, kick Christifori's butt, and then come back here to dig up the gems we came to find."

"You act more like a dirty merchant than a warrior," he baited. "I have no need for money. What matters is victory."

"Shut up, Norris," she said, even angrier than before, if that was possible.

"You cannot make me," he said.

"I will. You want a Circle of Equals? Fine. I'm no Clanner, but I'll clean your damn circuits and mop up the floor with you when I'm done."

"You will grant me a Circle?"

"Yes," she said, regretting her words instantly but too angry to take them back. "If it will end this squabbling."

"Excellent." He smiled wickedly. "If you are lucky, Snord, I may let you live." With those words, he turned his *Masakari* around and headed back to their command post.

Tasha looked down at her console and saw that their conversation had gone out on the broadband channel. Any Irregulars tuned in would have heard it. All of them would know about the fight. Her shoulders slumped for a moment, and she closed her eyes, half in anger at herself, half in frustration at Norris.

She reached out to close the channel. When she spoke again, the only one who heard her was herself.

"I'll beat you, Norris," she said. "My mother left Snord's Irregulars with me for safekeeping, and that's exactly where it's gonna be when she comes back."

Sitting in the back of one of the tracked supply trailers that followed the Avengers in the field, Archer stared at the metallic urn on the foldup table before him. The trailer resembled its mates, except for the black stripe that crossed the usual greens and browns of the camouflage paint scheme. This one was special; it was where the Avengers kept their dead.

Archer stared at the container of ashes and the white tag taped to it: "Hopkins, Darius, Sgt. Mjr., RA 16677615."

Archer had come here seeking some kind of help for the way things had gone on Odessa. It was what he would have done if Darius were alive—gone to him for counsel and reassurance. Nothing had gone according to plan, and Archer's soul felt like a volcano of frustration. The Avengers were doing well enough on the battlefield, but he had failed in his mission. He had also failed Darius Hopkins—failed so dismally that Hopkins had lost his life.

Archer dropped his head helplessly into his hands. "Damn it, Darius," he murmured. "I came to this cursed planet to negotiate. But all we've done since we got here is fight the people I came to recruit. I've wiped out the local militia, and I . . . I lost you."

He raised his head just enough to look at the cylinder. "Now, all I want is to make the Irregulars pay for what they've done to us—for what they did to you." He glanced at the other cylinders in their storage racks, their tags identical except for the names they bore. Underneath each one, carefully packed and labeled, were boxes with the personal effects of the honored dead.

"Katya and Gramash think this whole thing could be a mistake. We may have been suckered. But I've got nothing to go on, old man. And even if we do get some hard evidence, I'm not sure it would convince the Irregulars. Hell, I'm having a hard enough time believing it myself. I've been fighting as if it could bring you back, hoping I was honoring your memory. And right now, I'd kill to hear what you would say to me if you could."

The trailer was as silent as the tomb it was, and no voice came back to Archer from the dead. He stood and picked up the urn. The cool weight of the metal cylinder did not seem to belong to the man who had helped raise him. He could count on one hand the number of true failures in his life, and he knew that Odessa was becoming one of them.

He nodded to himself, still speaking silently to Hopkins. All right, old man, he said silently. The time has come to stop letting sheer emotion rule me. It's time I did this right.

He put the urn back in its rack, making sure it was secure. Then he stood there for a few moments longer, staring at the silvery object. His decision had been made. Now all he needed was a definite course of action, a plan that would lead him to that elusive victory.

As he was coming out of the trailer, he saw Katya Chaffee leaning against a nearby boulder, enjoying a few moments in the shade. He walked over to her, and she straightened, her eyes fixed on his.

"You spying on me now, Katya?" he said, thinking to lighten his dark mood with some levity, but the words came out harsher than he'd intended.

She'd been insisting on her theory that they'd been set up, coming at him like a swarm of Elementals over the past few days, and it was starting to wear on his nerves more than he liked to admit. He'd begun to snap at her, even though he knew she didn't deserve to be treated that way.

"You know better than that," she said, with elaborate politeness. "Gramash and I have just completed a little round of research that might interest you, sir."

"Not this theory of yours," Archer said wearily.

"It's the best we have right now. And it looks like we've got something." She held up a noteputer that showed a map of Odessa. "According to two of Gramash's local sources, there were indications of BattleMech activity about three hours south of here the night of the ambush. Some of the farmers found multiple 'Mech tracks in their fields, and the prints were headed in a southerly direction.

"After talking further with them, we narrowed the possible hiding places down to an abandoned commercial farming complex near the town of Gottfredson. It's large enough to hold 'Mechs and isolated enough to provide adequate security."

Archer looked at the map and then back at Katya. "So there could be a lance or even a company hidden there?"

"Right. Our field operatives working for Gramash have spotted uniformed troopers—at least two techs and eight others—in and around the facility."

Archer shook his head. "I know what you want, Katya. You want me to give the order to verify this. Well, I can't. I've got a siege under way here. I can't afford to pull a company off line so they can run off on some damn wild goose chase."

Her face reddened. "Permission to speak freely, sir?"

Archer nodded.

"We've failed in our objective here," she said. "We came to persuade the Irregulars to fight for the Prince. So far all we've done is pummel them."

Archer's nostrils flared. He didn't want to tell her about his own self-doubts. "In case you hadn't noticed, Katya, they attacked us."

"Yes, and they killed Darius. And I think sorrow over his death is clouding your judgment."

Archer bit back his anger. "I won't lie to you and tell you this hasn't affected me."

"Then give me a chance to put this right," she pleaded. "Thomas Sherwood's company is due in-system in two days. We can relay a signal-buoy satellite up at the jump point for him. We can tell him to drop on Gottfredson instead of here. If he finds nothing there, he can link up with us within two hours. Two lousy hours—that's all I'm asking for. If we don't find anything, I'll never say another word, and we'll finish mopping up the Irregulars."

Archer drew a long breath and looked at her intently. "You really believe they'll find 'Mechs hidden there."

"Including one elusive *Hunchback*."

Archer nodded. Somehow, he'd lost sight of his mission as well as the well-earned confidence Katya had earned from him. "Very well, Major. I'll cut the orders, and you beam them up to one of our data-buoy satellites. I'll give you and Sherwood a long leash to do this right. I can't keep operating from pure emotion. It's time I started acting like the CO you used to know."

She smiled, almost embarrassed. "Thank you, Archer."

"If they're there, get them. But I want to know exactly who they are, so we can make them pay. And if you're right, I'm going to need your help to end this little tiff with the Irregulars." Then, with a rare show of formality, he stood at strict attention and gave her a fast salute—a well-deserved sign of respect from a superior to a subordinate.

Katya saluted back, gave him a quick wink, and took off.

Tasha moved into the circle formed by her troops, ignoring the whispers and murmurs. Her dull gray T-shirt was soaked in sweat, but she didn't care. The air was filled with the stink of siege. They'd all stopped bathing and showering days ago to conserve water, and the running joke in the Junk Yard was that the Avengers would smell their base long before they got close enough to attack it.

Norris stood with his arms crossed, his thick muscles

slightly flexed, his expression full of contempt. In his arrogance, he seemed to look right through her.

"I know that we are not Clan," he said, "but in the end it is all the same. Your mother led us here in search of buried treasure, and your incompetence has left us penned up like cattle. You have led us in a way unworthy of your name. I challenge your right to command."

Tasha gazed at him levelly. "You're right about one thing, Norris. We're not part of the Clans. We are a mercenary unit, and we have a solid chain of command. My mother left me in charge, but you've been questioning my authority ever since she got injured." She took a step back and balled her fists. "So, listen up to this. You can say what you want about me, but you leave my mother out of it. No matter what, that ends here and now."

She expected sarcasm, but Norris simply gave her his version of a smile. "Agreed," he said, leaping into the air to attack even as he spoke.

Tasha twisted and sidestepped, but one of Norris's beefy fists caught her at the waist. The punch sent a ripple of pain through her side and lower back. Then he tucked, rolled, and sprang to his feet again as she circled to his other side.

Her heart raced. Many of the unit's officers and MechWarriors were cheering—some for her, some for Norris. The tension of the siege was wearing on everyone, and this fight was giving them a chance to release some of the frustration they couldn't blow off any other way. She lowered her stance and braced for Norris's next assault.

He was already rushing at her with a sweeping kick. She didn't jump to avoid it, but instead launched herself back at him. Her knee slammed into his jaw, and Norris reeled under the surprising attack.

She was just regaining her balance when he grabbed

her from behind in a bear hug. He had her arms pinned to her sides and was keeping her low to the ground instead of lifting her so she couldn't use her legs against him. He squeezed hard, and his sweaty arms were like steel bands around her arms and chest. She felt her ribs flex, and then there was a crack, a sound she recognized instantly as that of a bone breaking.

With her remaining strength, she bent at the waist, bringing Norris with her but not breaking his grip. Despite her pinned arms, she was able to wrap one hand around his right ankle. Before he could kick her free, Tasha snapped upright again, holding on to his ankle with all her might.

She yanked it forward between her legs, throwing Norris backward and falling on top of him. They went down in a cloud of dust, and the wind was knocked momentarily from his lungs. Sucking in a strained breath a few seconds before he did, Tasha twisted so that she was facing him. He flailed an arm at her, but she punched down with both balled fists at the base of his throat.

His neck muscles were powerful, but not strong enough to prevent the gagging effect of her blows. He reached instinctively for his throat as Tasha unleashed the pent-up fury in her blood. Her fists flew, hitting him in the face and the eyes. Then she aimed lower, slamming her right fist into his groin, which elicited a groan. Norris sat up, only to meet the full fury of four more rabbit punches to his face.

But he was not finished yet. He slammed the flat of his palm upward into her jaw, and she felt a tooth chip. Her head snapped back, but she held her position on top of him. Even when he slammed a cupped hand against the side of her head, popping one of her eardrums, Tasha still refused to be dislodged.

She finally rolled back and up to a hunched stance,

arms out to her side, ready for more. Norris was still lying on his side, curled into a ball of pain. Tasha stepped forward and kicked, this time at his lower back. Two kicks, then two more, each one more savage than before.

Norris moaned, a deep groan of pure agony. He raised his hand, waving it slightly to signal the end of the match. Adrenalin was pumping through her body, and Tasha stood straighter, sucking in air. She coughed and felt a coppery taste on her lips. She wiped her mouth with one dirt-encrusted arm, and it came away red-stained with blood. The ringing in her ear muffled the noise of the other Irregulars around her, their voices lost in a dizzy rush as she fought to maintain her balance.

"This is over," she said, not to Norris but to the other Irregulars around her. They looked shocked by what they had seen. "But the Irregulars will go on, no matter what happens with the Avengers or our contract."

She coughed again, painfully sucking in more air as the rush of combat began to fade. Her fingertips and feet were tingling with unspent energy.

"Anyone who doesn't want to be part of the unit can pack their gear and leave now. The rest of you have duties to perform."

She took an uneven step forward, trying to meet the eyes of as many standing around her as she could. "And just to make sure you all understand, I'm Major Tasha Snord—and I'm in command of the Snord's Irregulars. Who here will follow me?"

A roar of cheers filled the air as the Irregulars surged forward around her. Still cheering, they hoisted their battered but grinning commanding officer on their shoulders and carried her back to her dome.

Book Three

Old Soldiers Never Die . . .

Sure, we want to go home. We want this war over with. The quickest way to get it over with is to go get the bastards who started it. The quicker they're whipped, the quicker we can go home.

—General George S. Patton, Jr., addressing his
troops before Operation Overlord

19

DropShip Angelfire
Pirate Jump Point Baker, Odessa System
District of Donegal
Lyran Alliance
29 April 3063

"Are you sure about that reading?" Captain Lee Fullerton asked his sensors operator. The First Thorin DropShip *Angelfire* had arrived at a pirate jump point in the Odessa system less than a day's travel from the planet's surface, and the dimly lit bridge was abuzz with activity. The JumpShip that brought them had already left the system, leaving the *Angelfire* on its own.

"Confirmed, sir. Four DropShips on burn-approach to New Bealton. They appear to be two Overlord-class and two Union. In three days, we'll be right on their ion trail. I only had them on the sensors for a moment or two before the ionization kicked in and masked their signals." The young officer's face was lit by the myriad lights on his displays, and the impression was eerie.

Fullerton leaned back in his raised command seat. "Run it through the warbook. See if you can correlate the readings, transponder signals, and anything else you got with known ships and units. There can't be that many ships heading for Odessa, not if things are going the way General Christifori planned."

"Aye, sir," the sensors operator said. "It'll take a while for the enhanced vid-displays to confirm the names against Wolf Pack's Book of Mercenaries On-Line."

Just then a younger man with sandy hair entered the bridge, still adjusting the tight-fitting uniform on his narrow frame. "What's up, Captain?" Thomas Sherwood asked.

Fullerton shook his head in concern. "We'd just started our burn-in when we picked up several other DropShips heading for the surface."

"Did they scan us?" Sherwood asked.

"We don't think so. It was just as they hit the atmosphere."

"Captain, we have a secured data squirt from one of our satellites," the communications officer said. "Priority-coded for Captain Sherwood."

Fullerton and Sherwood looked at each other, then turned back to the comm officer. "Priority message for me?" Sherwood asked.

"Yes, sir. It's awaiting your command prefix code to open the cipher."

Sherwood stepped down to an empty workstation on the lower deck. He keyed in his private code word, and the data began to display. There was a message from General Christifori, data from Katya Chaffee, and a new set of orders. His eyes raced through the new commands and the targets, and the map of the area of operations.

"Shit," he muttered as he saw that the Irregulars and the Avengers were fighting each other.

"What have you got, Tom?" Fullerton asked.

"So much for a chance at R&R," Sherwood said. "We'll need to pipe this down to your Tactical Operations Room."

"Has General Christifori won over the Irregulars yet?"

Sherwood shook his head. "Quite the opposite. In fact, I think it's safe to say the proverbial shit has hit the fan."

The sensor operator spoke up from the far side of the bridge. "Captain Fullerton, I've got an ID on those ships we spotted."

"Go."

"The two Overlords were the *Celtic Warrior* and the *Rabid Hunter*. I only got confirmed ID on one of the Unions: *Roarke's Drift*."

Fullerton absorbed the information. "With what unit?"

"The three we spotted are from the Blackstone Highlanders—more specifically, the Wolverton's Highlanders. That means the other one is most likely the *Chard* or the *Emerald Piper*."

"The Wolverton's Highlanders?" Fullerton said in disbelief.

"We need to get that data, as well as projected landing zones, down to the general as soon as possible," Sherwood cut in. The comm officer was already pulling the data feed for a message. "I'd like you to come with me, Captain," Sherwood said.

"How bad is it?"

"Not bad yet. But we've just been handed an operation, and I need to get you and everyone else in the Foresters up to speed."

Colonel Robert Feehan, commander of the Wolverton's Highlanders, stepped down from his *Tempest* and surveyed his regiment's deployment on the outskirts of New Bealton. The city itself was still some distance away, but Count Fisk had ordered him out. He looked around. If the Avengers were nearby, they sure weren't showing themselves.

In the distance, he saw a ground vehicle approaching, kicking up a cloud of dirt and dust as it came. Feehan was sure he knew who it was. He'd been expecting this visit ever since his regiment began to deploy in the rolling hillsides around their DropShips. Recent hard times had all but forced his unit to merge with Scott Blackstone's Highlanders, where they were second-class citizens, but things could change now. If his people could prove themselves worthy on this mission, perhaps they could break away as an independent unit again. If nothing else, at least he might impress Colonel Blackstone with a success.

The hovercar and its two passengers pulled up near the legs of his *Tempest* and stopped. Feehan recognized Nicholas Fisk from the many holovids he'd seen. He tried not to be annoyed by the arrogant tilt of the man's head, reminding himself that his unit's future was in the hands of this pompous ass. He had to keep Fisk happy, though he never thought he'd see the day when the Archon would put combat units under the command of planetary nobles.

The other man walked with a cane. His limp was severe, yet something military still showed in his bearing. One eye was obviously artificial, ringed with the metal of a bionic replacement. As the two men approached, Feehan wiped his hands on his faded fatigues and stepped forward to greet them.

"Count Fisk," he said, bowing his head respectfully.

"Colonel Feehan," replied the Count, one hand holding the edge of his dark blue half-cape, which was being whipped about in the wind. "I am pleased that you made it to the surface without difficulty."

"I've been looking forward to meeting you, your Grace," Feehan said.

"May I present my son, Luther Fisk?" The Count indicated the younger man, who clicked his heels smartly. "He will act as my liaison with your unit while you are on Odessa."

Feehan tried to smile affably, but his stomach knotted at the news. The last thing he wanted was his employer's son looking over his shoulder. Beggars, of course, had no right to be choosers.

"I'm honored that you would post your son to our command," he said, "and I look forward to having him with us."

Fisk's lip curled slightly. "Good, Colonel, because I have a very special assignment for your Highlanders. As I'm sure you are aware, the First Thorin Regiment is on Odessa."

Feehan nodded. He'd gotten only dribs and drabs of data on Odessa since being obliged to "loan" two of his heaviest lances to the Count and his Loki operative weeks earlier. He still had been unable to reestablish contact with those units, and he'd lost more than one night's sleep wondering about them. He knew they had seen action and had incurred losses, but that was all he'd been able to find out. Worse, he already suspected how his men had been used, and the knowledge weighed heavily.

"As I understood it, Snord's Irregulars has been fighting them," he said.

Fisk nodded. "Yes, but matters have taken a turn that none of us could have expected. The Irregulars have been forced to withdraw to the ruins of Bealton and are under siege by Archer's Avengers."

"Do you want me to coordinate with them, your Grace?" Feehan offered quickly.

"In a manner of speaking, yes. The situation has been complicated by the fact that the Irregulars' contract expired as of midnight last night. Officially, they are no longer under my command or authority."

"And they have not renewed their contract?"

"Not yet," the Count replied casually. "But that will

not stand in my way. My main concern right now is that the First Thorin Regiment not leave Odessa intact. The Avengers are totally occupied with keeping the Irregulars bottled up. If you launch an all-out assault, you can hit their rear and take them permanently out of action."

Feehan nodded and found himself smiling. "Yes, m'lord. We're a light regiment, but they've probably lost both men and material if they've been fighting for a while. Once I get a full report, I will plan a detailed assault to break them once and for all."

"Excellent," the Count said. "My son should be able to provide you with any information you require." He turned and started walking back to the hovercraft.

"Your Grace?" Colonel Feehan called after him.

The Count turned back to him. "Yes, Colonel?"

"What about the Irregulars?"

"What do you mean, Colonel?"

"I assume you wish me to relieve them."

"Not necessarily," the Count said. "My other reason for bringing you here is to make sure the Irregulars either join the fight against Prince Victor or are left in no state to be of any assistance to him. If I were you, I'd make sure they help you bloody the First Thorin Regiment.

"What happens to them after the dust settles—well, that's up to you. If they were to accidentally shoot at you in the middle of the fighting and you took the opportunity to finish them off, who would protest? You could probably help yourself to whatever equipment and supplies they may have, though I doubt Major Snord would let you walk away without a fight. Of course, the choice is yours."

Feehan nodded, rapidly calculating the implications. What the Count was suggesting was unethical, bordering on illegal. Yet, he was also getting the message that he could do whatever he wanted with the unit. The prestige of rescuing a class-A mercenary unit had a lot of appeal. Even better, getting his hands on all that heavy gear, much of it Clan origin, would turn his rundown unit into a force to be reckoned with.

"I wish to go on the record as saying that the Highlanders have no desire to engage the Irregulars in battle," he said, testing the waters.

Fisk chuckled. "Of course. But it's a little late for that, Colonel. Your two lances have already tangled with the Irregulars and with Archer's Avengers. I wonder what Rhonda Snord would do if she were to find out? Not to mention your new commanding officer, Colonel Blackstone. As I recall, he didn't sign off on your 'loan' of those lances, did he? I'm sure he'd be interested to know that his newly acquired regiment was trying to break away on its own."

"Threats aren't necessary," Feehan countered icily. "I didn't know what you planned to do with those units."

"Don't play naive with me, Colonel. You knew full well how I was going to use them. My Loki operative is stationed with them now, and I can provide documentation to prove it, if necessary."

Feehan felt his face flush with anger. "I never—"

Count Fisk waved an airy hand. "Enough of this idle chatter, Colonel. Your hands are as bloody as everyone else's in this matter. If I were you, I would eliminate anyone who might make a case against you and your regiment . . . times being what they are."

Robert Feehan seethed silently at the veiled reference to his unit's diminished reputation. "I understand, your Grace," he said, softening his tone.

"I'm sure you do, Colonel. But mark my words. Don't let me down. I have little tolerance for failure." With that, Fisk turned to go, followed by his son. They headed back to the hovercraft that would carry them away from the Wolverton's Highlanders—and responsibility for anything that might result from the Highlanders' presence on Odessa.

Feehan stared at the vehicle as it rose above the ground, fans whirring. He wondered if he'd been wrong about this assignment. It had seemed to offer salvation for him and his unit, but now it looked like it might be their downfall instead.

20

Near Gottfredson, Odessa
District of Donegal
Lyran Alliance
1 May 3063

The old commercial barn was a five-story, oblong structure whose latticework metal roof had caved in here and there, probably decades before. Even from her concealed position on a nearby hilltop, Katya could tell that the structure was generally intact but far from sturdy. The tiny village of Gottfredson was also visible in the distance, but she and Thomas Sherwood were focused only on the barn, studying its every detail.

They had been planning the operation for the past day or so, and she had been impressed with the young Captain's energy despite his recent injuries. "You sure this is the best way to do this, Thomas?"

"No. But the general's orders were to secure the facility and all personnel to see whether we can find evidence that someone other than the Irregulars was responsible for the ambush. Frankly, that old barn could easily hold a whole company of BattleMechs and enough security to waste everything I've got."

She read the frustration in his voice, knowing the lives of so many people hung in the balance. "Well, you're the expert in special ops, Thomas. Gramash and I are only along to provide you with additional support if you need it." She looked around at their position on the hilltop. "Though I must admit that I would have expected something stealthier."

He lowered his binoculars and gave her a smile. "I would have been more creative if I'd had more notice." He pulled out his comm unit. "Time for some fun and games."

He activated the wrist unit and squinted down at the farm. "This is Forester One, all Foresters. Green, green, green."

With those words, an old farm truck began to approach the barn from the service road that ran nearby. Loaded with what looked like bales of spring hay, its wheels splashed up mud from potholes in the dirt road. As the truck turned and began to approach the barn, movement became visible near the barn doors.

Sherwood focused in with his enhanced binoculars, while Katya pulled out her surveillance gear so she could watch, too.

Two men had stepped out of the barn by now. Then two more appeared from the rear of the building and had begun jogging behind the truck. The first two signaled for the truck to stop. They were dressed as farmers, but odd bulges in their clothes suggested concealed weapons.

Katya watched as the "farmers" began talking with the truck driver as they began to casually circle the vehicle, examining the load of hay. Farther away, out of the view of the "farmers," a squad of troopers was moving in.

The driver had gotten out of his truck by now and seemed to be having a heated discussion with the farmers. Waving his arms in disgust, he stomped away from the vehicle, followed by two of the "farmers," still arguing.

A moment later, an explosion caved in a large portion of the barn's exterior, blasting the truck, the hay, and everything else nearby into the air. The two "farmers" who'd stayed behind disappeared in the blast. The two who'd followed the driver were thrown through the air. The driver, having set off the blast, had dived for cover even as the truck vaporized in a red and orange ball of flame. Now he pulled out a small autopistol and began to fire at the already felled "farmers," setting off a spray of blood mist.

While that was happening, gunfire erupted from the assault team on the far side of the barn. Smoke rose in the distance, followed by the appearance of three Avenger BattleMechs on the road. With a fast-moving *Hussar* in the lead, they charged through the gaping hole the truck-bomb had created in the barn wall. Katya heard the discharge of lasers and saw flickers of crimson and green light as the second 'Mech, a *Spider*, passed through the rent in the wall.

It was over in a matter of seconds. Her field communicator crackled, followed by a code phrase, repeated fast: "Blue, blue, blue." Operation successful.

Sherwood glanced at Katya and smiled. "My favorite part of these things is when they end."

Katya grimaced. "Easy for you to say. My work is just beginning." She slid down the hillside to join Gramash at the barn.

The Avenger 'Mechs stood guard while Katya and Sherwood went inside the barn, which was mostly dark despite the daylight outside. Along the far wall, across from the yawning hole, were two lances of BattleMechs. Two of the machines were more parts than 'Mech, having been stripped for salvage. All had been freshly painted in camouflage, including the insignia of a rabid wolverine against a blood-red disk, the mark of the Wolverton's Highlanders. They were also wearing the gray and black mailed fist of the Blackstone Highlanders, their parent unit.

The dozen prisoners who'd survived the explosion were on their knees, their hands held behind their heads with plasteel retraining straps. Gramash walked slowly down their line, looking at each one in the face. Some kept their heads down to avoid his gaze, but he used his cane to lift their faces up by the chin so he could look into their eyes.

"One of your men has already talked," he said quietly. "Quite an ingenious plan, too. Disguised, you strike at both sides and get them to beat the hell out of each other. But what I want to know is who ordered this?"

He stopped in front of one of them and smiled broadly. "Ah—I believe I've found our link, Major Chaffee," Gramash said. "Good to see you, old friend."

"You know him?" Katya asked.

Gramash nodded. "Oh, yes. We went to school together. Not the kind of school that any government likes to acknowledge, though—isn't that right, old friend?"

"I have nothing to say," the man spat out.

"What name do you go by now?"

"Does it matter?"

"Just curious. You always picked something with a 'v' in it. I'll get it out of you eventually. You know that."

"Don't bother," the man said, visibly swelling with anger. "I go by the name of Erwin Vester. That name will, of course, do you no good."

Gramash smiled. "Sorry to do this to you, old friend, but you know how the game is played."

"That's the difference between us," Vester snapped. "I don't think it's a game." His next words gave Katya a start. "You were once a member of Loki too. You know we never leave any evidence behind. So threaten me all you want—you won't get a thing."

"These BattleMechs are fairly incriminating evidence," Gramash said, gesturing to the line of 'Mechs along the wall of the old barn.

"Of what?" Vester asked coolly. "All of the battleroms are missing or have been purged."

"Really?" Gramash said calmly.

"That's right. A bunch of freshly painted 'Mechs doesn't prove anything. If there was ever any evidence, it's gone now. All you've got is a few 'Mechs, nothing more."

"Not entirely," Gramash said. "NAIS has come up with ways to track the individual signatures of fusion-reactor cores. We were able to get the research off New Avalon before the hostilities broke out. From the detailed scans we have of your failed attempt on the life of General Christifori, we have enough to match it against the signature readings from those reactors. They're better than retina or DNA scans."

"Bull," Vester said. "That technology doesn't exist yet."

"I guess you've fallen behind, what with the civil war and all," Gramash said equably. "Besides, I plan to torture the information out of you personally. Your confession will merely add to the technical evidence."

Vester laughed humorlessly. "I know that bluff as well as you do. You can't intimidate me."

"We'll see," Gramash said. He turned to Katya and pointed down at Vester. "Rip off his shirt and pants, but leave the restraints on. Cut his clothes off if you have to. Leave him naked right here."

There were murmurs of protest from the other prisoners, and Gramash motioned to the guards to escort them away. "Watch his hands. Don't let him touch any part of his body."

Easier said than done. It took three of Captain

Sherwood's infantry to hold the man, but he was soon naked and on his knees on the barn floor.

Gramash circled him slowly, examining the man's body clinically. Then, without a word, he reached down and tugged at the skin on Vester's rib cage. At first, it looked to Katya like he was going to literally rip off a piece of flesh, but what came away was a tiny, square, flesh-colored patch with fake hairs woven into it. He tossed it to Katya, who caught it gingerly and held it away from her like it was a dead bug.

"We call them QO's—quick outs," Gramash said. "If he'd gotten to it, a quick squeeze and the poison would've killed him in a few seconds. It's absorbed quickly in the skin. More important, it can spread through secretions in the skin to anyone touching the victim. He could've taken a couple of us with him."

Gramash used his cane again to lift Erwin Vester's chin, but this time the man's cockiness was gone. Katya put the patch in a small plastic container and sealed it. "You see—I do remember our training," Gramash told Vester.

"I'll never talk," Vester spat back.

"Please don't insult me with bravado," Gramash said coldly. "You'll talk. The medications Major Chaffee brought with her are enough to make you sing and dance in a tutu if I want you to." Without looking away, Gramash held out one hand to Katya, who immediately gave him a hypo.

"You've used triptipheno-xelic acid, haven't you?" Gramash went on. "I remember the session where they gave us that stuff. You'll talk, but the downside is that it melts your neuroconnections as it works. Permanently. You'll slowly lose control of your extremities, then your internal organs will begin to misfire.

"Fortunately, it's genetically engineered to keep your vocal cords and brain intact and functional until the very end. But you know that, don't you? Smaller doses are not as lethal, but just as painful. Messy stuff. Hell of a way to die." He shook his head and leaned forward on his cane. "But you will tell me everything first."

"You wouldn't use that on me," Vester said.

"And why not? Because it's inhumane?" Gramash frowned. "In our line of work, sometimes people have to die to get what we need. Maybe I don't like doing this, but I will if I have to."

Vester said nothing for a while. Then, "I'm worth more to you alive than dead."

Gramash cocked an eyebrow. "What makes you say that?"

"I can hand you Odessa, or at least Count Fisk. I know where some of the evidence is buried—not just here, but on other worlds. You won't use the drug, because you'd never get everything I know out of me before I died."

Katya watched, something in her rebelling as the drama played out. She believed what Gramash was saying. It would take time to torture him through normal, "conventional" means—time the Avengers didn't have.

In the past, Gramash probably would have bluffed about injecting Vester until he broke. Now, though, a civil war was raging and Gramash himself had nearly died as the result of Vester's spy activities.

With one quick movement, the young officer stabbed the needle into Vester's neck. "Even the most devoted agent breaks under this kind of pain," he said simply. "Pretty soon you'll be begging me to kill you."

Vester's eyes flared in horrified disbelief. He never thought Gramash would do it, and now it was too late for him to be so wrong.

The screaming had gone on for so long that Gramash had become numb to it. Vester struggled to hold out, but in the end, he broke. Within an hour, Gramash and Katya had everything they needed. As Vester talked and screamed and begged, Gramash recorded his words. Finally, he stabbed him with another hypodermic.

"Death at last," Vester said through a sweaty haze.

"No," Gramash said. "Triptipheno-xelic acid would have killed you. I used a derivative of ceniyo-choloratic. It duplicates the effects of the acid, but not permanently. You've been given just enough neutralizer to keep you too weak to move."

"You tricked me?"

Gramash smiled thinly. "I don't enjoy torture, but it does work, even against the best minds."

"I'll kill you," Vester said weakly.

"No, you won't. You tried that once and failed. You'll remain a prisoner of Prince Victor until we can squeeze every bit of useful data out of you. You, Vester, are a prize asset."

Vester slumped. He'd been duped and tortured at the same time, his mind and body broken. Several of Archer's specially trained infantry began powering up the barn's BattleMechs. They would take them to the First Thorin's command post, where the machines would be welcome reinforcements. The prisoners and anything else of use in the barn were removed for relocation, in preparation for the fire that would consume it. Just before the charges were set off, Katya stopped Gramash in the doorway.

"One thing, Sergeant," she said, keeping her voice low so the others wouldn't hear her.

"Of course," he replied.

"I didn't know about the reactor-signature matching. Where's the hardware for it? That kind of technology would sure be useful down the road."

Gramash smiled. "Sounds cool, doesn't it? Too bad NAIS still hasn't been able to pull it off."

"Another lie?"

He broadened his grin. "No. Misinformation. A good tool, don't you think?"

"I never want to use torture like that," Katya said.

Gramash gave a helpless shrug. "I had no choice. Things have changed, Katya."

"Things?"

"*I've* changed."

Katya stared at him for a moment. "I guess war does that," she said, "even to spies."

21

Hill 403, Odessa
District of Donegal
Lyran Alliance
2 May 3063

"So that's it?" Archer asked as he stared at the image hovering in the space over the portable holo-projector in his field tent. The fight being played out from the point of view of the cockpit camera showed the *Anvil* savaging Rhonda Snord's *Highlander* from the rear flank.

For the second time since reviewing the battleroms, he saw the *Highlander* fall under wave after wave of fire from several BattleMechs. He had closed the data-display windows showing the damage done to the 'Mech. He didn't need them—the images told him everything.

Rhonda Snord had been ambushed just like he had, and by the same people. It was a Loki-inspired trick to plunge the two sides into battle with each other. And he was sure the attack could only have been planned, financed, and sanctioned by Count Nicholas Fisk, who had used another mercenary unit as his tool of destruction. Fisk's fingerprints were everywhere, but in the end, Archer placed the blame higher—on the Archon herself.

"That's it, General," Anton Gramash said from where he sat in one of the tent's folding chairs. "Snord's Irregulars were attacked almost at the same time that we were."

"And we have a battlerom of the attack on the Rotunda, as well as Erwin Vester's testimony implicating Count Fisk," Katya added. "Combined with the other intel we've gathered, I'd say we've verified our theory."

Archer shut off the holoprojector. "My hat's off to you, Katya," he said. "In fact, I don't see how the case could be more solid against the Wolverton's Highlanders and Count Fisk. Now we know why we haven't seen Rhonda Snord and why the Irregulars have been fighting with such ferocity."

"From what Vester told us, Snord is alive but in a coma," Gramash said, rubbing his arm at the memory of the ambush. "He also confirmed what Captain Sherwood witnessed: the rest of the Wolverton's Highlanders have dropped on Odessa. The Count plans to use them against us as well."

Archer nodded. "Alesia," he said softly, more to himself than aloud.

"Sir?"

"Caesar's epic battle of Alesia. I was fascinated by it when I was at NAIS. Caesar had the Gauls in their fort surrounded on all sides, totally encircled and pinned down. Then he was attacked by a relieving force attempting to break in to free the Gauls, and they surrounded him. Caesar was forced to fight in both directions, inward and outward."

Katya's eyes narrowed. "That was an awful long time ago. How'd it end?"

"Caesar won. He built fortifications facing both in and out and beat both sides. Like Caesar, we've got the Irregulars bottled up, and now we're going to be hit by a force on our backsides. Hell of a way to fight a war, don't you think?"

"Caesar won, though."

Archer frowned. "I might be a general, but that doesn't make me Caesar. I don't want to end up in that kind of fight. Even if we won, there wouldn't be enough of us left to be a viable force for months to come—if ever."

"We've caught Count Fisk with his pants down and have enough evidence to convince anyone," Katya retorted. "It seems to me we've got the upper hand for a change."

Archer nodded. "The evidence is good, Katya. But getting it to the Irregulars is another story. Tasha Snord will probably think we fabricated the whole thing to lure her out. You got me the proof, and that's incredible. But making it stick is going to require one hell of a tap dance on my part."

"I'm sure Major Snord will listen," Katya said, though she saw Gramash cross his arms and shake his head.

"The general is probably right," he said. "We've had the Irregulars under siege for a while now. We've gone head to head with them for every mound of rubble we've been able to secure. Most mercs would have folded by now. From what Vester told me, their contract with the Alliance finally ran out a few days ago. People on both sides have been killed or injured. If they're hanging on now, it's because it's gotten personal."

"I agree," Archer said. "They didn't get that A-class merc rating by being quitters."

"So how are you going to get through to Tasha Snord?" Katya asked.

"I'm going to have to make sure she actually sees our evidence, not just try to get it to her. For that, I'll need your help."

"Anything," Katya said.

"You'll be in command of the regiment in my absence, with instructions about what to do if I don't come back."

Concern rippled across her face. "You're not going to do anything stupid, are you?"

Archer smiled in spite of himself. "If I told you, you'd just try to argue me out of it. Besides, right now, it's still just the germ of an idea. I need a few hours to turn it into a plan. Suffice it to say I'll be going out on a limb, and I need you here in case I crawl out too far and can't get back."

"You've got to rest, sir," the medtech said as he tried to get Rhonda Snord to lie back. She resisted, and with more strength than he would have expected.

"Rest? I've been out for days," she said hoarsely, pushing the man aside "Did you inform the major that I'm awake?" she asked, suppressing her weariness and drawing a long breath.

Before the man could answer, Tasha hurried in, rushing to her mother's side and grasping Rhonda's right hand in both of her own. "I came as soon as I heard. How are you, Mother?"

Rhonda took a sip from a glass of water the medtech handed her, wincing as the liquid stung her dry throat. "That's not important. My friend here gave me the short version of what's been going on. You fill me in on the rest."

Rhonda knew only that the unit was under siege. Though she certainly didn't blame Tasha, she saw the look of shame that crossed her daughter's face. The girl was always too hard on herself, Rhonda thought.

The briefing took well over thirty minutes, and little of the news was good. Rhonda listened intently, fighting the lure of her weakened condition that was begging for sleep.

She fixed her gaze on Tasha, devouring her words, reconstructing the battle in her mind. Her unit had been hard hit, taking casualties of almost fifty percent. The news of Shorty Sneede's death pained her the most. He'd been with the Irregulars back when her father had commanded. His loss felt like a heavy stone on her chest, crushing her against the bed. She would have to get a message about Shorty to her father, who by now would be back on Clinton. She dreaded it.

Tasha looked even wearier than Rhonda felt by the end of the briefing. It was the burden of command, and there was no escaping it.

When Tasha finally finished and let out a long sigh, Rhonda sat up and caught her daughter's eyes. "So here we are, penned up, surrounded, almost out of supplies, ammo, and food. Other than that, how are *you* doing?"

"What?"

"You. How are you holding up?"

Tasha managed a wan smile. "I haven't had time to think much about myself. Besides the Avengers, I've had to fight some of my own officers who want to run the unit differently. There are also the supply problems that have no hope of getting better.

"So, how am I holding up? I really don't know. I *am* thankful as all hell that you're finally awake. Running this unit has stretched me pretty thin." Tasha paused and glanced down at her dirty T-shirt and frayed shorts. "Frankly, I'm looking forward to a real shower more than anything else."

Rhonda leaned back in the bed. "It'll be a day or so before I'm up and about. Before I can jump back into the cockpit of a 'Mech, the medtechs have to make sure that blast of neurofeedback didn't do any permanent damage."

Tasha looked shaken by her words. "But you're awake. Command should return to you."

Rhonda smiled weakly. "It's never quite as easy as you hope, Tasha. You're still in command for now. You know the terrain and the current state of the unit better than I do. "

Tasha's jaw dropped, but Rhonda didn't give her time to protest. "I know what you're going to say, but I'm getting old, Tasha, whether you want to see it or not. A decade or two ago, I would've shaken off these injuries. Now, my joints and bones ache, and my head is pounding like a drum."

"You've been running this unit since before I was born," Tasha protested. "Everyone looks up to you— they respect you."

"They'll respect you over time as well. But only if you remain in command," Rhonda said firmly. "I'll be on hand to give you advice, but I need a day or two to get back in the saddle. When the time is right, I'll jump back in. But that's my call to make, not yours. A commanding officer sometimes has to deal with situations she cannot control. You've done very well thus far. I'm not going to take that away from you."

Her daughter shook her head. "I haven't done well. I've had to order retreats and I've gotten us bottled up in these godforsaken ruins. From a pure logistics sense, the unit is pretty strapped. Everyone is on edge."

Rhonda chuckled. "It's no different when I'm at the helm, Tasha. You just don't see it. If you were doing a bad job, the officers would be rebelling against you."

Tasha opened her mouth to say something, but a rap on the door of the medical dome cut her off.

Captain Norris entered and gave a quick salute to Rhonda and a brief nod of acknowledgment to Tasha. Rhonda could see bruises under his eyes and under the stubble of hair on his skull. The look in his eyes was sullen, but his attitude was crisp and military. "Colonel Snord, it is good to see you."

"Norris," she said, gesturing to his bruised face. "You've looked better."

Norris glanced quickly at Tasha, who said nothing, then back at Rhonda. "A minor disagreement regarding command priorities. It is not a matter that need concern you. I believe everyone will be pleased to see that you are up and around again, Colonel."

"Don't get too excited, Norris," Rhonda said. "I need another day or two."

"Very well," he said, then turned to Tasha. "Major Snord, one of our teams has uncovered a tunnel under these ruins. Apparently, it was part of a mass-transit system. From our initial survey, it is large enough to contain BattleMechs if they move carefully."

"Where does it lead?" Tasha asked eagerly.

"We are still exploring it. It is filled with rubble that must be cleared, of course, but the tunnel appears to run south for at least three kilometers before it is totally blocked. I have ordered a platoon of infantry to explore it fully. They believe that they can successfully blast through with shaped charges."

Tasha nodded. "If it does go that far, it would put us right behind the Avenger lines. We could hit them from two directions at once."

"Aye," Norris said, allowing himself a brief grin.

"Check it out," Tasha said. "I want to make sure it's safe before I send in a full company on a raid."

Norris bowed slightly. "I will handle it, Major," he replied, then turned and left the medical dome.

"Mother . . ." Tasha said apologetically as she took a step toward the door.

"I understand," Rhonda said. "But before you go, what happened to Norris? Those don't look like the kind of injuries someone gets in a 'Mech cockpit."

Tasha smiled sheepishly. "Maybe I missed some details in the briefing, but he's all right now. All that matters at the moment is that you're okay. If you managed to survive this thing, so can I, and so can the Irregulars.

"All that's left now is to win."

22

Wolverton's Highlanders Mobile Command Post
South of New Bealton, Odessa
District of Donegal
Lyran Alliance
2 May 3063

The brilliant Odessan sun was just coming up outside the Highlander mobile command post, the morning dew turning to mist as the sun's rays warmed the grasses. Inside, Colonel Robert Feehan stared nervously at the holomap on display. Odessa was a beautiful world of only twenty million people, and among those millions were two combat units—Archer's Avengers and Snord's Irregulars. As he studied their positions to the far north of his own base camp, he contemplated how exactly he would deal with them.

The Wolverton's Highlanders were primarily light and medium 'Mechs, built more for speed than brute force. The best way to leverage that, to his mind, was to punch through the ring of Avengers that had the Irregulars trapped in the city. By cutting the First Thorin regiment in half, he could turn their flanks and wipe them out piecemeal. It would be a coup de grâce, and he looked forward to it. A battlefield success against the Avengers would end a long and painful chapter in his unit's history.

But that still left him with the problem of what to do with the Irregulars. A lot depended on how bad the unit had been hurt during the siege. Feehan had decided to see if he could convince Major Snord to break out at the same time he attacked. That way, whatever was left of her unit would draw the Avengers' fire until he got through. Then he could make his choice: relieve his fellow mercenaries, or simply wade into them and finish them off in the heat of battle.

Oddly enough, the second option was the one he was favoring. If he didn't destroy the Irregulars, he risked them finding out that his people had been responsible for the ambush on Rhonda Snord. He didn't relish the prospect of a unit like that out for his head. Wiping them out would eliminate the problem entirely. The only thing he disliked about the option was that it was also the one Count Fisk favored.

He'd figured it out, and on paper, it looked like he had the firepower to take out both units. In fact, he thought at least facts actually shifted the odds in his favor. First, his troops were fresh, while both of his intended targets were exhausted from battling each other. Second, he had the advantage of surprise. The First Thorin would be caught off-guard, and he'd be hitting them from the rear. And the Irregulars would never expect their rescuers to turn on them. He was also counting on the fact that both units would be so weakened that they'd capitulate rather than fight to the death. Victory for the Wolverton's Highlanders was entirely possible.

Luther Fisk limped into the planning room of the mobile HQ, looking a little annoyed. He had been out inspecting the troops, with orders to bring back the two lances his father had "borrowed" for his ambush on the Avengers and the Irregulars. That had been five hours ago. His return meant that the Highlanders were back together again.

"I trust my Highlanders met your expectations?" Feehan asked as Luther leaned forward to study the holographic display where he was working.

"Yes, Colonel. I was impressed. Given the unit's recent history, I expected to find them in a more dilapidated condition. I was pleasantly surprised."

"I'm glad," Feehan said evenly, ignoring the insult.

"But why didn't you tell me you had relocated those 'Mech lances my father and his Loki man were using?" Luther demanded. "It would've saved me a trip out to the middle of nowhere."

Feehan felt his senses suddenly scream. "I didn't relocate those 'Mechs," he said.

Luther Fisk's face fell slightly, then turned red. "When I got there, I found the site recently burned down. There were some 'Mech prints, but most were obscured. There was no evidence of a battle, so I assumed you'd moved them and burned the site to cover your tracks."

Feehan shook his head. "Not me, damn it. Is it possible this agent working for your father might have moved them?"

"Vester?" Luther shrugged slightly, looking dubious. "It's possible, I guess, but I think my father would have said something. Of course, with Loki, who can tell? They tend to play by their own of rules."

"So we don't know?" Feehan insisted.

"I'll check with my father," Luther said.

"You do that," Feehan said shortly. "Because if he didn't relocate the 'Mechs, it had to be either Snord or Christifori who did. Which means they may have learned of my unit's involvement in those ambushes. I don't want this battle to turn against me before it even begins."

Luther laughed dismissively. "The odds of that are pretty slim, but I'll follow up on it. The last thing my father wants is for you to lose the advantage of surprise."

He gestured to the holodisplay. "Besides, Snord's Irregulars certainly aren't going anywhere. They're bleeding to death in those ruins. As for the Avengers, I don't think they could pull enough forces away from the siege of Bealton to capture that many BattleMechs without leaving traces of a pitched battle. Relax, Colonel," he concluded. "Everything is under control."

"Those men and women report to me," Feehan said. "I'm responsible for them. Check with your father and find out, Fisk. I need to know if our security has been compromised."

Katya's last words still rung in Archer's ears as the old J-27 transport bumped through the trees. "This is a mistake," she'd insisted. "It's too risky."

As he approached the clearing that separated the woods and the ruins of old Bealton, Archer wondered if she was right. He slowed the munitions carrier to a crawl and stared with no little apprehension across the no man's land between his forces and those of the Irregulars. He just hoped to hell she was wrong.

He'd been pressing his luck ever since the day he got into the fight against the Archon. Back on Thorin, outnumbered and outgunned, he'd split his forces and also attacked Katherine's people on Muphrid, a scheme that had worked despite the fact that it made no real military sense. The press, especially Victor's supporters, had played it up as if Archer were some kind of strategic military genius. The truth was that he'd acted from sheer desperation because his choices were so limited.

He brought the transport to a halt and reached out through the open armored hatch to make sure the makeshift flag was still in place on the side of the vehicle. It was white, the color of truce or surrender.

Leaving the J-27 idling, he sat back and let out a long sigh of pent-up tension. Back in his regular army days, he'd never been obliged to deal with politics. Now, as a general, politics had become a way of life. He would much rather have visited the Irregulars in a BattleMech, but it was important that he not be perceived as a threat. He took hold of the yoke and throttled the transport forward again.

The vehicle had just rumbled over a rocky outcropping when his sensors—mere toys compared with those in his *Penetrator*—told him that a 'Mech was moving to intercept him. From the readings, it was a *Masakari*. Good. He was looking forward to meeting the MechWarrior who had stormed through the middle of his command post.

The *Masakari* came up over a hillside and leveled its weapons pods at Archer. Even at this range, he knew the MechWarrior could see the white flag. Besides, the old munitions carrier was unarmed.

To his total surprise, the *Masakari* fired a brilliant blue-white blast of PPC fire down at him. His cockpit glass shattered, and Archer was thrown back with such force that the wind was knocked from his lungs. His vision tunneled for a second, and then he passed out. His last conscious thought was that Katya Chaffee had been right after all.

23

The Junk Yard, Bealton ruins
Odessa
District of Donegal
Lyran Alliance
3 May 3063

The air was rank with sweat, dust, and the smell of humans living in the wilderness. The beefy hand of the MechWarrior who had captured Archer pushed him forward, knocking him off-balance. It didn't help that his own hands were bound behind his back, but he didn't complain. If their roles were reversed, he'd be acting the same way. They'd kept him overnight in a makeshift jail in the ruins of an old building, and this morning the big MechWarrior had come and brought him to Rhonda Snord's field tent.

"General Christifori," she said, her voice strong despite the fact that she seemed to need to hold onto a table to stay steady on her feet. "This is an honor we had not expected."

Archer gave her a slight bow. "You probably won't believe this, Colonel Snord," he said in an equally formal tone, "but I'm glad to see you're well." He noticed that Tasha, the younger Snord, frowned and crossed her arms as he spoke.

"That is hard to believe," Rhonda said, "considering what you did the last time we were to meet face to face."

"That is why I'm here, Colonel," he said, thinking she had no idea how much he, too, had lost that day.

"What was in the transport you captured, Norris?" she asked the big MechWarrior.

"Rations, water, and an officer's order case," he said, tossing the black metal briefcase on the table. "Our people are analyzing the food and water to confirm that it is not poisoned."

Archer looked down. He couldn't help but feel shame that anyone would suspect he would stoop to poisoning an enemy.

Tasha snapped open the case, picked up the circular black chips inside, and eyed them with some degree of skepticism. "Battleroms," she said to Rhonda, tossing them back into the case.

Archer stood as straight as he could with the one called Norris still holding the strap that bound his wrists. "I came here under the flag of truce for a reason. We were both set up, Colonel. I was attacked at the same time you were that night. In fact, it cost me the life of a comrade who meant a lot to me."

"And who was behind this attack? The Combine?" Tasha probed.

"No. It was ordered by Count Fisk, using troops from the Wolverton's Highlanders. They were disguised and sent to attack us at the same time. The plan was to kill the two of us and leave our junior officers to beat the snot out of each other."

"The Wolverton's Highlanders were absorbed by Scott Blackstone's unit," Tasha said.

Archer nodded. "I think Feehan must be running his own game. I met Blackstone once, and I can't believe he'd ever get involved in a dirty scheme like this."

"What motive would Fisk have?" Norris asked from behind him.

"Your contract was coming due with the Alliance," Archer said to Rhonda, ignoring him. "Everyone knew you wouldn't get involved in a civil war. But Fisk must have figured if you were assassinated, Major Snord would jump in for revenge's sake."

"And you really expect us to believe this?" Tasha asked.

"The only reason I came to Odessa was to negotiate with your unit, in hopes of persuading you to work for Prince Victor instead of Katherine. But even I got fooled. I was pulled into this along with my whole regiment. We've been beating each other senseless all this time, while the only people benefitting from it are Count Fisk and Katherine Steiner-Davion."

Rhonda looked at Archer evenly for several moments. "So what do you want from me now, General?"

"We discovered proof showing how the Wolverton's Highlanders were used against us. We recovered the 'Mechs they used, the Loki agent who was running the show for Fisk, and even two of their battleroms. The 'Mechs that attacked you weren't from my unit, and I have evidence, including the holovid recording of the Loki agent's confession. It's all in that case."

Rhonda didn't even glance at the case. "You still didn't answer my question, General. Why are you here?"

Archer felt his face tighten. "The rest of the Highlanders have arrived on Odessa by now, and they're planning to attack us at any moment." He saw Rhonda and Tasha exchange wary glances. "Frankly, Colonel, I have no desire to fight both you and them. And based on what I know now, they are my real enemy, not you. I got suckered into fighting you, mostly out of a desire to avenge my old friend's death. But I came to Odessa to recruit you, not to fight you."

"Why not simply transmit the data?" Tasha probed. "Why come in person?"

Archer shook his head once, heavily. "You don't want to believe me now, even with the physical evidence in hand. You'd never buy the story if I'd merely sent it to you. No, this required a personal visit."

"And the rations and water?" Rhonda asked, her tone softer.

"You and I have been MechWarriors for a long time. I have a pretty good feel for your condition. You've got to be running low on both food and water by now, no matter how much rationing you've done. I'm also returning the J-27 we captured from you. It's a good thing I left its ammunition behind, though." He turned to look at the one called Norris. "Considering this fellow's reaction, I'm just lucky the vehicle wasn't loaded."

Rhonda listened intently, her face betraying none of her thoughts. Tasha, on the other hand, looked at him angrily, as a man who had cost her a great deal. Which was true.

"And why you?" Rhonda asked. "Why not send one of your officers?"

This was the crucial moment, the one Archer was counting on to sway Rhonda Snord. "I am the commanding officer of the First Thorin Regiment, Colonel. For better or worse, I'm the man responsible for my unit. To tell you the truth, I didn't put much store in the theory that we'd been set up when my own people started to ask questions. To prove my sincerity, I'm surrendering conditionally to you and the Irregulars. You can hold me hostage, slap me in irons, whatever. I'm willing to put my life on the line to back up what I've told you."

He turned to Tasha. "And just so you know, Major,

I've ordered Major Chaffee, my XO, to pull the Avengers back. We're turning around to face the Wolverton's Highlanders. Some of our civilian contacts have given us a pretty good picture of their movements. I left standing orders to exchange no further fire with the Irregulars."

"So, we can just walk out of here if we want?" Tasha asked skeptically. "Is that what you expect us to believe, General?"

"Major Snord, you can do whatever you want," Archer said patiently. "My hope is that we can fight together against a common enemy who has already cost us good people and valuable equipment. If you want your pound of flesh from my people, you can get it, but you'll gain no honor from hitting an enemy that won't fight and has its back to you. The choice is yours."

Rhonda Snord motioned for Norris to lead Archer to a chair while Tasha picked up the case and tucked it under one arm. Norris called in another guard to watch Archer, then he and the two Snords left the tent.

Archer watched them go, then leaned back in the chair as best he could with his wrists tied and closed his eyes. He was exhausted but also very glad that he had made it at least this far.

"So you think these battleroms are authentic or else the best damn fakes ever forged?" Tasha asked the technician hovering over the reader in the command dome.

"Major, I just call 'em as I see 'em," the man replied. "If they're forgeries, they're the best I've ever seen."

Tasha nodded. "That will be all," she said, dismissing the man.

She looked over at her mother, who was sitting next

to the table that held the reader. Tasha thought she looked pale, probably from pain. "So, I guess the question is whether or not we believe Christifori."

Norris stepped forward, speaking before Rhonda could. "Anyone who would use such treachery and deceit against us and the Avengers must be dealt with. They must atone for their lack of honor."

Tasha thought he sounded like a judge pronouncing sentence, which surprised her. She had thought he would oppose Christifori and call for a strike against the Avengers.

Captain Deb H'Chu of the First Battalion, who had joined them at Tasha's behest, sat forward in her chair. "Christifori's story sounds pretty far-fetched to me. We've been working for the Lyran Alliance for decades. I find it hard to believe they would suddenly turn and stab us in the back."

There was a momentary silence in the room, and Tasha looked again at her mother. "You've haven't said a word yet, Colonel. What do you think?"

Rhonda raised her head, and the dark circles under her eyes betrayed her weakened state. Her injuries, especially the neurofeedback damage, had taken a lot out of her.

"It all boils down to who has the most to gain," Rhonda said. "Christifori and his people came to Odessa to get us to join them. We hadn't even begun to talk when I was ambushed. In hindsight, it seems like we should've started questioning the whole thing then and there."

"So you believe we were suckered?" H'Chu asked.

Rhonda nodded. "If Christifori hadn't shown up here in person to surrender himself, I probably wouldn't have. But he took a big risk showing up here unarmed. And from what our scouts say, the Avengers have all pulled back, as promised."

"He did bring food and water. If he wanted to defeat us, all he had to do was to hold out a few more days, and we would've been forced to negotiate with him. That counts for something, too," H'Chu said.

Tasha slumped in her chair. "After all these years—to be double-crossed by the Lyran Alliance," she said, shaking her head in disbelief. "I wonder if the Archon-Princess knew?"

"It does not matter," Norris retorted. "The Count answers to her. Katrina Steiner-Davion is as guilty as the man who did this."

"So what do you want us to do, Colonel? Should we fight alongside the Avengers or simply bug out of here?" Tasha asked.

Rhonda waved away the question. "It's your call. I'm still not fit enough to command. You're the boss of the Irregulars."

"But what—"

"No, Major," Rhonda said with unusual formality. "I've given you my assessment of the situation. A leader can ask for advice, but in the end, you have to set our course and get us there. I trust whatever decision you arrive at, and that should be enough."

Tasha put her elbows on the table and stared into her mother's tired eyes for a few moments. "Okay, then," she said finally. "Let's go talk with the general."

Archer looked up as Rhonda and Tasha Snord, Norris, and another older woman with jet-black hair and Asian features came back into the tent.

"General Christifori," Tasha Snord said solemnly. "We've reviewed the data you brought us."

Archer tensed as she pulled a knife from her web belt and took a step toward him. Then he relaxed when she bent to cut the restraint holding his wrists. His fingertips tingled as the blood started flowing back into them. He brought his hands in front of him, rubbing his wrists.

"I wish to extend to you an apology. It appears we were deceived by the same people who tricked you," she said.

Archer rose slowly and saluted, which all the others returned. Then he extended his hand, which Tasha clasped firmly. "I regret the pain and loss this whole thing has caused us both," he said.

Tasha nodded sadly.

"I fully understand if you don't want to fight alongside us," Archer went on, "after all that's happened. My Avengers should be able to beat the Highlanders on our own, but we could beat them a lot faster and more effectively if we fought together. Till now, they used the advantage of catching us off guard and hitting our rear."

Tasha glanced at her mother. "The Irregulars' contract with the Lyran Alliance has lapsed, General Christifori. That makes us free agents of sorts. I think I speak for all of our people when I say we would be honored to fight alongside you."

She glanced at the other three, who nodded their agreement.

"Good," Archer said, smiling now. "Where do we begin?"

"We need repairs, ammo, spare parts, and any of our MechWarriors you captured . . . and their 'Mechs, if that's possible," Tasha said immediately.

"Done." Archer knew this was a test to see how they could trust him. "I've got some ideas of how we can get Fisk and Colonel Feehan, too. I think we could pull off a little hoax of our own." He looked over at Rhonda Snord. "I'll need your help, Colonel Snord."

She raised an eyebrow. "I'm not in the best shape to help anyone, General."

"You don't exactly have to do anything," he said.

"But your death—now, that would be something we could leverage." The faces of the other two officers darkened angrily at his words, but Archer saw the fire in Rhonda's eyes as she caught his meaning.

"That I can do, General Christifori," she said, a smile spreading across her weary face. "I can definitely die."

24

The Junk Yard
Bealton, Odessa
District of Donegal
Lyran Alliance
4 May 3063

Major Tasha Snord stood near the field holoprojector
in the cramped space of the portable command dome
communications office, where the comm officer nodded to indicate that the linkup was complete. The projector was a dull black circular disk a half-meter in
diameter and five centimeters thick. A faded yellow
light flickered to life in the air above it, followed by
a static-filled image of Robert Feehan.

He was a man of average height, with dull blond,
prematurely graying hair. His mustache was tinged
with gray as well, with its ends curled up. He wore a
fatigue jumpsuit, with his rank insignia on the
epaulets.

In contrast, Tasha's clothing was covered with a thin
layer of dust and dirt. Spots of green 'Mech coolant
stained her shirt, and her shorts were smeared with
lubricant where she'd used them to wipe off her hands.
Wet spots of sweat stained her shirt collar and under-
arms. Her hair hadn't been washed in days and was
slicked back, leaving only the neuroconnection points

along her hairline to mark her as anything more than a field tech.

"Colonel Feehan?"

"Major Snord," he said formally.

"I understand you are on Odessa?"

"Yes, Major. Count Fisk ordered us here. We are fully staged to move out with our entire regiment in the next three hours. We're about thirty kilometers due south of your position."

"Move out? What are you planning?"

"The Count has asked us to rescue the Irregulars, Major. We will strike at the First Thorin Regiment, then punch through to you in old Bealton. Be ready to evacuate your wounded and noncombatants, especially Colonel Snord." He lowered his eyes almost reverently, and Tasha gave a silent snort of disgust at his hypocrisy.

"There have been a few changes in the last day or so, Colonel. My mother . . . my mother passed away yesterday."

"My condolences, Major," Feehan said after a slight pause. "I guess that puts you in permanent command of the Irregulars."

"Yes," she said, looking straight at the half-size holographic image hovering in front of her. "The First Thorin penetrated our perimeter and hit our command post. We've suffered extensive injuries."

"I'm sorry, Major."

"It's not all a wash, though," she said, nodding to Norris. He stepped forward, pushing a man in front of him into projector range. The man's hands were bound behind his back, and he was soaked in sweat. He looked like a beaten man. "We were able to capture the man responsible for my mother's ambush and death. Colonel, allow me to present General Archer Christifori."

Feehan looked surprised, then smiled broadly. "You captured him alive?"

"See for yourself," she said, gesturing to Archer, who refused to make eye contact with Feehan's image. "We're counting on his capture to take the fight out of the Avengers. I don't think we'll be needing any rescue. We can use our esteemed prisoner to get us out of this siege."

Feehan looked stunned. "Major Snord, the First Thorin is not likely to just let you go," he said, recovering. "I think it's best that I continue as planned. Together, we can not only defeat them but destroy them."

Tasha shook her head. "I won't be needing your help."

Feehan smiled. "Oh, but Major, I insist. Your unit's value to the Lyran Alliance is immeasurable. All you have to do is initiate a raid or draw the attention of the First Thorin in some other way, and we'll cut them to pieces."

"You won't change your mind?"

"No. My orders come from Count Fisk. This might be a good time for you to renew your contract with him, Major. The Count tells me that your mother opposed getting involved in a civil war, but you've done an outstanding job against the First Thorin."

"Thank you," she said evenly.

He offered an informal salute, which she returned. "Remember, Major, we strike in three hours. It would be a pity if you weren't able to show up for your own rescue."

The image disappeared, and Tasha turned to Archer Christifori. He stood up and brought his hands out from behind his back, discarding the pretense of restraints.

"How are the repairs going?" she asked.

"Major Chaffee tells me your damaged 'Mechs will

be ready to go by the time the Highlanders attack," Archer said.

"Good. I've arranged for our ground staff to set up a base with yours on Hill 403. Oh, and I appreciate the ammunition and parts, General."

"Now you'll be in a better position to employ your aerospace elements," Archer said.

"Sounds like this Feehan is planning to wipe your unit out."

Archer shrugged. "Fisk's just playing with his head. In many respects, Feehan's just a pawn in all of this. Besides, from the sound of it, he's going to try to improve his unit's rating by supposedly saving your butts." Thanks to Gramash's interrogation of Vester, both commanders knew of the mercenary colonel's true intentions.

Tasha frowned. "First he ambushes us, and now he's trying to pretend to be the cavalry riding in to save the besieged homesteaders. That innocent act was laid on a little too thick for my taste."

"I hope you found my performance adequate," Archer said with a small laugh.

"You're no Immortal Warrior, but you do play a good prisoner, General," Tasha said, smiling back. "Feehan thinks that by suckering us into a fight, his Highlanders will be the only ones still standing."

"We'll make sure his plans take a little turn for the worse," Archer said.

"Yes," said Rhonda Snord as she entered the command dome and caught the last couple of words. "That is exactly what we'll do."

Count Nicholas Fisk's holographic image, though smaller than life-size, was still imposing in Feehan's cramped mobile HQ. "My people have had no luck in locating either my Loki agent or the missing Battle-Mechs, Colonel Feehan," the Count said, his tone menacing as he paced back and forth. "I suppose you've had no luck, either."

"No, m'lord," Feehan replied.

"Then we must assume the agent has been captured or killed. Chances are he took his own life when they tried to make him talk. He was supposed to have removed the physical evidence of our involvement in the ambush."

The word "our" stung Feehan. *His* involvement had been superficial at best, amounting to nothing more than turning a blind eye. Now, suddenly, he was as deeply implicated as his employer.

"We can't rely on that," he snapped. "And if the First Thorin Regiment has captured any of my people, they'll learn about my unit's involvement anyway."

"I guess that means there's only one thing you can do," the Count said thoughtfully. "You must attack now—strike before they can act on that information."

"Preparations are complete, sir. Based on my communication with Major Snord, I don't think she'll join in the attack. She didn't give any indication that she knew about this Vester fellow or what really happened in the ambush."

"By this time tomorrow, it won't matter," the Count said flatly. "You must move out as soon as possible and destroy the Avengers. Do you understand, Colonel?"

Feehan nodded. "Perfectly, m'lord," he said, bowing slightly to the holographic image.

"The death of Rhonda Snord will have her unit in disarray, commanded by an inexperienced girl. I'm sure you'll be able to turn that to your advantage."

"Snord was an outstanding field commander in her time," Feehan said with real sincerity. Snord's Irregulars were known throughout the Inner Sphere, and even among the Clans.

The Count seemed to puff up his chest slightly.

"Yes, she was, but like many mercenary commanders, a little shortsighted. That is where men like me come in. We provide the vision that a military man often cannot."

"I appreciate the opportunity you've given me and my unit, sir," Feehan said.

Fisk ignored the veiled sarcasm. "Don't fail me, Feehan," he said coldly. "You'll find I have little patience with those who let me down." With that, the light flickered yellow and the Count's image vanished back into thin air, leaving Feehan alone in his tiny communications room.

Piloting his *Axman,* Captain John Kraff led his lance to their predesignated coordinates. Looking around, he thought the rolling hills and tiny stands of trees were a lot more pleasant than the endless monotony of the siege area around old Bealton. His destination was a ring of hills to the south of the command post now shared by the Avengers and the Irregulars. Somewhere, several kilometers farther south of them, was the vanguard of the Wolverton's Highlanders. And from what the general had said, they were headed this way.

"Rangers, fan your fat asses out," he said. "Make sure we link up with our flanks. I don't want any freaking gaps in the firing line." He stopped the *Axman* and adjusted the controls for his long-range sensors. His secondary display showed another lance of four 'Mechs whose IFF transponders tagged them as Irregulars.

He checked the data display to read the ID of the lead 'Mech, and said, "Ranger One to Scavenger Two. We are on your right flank. I suggest you take advantage of that rise to the left, the one with the rocky outcropping. Anyone charging over the top would be in for one hell of a surprise."

"We know our deployment pattern, Ranger One," a curt voice answered over the commline.

Kraff twisted inside his cramped cockpit and looked at the sensor readout for Scavenger Two. "Just trying to be friendly, partner," he said.

"We exchanged shots a few days ago, you and I."

"Well, we're on the same side now," Kraff said.

"It is awkward. But I have learned to adapt."

"Me, too."

"We are deploying as ordered, Ranger One. Since you have lighter 'Mechs with some longer-range sensors, I suggest you deploy them farther forward, aff?"

Aff? Kraff checked the 'Mech type and winced. A *Masakari*? "You're a Clanner, aren't you?" he couldn't resist asking.

"I am Captain Norris, acting commander of the Second Battalion. I am no longer Clan," the man said curtly.

"Captain John Kraff here, commander of the Muphrid Rangers."

"Indeed."

Kraff sent off a fast message for Corporal Mbenga's *Firestarter* to deploy farther forward, at the advice of his new comrade in arms. There was a long silence as he settled deeper into his seat and double-checked the *Axman*'s heat-sink controls and target interlock circuit settings. He jumped slightly when an alarm shrilled in his neurohelmet's earpiece.

"Ranger Five to all commands," Mbenga said. "I have movement on the outer marker. I paint two companies in the lead, three following in column formation. They are in sector 539 and closing fast."

Kraff could see that Mbenga was starting to pull back, not wanting to be the only 'Mech facing the attack force.

"You hear that, Captain Norris?" he asked as he throttled his *Axman* to life.

"Aye, Captain," came back the expressionless voice of Norris. "On my command, you sweep to the left flank. I will do the same on the right, and we can catch them in the crossfire."

Kraff frowned. "Damn it, who put you in charge of this operation?"

"Logic put me in charge," Norris replied. "Even you can see the merit in the overlapping fields of fire."

Knowing that Norris was right, but irritated by it, Kraff glanced at his tactical display and started moving to the left.

"Rangers, wheel to the left by lance," he commanded on his own channel, then turned on the command frequency. "I agree with you, Norris, but I sure as hell hate to admit it," he said.

Then he switched to the regimental command frequency. "Specter One, this is Ranger One. We have the enemy approaching in numbers. They have crossed the outer marker at five-three-niner. Transmitting tactical data now." He could see the first of the approaching Wolverton's Highlanders almost in range.

"Specter One to Ranger One and Scavenger Two," came back Christifori's voice. "Hit them hard and slow them down. We've got a few surprises inbound to your position now."

Kraff smiled as a green-painted *Assassin* crested the rocky hill and swung its medium pulse laser around toward him. His autocannon went on-line first and poured a stream of shells into the Highlander 'Mech's right arm. The *Assassin*'s shot went wide as the large-caliber AC rounds tore off its arm and sent it flying into the rocks. There was a rippling explosion as the 'Mech's long-range missile ammo cooked off, and the 'Mech went spinning and then stumbling down the hillside.

"Gonna be one hell of an afternoon, Norris," he said, more to himself than to the other MechWarrior.

To his surprise, the former Clansman answered him. "Aye, Captain Kraff. One hell of an afternoon."

25

South of Hill 403, Odessa
District of Donegal
Lyran Alliance
4 May 3063

"I've got them closing at one point five kilometers," came the voice of Tasha Snord over the commline as Archer took his *Penetrator* toward a semi-covered ledge on the hillside. "I'll say this for Feehan—he knows how to use his people. He pushed right past our advance companies with the faster 'Mechs. I'll bet Norris is pissed."

The Highlanders were coming at them with slightly less than a regiment, while the Irregulars and Avengers combined were more than a full regiment, and mostly heavier machines. The odds were in their favor.

"Stand by," Archer said. "Specter One to Sledgehammer and Spider One. Have your artillery units ready for the coordinates as we mapped them." Alice Getts and Paul Snider both confirmed as they prepared their units to deliver a deadly barrage of artillery fire.

Tasha Snord then came on-line, her *Spartan* moving to his left. "I've got my pair of Padillas ready as well, though we're running light, even with the reloads," she said.

"Right," Archer said, checking his sensors. The number of approaching 'Mechs was not encouraging, despite the fact that they were lighter-weight classes. Feehan was driving his machines straight at Hill 403 with a vengeance, and there was a good chance they might actually get through. For a moment, his thoughts turned to Katya and the other noncoms there. It worried him.

The advancing Highlander lances seemed to skim along the grassy slopes until they entered the marked artillery zone. "Light up the TAG units," Archer called over the open channel. "Artillery, fire at your discretion. Fire for effect!"

The waves of Arrow VI and long-range missile fire sounded like the rumble and roll of thunder coming from behind and above him. The enormous salvo stabbed at the advancing wave of 'Mechs, the missiles trailing smoke streams from their exhaust as Archer began to precharge his own extended-range large lasers. Out in the distance, five explosions ripped the air, marking the smoldering graves of five BattleMechs. The missiles switched from target to target, and for a short few seconds, the ground in the target sector churned as if a giant plow had been taken to it. The smoke obscured his vision, but his sensors told him the Highlander attack had blunted some of the onslaught.

The first wave of 'Mechs emerged from the haze, a dull-gray *Wolf Trap* leading a pair of *Jenner*s. A fluorescent green fluid belched from a hole in the lower torso of one of the *Jenner*s, the result of an Arrow missile hit.

Archer yanked his joystick just as the *Jenner*'s SRMs and medium lasers lanced out at him. A splatter of autocannon rounds also tore into his right-leg armor, shaking the *Penetrator* as if it were caught in an earthquake. His shoulders and lower back ached from being tossed so hard against the restraining straps of the ejection seat.

Armor sizzled off the *Penetrator*'s torso and arms as he turned, bringing his arm lasers to bear on the *Wolf Trap*. One shot hit each of the enemy 'Mech's arms, ripping off armor from the wrist to the shoulder actuator. The 'Mech's run slammed to a halt, and it tottered backward under the fury of the assault as the *Jenner*s continued past it. Archer fought to ignore the wave of heat, and was just bringing his medium pulse lasers to bear when he saw a white-hot flash of PPC fire tear into the *Wolf Trap,* hurling it against the rocks. The 'Mech skidded back nearly five meters, digging a small trench in the ground as it went.

He turned and saw Tasha's *Spartan* off to one side, its PPC hissing hot as it turned to another target. "Thanks, Major," he said, then unleashed two of his medium pulse lasers into the side and leg of one of the *Jenner*s as it raced past.

"No problem, General," she said while bringing her medium pulse lasers to bear on the other *Jenner*. Both Highlander 'Mechs were riddled with fire, but instead of slowing down to stand and fight, they ran right past.

"They're headed for the command post," he said.

"Roger that."

Archer switched comm channels. "Brain and Jailhouse Rocker, this is Specter One," he said even as a gray-green *Panther* also ran past him, firing its short-range missiles into the chest of Tasha Snord's *Spartan*. "They're overrunning our position. We're going to move east and regroup. Abandon the command post or brace yourselves for attack."

"Copy, Specter One," Katya said. "I've got our air support en route. We'll see if we can hold 'em."

"Take care of yourself, Katya," he said, unable to hide his concern.

"If she doesn't, *I've* got my eyes peeled," put in the deeper voice of Colonel Rhonda Snord.

Archer didn't waste another instant. He turned his *Penetrator* and broke into a run after a Highlander *Centurion* that was attempting to press his flank.

"Have at 'em," Snord called as he went. "We need a killing blow."

Katya was snapping out commands to the communications officer, who was climbing aboard the already crammed Blizzard armored transport. As the side door hissed and clanged shut, she scanned the area, making sure that everyone was clear of the site. In the distance, she could hear the rumble of missile and autocannon fire, and it was getting closer. She knew the sounds well, and the vibrations shook her bones as much as they stirred her blood. Satisfied that the command post was clear, she turned and saw only a single lance of 'Mechs standing on the flat top of Hill 403.

These were the last of the BattleMechs to be refitted, repaired, or manned—some Irregular, some Avenger. Most were not completely ready but were probably operational. Everyone knew them for what they were—the last line of defense.

The vehicles were clear and moving to the rear, but Katya still felt horribly exposed. She was in the middle of an approaching storm of combat, with no weapon and no defense. She watched while two MechWarriors climbed up the handholds to the cockpits of their towering machines.

Someone touched her shoulder, and she turned quickly. Standing in front of her was a woman in a battered old neurohelmet and cooling vest. At first, Katya didn't recognize her face through the helmet's small frontplate. Then she made out the well-known features and red hair of Colonel Rhonda Snord. The older officer thrust another neurohelmet and a rubbery cooling vest into Katya's hands.

Katya stared down at them for a moment. It was only ten or twelve years, but it seemed a lifetime since she had been a MechWarrior. She had taken a nearly fatal burst of neurofeedback in a cockpit hit on Tukayyid. It had so damaged her balance that at the longest she could only sustain very short outs at the controls of a 'Mech. Humbled but not wanting to give up the military, she had put her 'Mech piloting days behind her and transferred to intelligence. Like Archer, she had retired at the end of the Clan invasion, becoming a civilian and a weekend warrior in the Thorin Militia.

"Can you pilot a 'Mech?" Snord asked in a voice muffled by her sealed neurohelmet.

"It's been a while," Katya said nervously, holding the helmet and vest as if they were alien artifacts. "I'm not sure I still know how."

Snord pointed at the remaining 'Mechs behind her. "You can do it. It's in the blood. That *Hunchback* doesn't have a MechWarrior. Mount up. The techs said they purged the battle computer's security system, so you won't have any problem with start-up."

Katya stared up at the 'Mech and almost automatically pulled on the neurohelmet. Memories flooded back as she secured the chin seal. A part of her dreaded what might happen once she was back in the cockpit. Yet, this was the *Hunchback* they had recovered from the Wolverton's Highlanders—the one that had killed Darius Hopkins and was intended to take Archer's life as well.

What if she couldn't do this? What if she couldn't keep her balance or the 'Mech's? The *Hunchback* seemed to loom over her like a golem.

"Come on, Major. Let's move it," Rhonda Snord said, walking toward her *Highlander*. As if in a daze, Katya Chaffee began the long climb up the leg and torso of the *Hunchback*, and it felt like she was traveling back in time. The sounds of battle—no longer just the rumble of explosions but the whine of lasers and the crack of PPC fire as well—were coming toward her.

The interior of the cockpit seemed even smaller than she remembered, not to mention much lonelier. It wasn't the first time she'd been in a 'Mech since her injury, but she had never been alone, and it had never been as the pilot. The combined scents of old sweat, cleaning fluid, metal, and other familiar scents stung her nostrils. Slowly, apprehensively, she slid into the seat, plugged in her neurohelmet, and adjusted her cooling vest. In the distance, she saw erratic fire coming closer to her position.

"You okay over there, Major?" asked Snord.

Katya stared at the sea of controls in front of her and activated the commline. "I'm here. It's just that I haven't done this in a few years."

"You'd better learn fast," said Snord from her *Highlander*. " 'Cause in thirty seconds you're going to be sitting in the second biggest target on this hilltop."

Colonel Robert Feehan landed his *Tempest* on an exposed slab of granite, and felt its feet slip a half-meter on the smooth rock. Charging at him was a Star League-era *Sentinel,* and he swung his large pulse laser in line with it. Unimpressed, the *Sentinel* unleashed its ultra-autocannon, sending a storm of shells ripping into Feehan's right torso. The autocannon chewed up the armor plating there and rocked his 'Mech, making it harder to maintain his target lock.

He fired his pulse laser as the *Sentinel* continued to close. A line of emerald-green bursts laced into the enemy 'Mech, ripping its right arm clean off. The *Sentinel* twisted slightly under the assault, but continued to run forward as if the loss of the limb meant nothing.

Fight on, little one, Feehan thought. Victory is only a few hills away.

The *Sentinel* fired its medium laser, and the crimson beam sliced into the *Tempest*'s chest while a pair of SRMs snaked through the dwindling distance and slammed into his right arm. Feehan's *Tempest* weathered the assault, losing only a little armor.

Feeling a little nervous about the closing distance, he unleashed his short-range missiles, followed by his trio of medium lasers. The heat in his cockpit rose as the weapons discharged, the lasers whining as their capacitors discharged. Two of his missiles missed, but everything else hit home, riddling the *Sentinel* even as its pilot continued to charge at him.

Feehan took a step back as the *Sentinel* again fired its autocannon, the last weapon it would have time to discharge before it physically slammed into him. The line of deadly shells lanced into his chest, further mangling the armor there. The next instant, the *Sentinel* itself plowed into him.

Feehan's *Tempest* outmassed the smaller 'Mech by twenty-five tons, but the *Sentinel* had smashed into him at a full run. Armor plating ground up under the charge, and the *Tempest* rocked backward, threatening to fall over. Feehan struggled to stay upright, sidestepping slightly to let the *Sentinel* fall at his feet.

He checked his damage display, and saw that he had lost some chest armor. The *Sentinel* was out of the fight, half-rolling as it fell, its reactor powered down from the damage of the charge. Feehan saw the symbol of a buffalo nickel on the fallen 'Mech's right torso, and his eyes widened.

Snord's Irregulars? he thought. Fighting alongside Archer's Avengers?

A hollow seemed to open up in the pit of his stomach as he digested the implications. Did they know what the Wolverton's Highlanders had done to them?

"Colonel," he heard Luther Fisk say in his headset. "Your forces seem stalled." Feehan had persuaded the younger officer to stay with the mobile HQ rather than ride along with him. The last thing he needed was a back-seat driver.

"We're not fighting just one beat-up regiment here, Fisk," he snapped. "The Irregulars and the Avengers are fighting together."

"Damn!" cursed Luther.

"I'm ordering my people to fall back," Feehan said.

"You've got to hang in," Fisk said.

"Easy for you to say," Feehan retorted as his *Tempest* shuddered under another medium pulse laser hit from an enemy he had yet to even target. "You're sitting in the HQ. I suggest you have the command post fall back to position bravo. I'll rendezvous with you there."

"Colonel . . ."

"Shut up, you ass. If Snord and Christifori know what we did to them, we're in deep trouble."

No, I'm in deep trouble, he told himself. He cut off the radio and started to fall back in a long, running arc. As he turned, he saw something in the distance that sent a chill down his spine: a *Highlander* BattleMech. He knew from intel reports that there could be only one of those on the battlefield: the 'Mech belonging to Colonel Rhonda Snord. What was going on here? Wasn't she supposed to be dead?

Feehan's mind raced trying to figure out how he could turn this fiasco into a victory even as he began to withdraw at a full run.

Archer, Tasha Snord, and a handful of Avenger 'Mechs moved along the flanks of the Wolverton's Highlanders. They were keeping Feehan's people boxed in, channeling them toward Hill 403.

As he came over a small crest, he saw the site that

until recently had been his acting command post. Four 'Mechs were downed, while two damaged 'Mechs were still fighting at the top of the hill. One he recognized instantly as Rhonda Snord's *Highlander*. He watched as it fired its gauss rifle at an approaching *Clint*, sending the Highlander BattleMech flying back eight meters and onto its back.

"Specter One to Jailhouse Rocker One," he said. "Looks like you blunted them here, Colonel."

"They seem to be pulling back, General," Snord answered. "I'd say they've had enough." She swept her *Highlander*'s LRM rack at a target somewhere out of Archer's line of sight, and a wave of long-range missiles streaked away into the distance. Then he spotted a *Tempest* running along the hillside, turning as if to flee the battle. He brought his extended-range large lasers to bear on it, and one missed by a maddeningly wide margin. The other sliced into the 'Mech's thin rear armor, blazing a nasty black scar diagonally across the 'Mech's back.

"My sensors show them withdrawing in apparent good order," Snord reported.

"They did a hell of a lot of damage," Archer said, taking off in pursuit of the *Tempest* in hopes of getting another clear shot.

"Do you still have those special forces boys of yours on-line?" Snord asked, coming up alongside him. With her was a lumbering *Hunchback*, scarred from several missile hits along its chest.

"I'm with you," Archer said, then called, "Specter One to Sherwood Foresters." He was unable to suppress a smile. "You are a go with your mission."

"Copy that," Thomas Sherwood said.

The next voice he heard was Katya's, over the command frequency. "Chances are that Feehan is moving his mobile HQ by now," she said. "I'll order some fighters to sweep the area on their way in. Maybe they'll get lucky and spot the Highlander HQ in transit."

"Brain, where are you?" Archer asked, puzzled.

"In the *Hunchback*, General."

Archer's mouth opened in surprise, and he twisted the *Penetrator*'s torso to the right to see the *Hunchback* more clearly. "You're piloting a BattleMech?"

"It was Colonel Snord's idea. It's all coming back to me—just like riding a scooter," Katya said proudly.

"Move up along my right flank then," Archer said, slowing his pace slightly as Rhonda Snord moved up on his left. "Let's see if we can turn this retreat into a full-blown rout."

26

Southwest of New Bealton, Odessa
District of Donegal
Lyran Alliance
4 May 3063

"This is Count Fisk to Major Snord," Fisk said into the mouthpiece of his field transport's transmitter, as the vehicle raced along the sloped plains southwest of New Bealton.

He was on his way to the command post to inspect the rapidly deteriorating situation. He should have known better than to leave it in the hands of his son—now he would have to step in and clean up the mess.

The voice that came back was not the one he'd expected, but somehow he wasn't surprised. "I'm afraid the major is tied up right now, your Grace. This is Colonel Rhonda Snord. Is there anything I can do for you?" Her voice dripped with contempt.

"Colonel Snord, what a pleasure to discover that reports of your death were premature," he said, more smoothly than he felt. With Snord alive, it meant the Irregulars were being led not by a novice girl but a seasoned vet. He had heard that the Avengers and Irregulars were fighting together; now a ghost was challenging him on the commline.

"I bet," she said.

"I hear that your Irregulars are fighting alongside Archer's Avengers, and I must admit that I find that turn of events disturbing. As your direct link with the Lyran Alliance, I must ask that you pull your battalions out of this fight. This is between the First Thorin Regiment and the Wolverton's Highlanders."

There was a pause and a small crackle of static, then Rhonda Snord's voice returned just as his driver hit a rough patch of road that shook the entire touring vehicle.

"Don't play games with me, Count. I'm far too old for this sort of foolishness. I saw the evidence. The Wolverton's Highlanders tried to kill both me and Archer Christifori. This, Count Fisk, is personal. Between the Highlanders, us, and eventually . . . you."

"I assure you, Colonel Snord—" the Count began.

"Don't insult my intelligence," she cut in. "Now, you'll have to excuse me. I have to go. We're about to finish off the Highlanders, and I never like to miss a good party."

"I remind you again, Colonel, that I am the holder of your contract. I order you to withdraw."

Rhonda laughed. "Our contract is up. From what Tasha tells me, you let it lapse and hung my unit out to dry. I stopped taking orders from you the minute I came out of that coma, Count Fisk. There isn't a safe place on this planet for you right now."

Fisk threw the wireless microphone so hard against the window that the small plastic device shattered into dozens of little black shards that rained down onto the floor of his vehicle.

Colonel Feehan arrived at the mobile headquarters unit as it traveled along with the other vehicles carrying the regiment's ammunition, supplies, parts, and other materiel. The mobile HQ was essentially a large wheeled vehicle, armor-plated and topped with satellite dishes, antennae, and other sensors. This one was an older version, weather-worn and patched many times in its long and less-than-illustrious history.

He angled his *Tempest* to intercept, and the convoy slowed to a stop as he and other elements of his regiment fanned out along the road and beyond, kicking up small clouds of dust as they went.

Feehan had pulled his entire regiment back, and with good reason. The light and medium 'Mechs of the Wolverton's Highlanders had hurt the Avengers and the Irregulars, but they could not maintain their momentum. The combined units facing him had longer staying power, and in the end, it was either withdraw or face total destruction. If it had been just the Avengers, he was sure he could have wiped them out. But combined with the Irregulars . . . well, the hope of victory was faint, but it was still possible. He just had to choose the right ground to make his stand.

He brought the *Tempest* to a halt and left it in low-power mode rather than shutting down totally. Feehan climbed out of the cockpit and down the 'Mech's handholds, seeing up close the damage it had suffered. The armor plating on its chest and legs was ripped and torn, and the smell of smoke mixed with ozone from laser fire stung his nose. He dropped the last bit of the climb onto the sparse grass alongside the road, then jogged over to the exterior hatch of the mobile HQ and entered.

Chaos reigned in the comm room. His regiment was still somewhat scattered and in the process of trying to break off combat with the combined Avengers/Irregulars. He made his way through the narrow passage into the planning room, where he saw the hunched-over form of Luther Fisk staring intently at the illuminated holomap.

"Colonel Feehan," Fisk said firmly. "We can't stay here, out in the open like this."

Feehan shut off the manual-flow control valve on his cooling vest and wiped the sweat from his brow. "Do you think I don't know that? I was commanding in the field before you even dreamed of being a MechWarrior. We've got to pull back and regroup. Many of my companies are mixed, and we've taken a lot of casualties."

"Are you certain the Irregulars and Archer's Avengers are working together?" Fisk asked.

"Archer Christifori's *Penetrator* shot up my backside when we started to fall back, Fisk," he said contemptuously, "and my sensors picked up a *Highlander* in the fight as well."

"Rhonda Snord," Luther said slowly. He'd also heard the rumor that she'd survived.

"Damn straight," Feehan snapped. "I suggest we pull back to the outskirts of New Bealton. There are some woods there, some sort of park. We can use that for cover."

"I'm afraid the course of action you're outlining doesn't meet my objectives," a voice said from behind him. Feehan spun around and saw Nicholas Fisk standing in the doorway.

"Count Fisk," he said. "This isn't the time or place for this kind of discussion. My regiment has to fall back, rearm, and regroup right now. Initial losses are nearly fifty percent."

"And what of the Avengers and the Irregulars?" the Count asked coolly.

"Hard to say. Much of their forces were already battered. I'd say they've suffered about thirty to forty percent overall."

"Your troops are still comparatively fresh," the Count said. "Retreating will not solve anything. The situation on Odessa must be decided on the battlefield."

"It would be best to pull back and engage the enemy on ground of my own choosing," Feehan said, sweat breaking on his forehead again, this time from tension.

"I understand, Colonel," Fisk said, his jaw clenching as he held his anger in check. "But you seem to forget that your lances were the ones that attacked Christifori and Snord. If you fail to take them out, there isn't a government in the Inner Sphere that will hire the Wolverton's Highlanders. Falling back into a defensive stance is not the way to wipe out these units. You've got to be aggressive—take what you have back into the field."

"M'lord," Feehan said, almost pleading, "I appreciate the political sensitivity of all of this. My forces are rearming and carrying out field repairs right now. But we are lights and mediums against a full-force mix of all weight classes, ground armor, and infantry. I got strafed twice on the way back here."

"I appreciate that," the Count replied. "But you don't have to take them all out. Kill Snord and Christifori, and both units will scatter. That was the original plan—if your people had done their work right the first time, we wouldn't be here now."

Feehan felt his face get hot with anger, but somehow he held his tongue. "Sir, what are you proposing?"

Count Fisk smiled slightly. "Send your troops straight at those two targets. Take them out. Kill Snord and Christifori, and this fight will be over."

Feehan couldn't help the sense of shame that swept over him. The tactic Fisk was talking about was known as "headhunting." It wasn't unheard of, but it was certainly not considered honorable.

Yet his people had already been drawn into much worse by the Count. For good or ill, he couldn't turn back now. As much as he hated Count Fisk, he knew that if the Irregulars or Archer's Avengers survived the coming fight, they would come after him and hunt him down. The black hole into which the Wolverton's Highlanders had been drawn suddenly seemed to get deeper.

"We'll finish up our field repairs, then we're out of here," he said in an almost-lifeless tone.

"How long will that take?" the Count pressed.

"Twenty minutes," Feehan said, squeezing past the Count and heading for the door of the mobile HQ.

"I've painted the target in sector 1551 'F,' as in Foxtrot," Captain Thomas Sherwood said into his wrist communicator. "Only one problem, General," he added, using the enhanced binoculars again to confirm what he had been watching from behind the small clump of trees for the past few minutes.

"What's that?" Archer replied.

"I think just about every surviving Highlander is here. Lots of rearming and fast repair work. I think they aim to—" He stopped and stared intently through the image finder. "Hang on, it looks like they're moving out. Heading due west, right back at you and the Irregulars, sir."

There was a pause. "I understand, Thomas. Stay hidden. Wait until they're well on their way, and then take out their base."

"Sir, you've got well over a battalion heading your way, and they're moving pretty fast."

"Don't worry about us," Archer replied. "I think we can handle them ourselves."

27

Southwest of Hill 403, Odessa
District of Donegal
Lyran Alliance
4 May 3063

Captain Joey-Lynn Fraser moved up ahead of the regimental command lance, pausing her *Gallowglas* on the slope of the hill near an opening in the brush. The hillside swept down and away for nearly two kilometers. The glare of the sun was muted by the storm clouds that had rolled in as well as by the polarized glass of her cockpit. From where she stood, it was a flat run downhill.

"Good to have the White Tigers here," she heard General Christifori say in her earpiece. He had had them posted on the far-left flank, but the time had come to pull them in to the center.

"Glad to be here, sir," she said, longing for a cigar. Time enough for that when all this was over, she told herself. "You sure they're headed this way, General?"

"Pretty sure," he said. As if on cue, her long-range sensors started painting targets in the distance on the circular display. From their IFF transponders, they were not Irregulars or Avengers. It was a fast-moving wave of the Wolverton's Highlanders.

"I have incoming bogies," she barked out.

"Confirmed," another voice said, this time from a *Thug* off to her side, one Snord's Irregulars. "They seem to be headed straight at us, sirs."

"All right, then," Archer said calmly. "White Tiger Company, advance on the enemy through the center."

Joey heard another voice that she assumed belonged to Rhonda Snord. "First Battalion, Shake, Rattle, and Roll company, you have the White Tigers along the hillside to provide crossfire."

As Joey started her BattleMech into a slight trot, she saw a battered but still intact company of Irregulars also sweeping down the hillside off to one side. Some were jumping; others were breaking into a full run.

In front of her, the lead elements of the Highlanders were starting to come in range. A fast-moving *Jackal* slowed long enough to discharge its extended-range PPC up the hill past her. The azure energy sliced through the air, winging past her shoulder. The rotund little *Jackal* didn't wait for return fire. Its jump jets ignited, and it began to rise as if it were going to jump straight over her head.

Joey-Lynn slowed and fired her pair of large lasers. The crimson beams seared through the air and hit both of the rising 'Mech's legs. Armor flew off in every direction, raining down over the hillside, but the course of the *Jackal* did not waver. It came down to one side of her, landing about forty-five meters away.

The Irregular *Thug* she'd seen earlier rushed up to meet it. The *Thug*'s right arm drew back and then let go like a jackhammer, punching squarely into the *Jackal*'s head. Armor plating and ferro-fibrous internal structure collapsed inward. The punch was so powerful that what was left of the *Jackal* did not pull free from the massive fist until it fell backward down the hillside.

"One hell of a punch there," Joey said on the open channel.

"Thanks. I'm Captain H'Chu," the *Thug* pilot said.

"Captain Fraser," Joey returned.

"Very well, then, Fraser, watch out—you've got a *Spider* on the left," H'Chu warned.

Joey pivoted her torso and saw the *Spider* standing almost at point-blank range, firing not at her but back up the hill at the regimental command lance's position. A staccato of emerald bursts from its medium pulse lasers peppered the hillside, aimed at a target she could not see.

Just as H'Chu had done, Joey pulled back her *Gallowglas*'s fist and punched with all her might at the *Spider*. The tiny, thirty-ton 'Mech took the blow on its left arm, which crumpled under the blow and hastily retreated down the hillside.

She turned and saw another full lance of 'Mechs racing up the hill. "They don't seem interested in us at all," she muttered to herself.

"Roger that," H'Chu said. "Command lance, it looks like they're gunning for you. Recommend you and the general pull back and give us some room to work." Then she unleashed the raw energy of her PPCs down the hill.

Archer sidestepped the charging *Lineholder*, evading its ramming attack by less than a meter. His armor was already badly savaged by long-range missiles and laser fire from farther down the hill, as was the larger *Highlander* piloted by Rhonda Snord. The fight had been raging for almost an hour, and his nerves were starting to show the strain. The Highlander *Lineholder* tried to turn and resume the attack but wasn't fast enough. Archer opened up at point-blank range with his five remaining operational medium pulse lasers. The thin slice of space between the two 'Mechs suddenly came alive with green pulses of light. Melted globs of ferro-fibrous armor splattered against his cockpit glass and sizzled as they cooled.

The *Lineholder* quaked under the pounding he was giving it, but it remained standing and ready to renew the attack. Two of its medium lasers fired, one barely missing, the other slicing a scarlet lance of energy across his *Penetrator*'s right shin, melting his armor there.

Archer stepped to the side and waited a moment for the heat to fade as he kept his targeting reticle on the *Lineholder*. It took a step backward, as if seeking more room. Archer was about to fire when a shot whizzed over his 'Mech's shoulder and tore into the already-mangled center torso of the Wolverton Highlander. The gauss slug dug past the remaining armor, punching deep into the guts of the BattleMech. The *Lineholder* reeled backward under the attack and then wobbled uneasily, its legs buckling. The upper torso of the *Lineholder* bent at the waist as the MechWarrior strained to keep it upright. It must have suffered a gyro hit. Like a staggering drunk, the *Lineholder* sagged and fell face down on the hillside.

He turned and saw Rhonda Snord in her *Highlander* BattleMech farther up on the hill. "Thanks, Colonel."

"Don't mention, General," she said. "What are friends for?"

The mobile headquarters of the Wolverton's Highlanders had gone nearly four kilometers, followed by its convoy of spare parts and ammunition, when Sherwood decided it was time to attack. Most of the 'Mechs were already long gone thirty minutes ago. Only those that were not battle-ready remained, and four of those were laid out on Prime Haulers, being taken somewhere for more permanent repairs.

"Sherwood Foresters, this is Forester One," he said over the commline. "I want this done by the numbers.

Sprint Lance, you sweep in and make sure the HQ is captured. Take it intact if you can. Sergeant Holt, you and your infantry secure the HQ once it stops, and then secure those transports. Command Lance, form up on me. We'll take out the lead vehicle as roadblock; then provide cover fire on the HQ.''

He paused and checked his watch. Switching to the command frequency, he called the general. "General Christifori, this is the Sherwood Foresters. We are engaging the enemy.''

There was no response. Things back at the HQ must be hectic. "All right, Foresters, sweep in now!" he ordered.

Sherwood angled his *Nightsky* out from behind the trees and fired at the hauler at the head of the column, his pulse-laser array spitting forth a wall of green death as he broke into a run. The hauler must have realized its plight and tried to accelerate, but it lacked any real armor or weapons. The laser blasts gutted the side of the huge commercial vehicle, and it ground to a dead halt.

Then the entire column slammed to a stop. Off in the distance, Sherwood saw Sprint Lance—four lightweight Savannah Masters—race down the line of vehicles. In the dim evening light, he saw them concentrate their fire on the mobile HQ with their tiny lasers, delivering a stunning series of blows. The HQ vehicle's machine guns leapt into action, but the Savannah Masters were lightning fast and hard to hit. They spun and danced around the puffs of fire like dervishes.

One of his other 'Mechs, a *Scarabus,* bounded from cover and fired its pair of medium lasers at the J-27 directly behind the mobile headquarters, slicing into the thin side armor. The vehicle reeled under the flank attack, rocking hard to its right. Sherwood first saw a crack in the armor, and then it glowed orange for a millisecond. Then, before he could react, the J-27 and its cargo of ammunition exploded. The cab of the carrier slammed into the rear of the mobile HQ, mangling its armor. The transport behind it turned slightly, its front blackened by the flames, and drove off the road straight at him.

"Watch that fire," he said to his unit. "I'd like to get some of these people alive if we can." Then he saw it: a commercial ground transport, obviously civilian, moving to the far side of the mobile HQ. But what was a civilian vehicle doing at a military base?

"Sprint Lance, make sure that transport doesn't get away. Blast out its tires," he said calmly as he leveled his weapons at the cab of the mobile HQ. He just hoped to hell this would work . . .

Archer's *Penetrator* staggered back another five meters under the withering charged-particle blast. The outline of his BattleMech on his sensory display was covered with mostly yellow and a few red spots, indicating the damage he'd sustained thus far. His head throbbed as he fought the gyro controls to keep the *Penetrator* upright.

One thing had become certain: he and Rhonda Snord were the intended targets of the Highlanders' assault. At his feet was a debris field of armor, broken and battered 'Mechs, and the occasional 'Mech arm or leg still kicking out smoke. Seven times the Highlanders had ground their way up to point-blank range with him or Snord. Seven times they had been driven back. Now, most of the shots came from farther away, but Feehan's assault did not seem to be slowing.

Archer's cooling vest was working overtime as he leveled off and swept for targets, then spotted a fast-moving *Panther* snaking its way up the hillside, using the clumps of trees for cover.

"You still with us, General?" Katya asked. She sounded worried.

"My frontal armor is more memory than protection," he said, sweeping the joystick to achieve a lock on the elusive *Panther,* "but I'm still in the game."

He dropped the targeting reticle on the brown-and-green-striped BattleMech and heard the tone of weapons lock. He unleashed his ER large lasers—first one, then the other. The waves of heat made his skin tingle, but he fought it off. One of his shots slammed into the *Panther*'s right leg, while the other hit its right torso. Melted armor splattered off as the enemy MechWarrior fought to maintain control.

At his side, Rhonda Snord opened up with her last salvo of long-range missiles. Most of the twenty warheads rammed into the tiny *Panther,* riddling its legs with holes. Armor flew off in every direction, and three missiles exploded inside the gouge he'd dug in the *Panther*'s thigh. Green coolant splattered out like blood from an arterial wound as the 'Mech contorted and fell, its knee actuator either locked up or destroyed.

Archer turned his head and glanced over at Snord's huge *Highlander*, which had also taken a lot of damage. Its legs were ripped open like gaping wounds, and its head was blackened from a flamer attack at nearly point-blank range. Three gauss rounds had destroyed most of her chest armor, leaving massive pits where the nickel slugs had exposed myomer muscle bundles. Still, the centuries-old war machine was still in the fight.

"Another wave is coming," Katya said over the broadband channel. Archer turned to look down the hill as a pair of *Cicada*s broke from cover, firing up in his direction and ripping up the rock formations near the feet of Rhonda's *Highlander*. The rock exploded like shrapnel in the air.

Archer moved to the right and torso-twisted the *Penetrator* to keep the assaulting 'Mechs in view. Then he spotted the real threat. Not the *Cicada*s. They were too small, too lightly armored.

The threat came from another pair, a *Tempest* and a *Vindicator*, which had moved in behind the *Cicada*s. As if to reinforce his assessment, Katya piloted her *Hunchback* forward and leveled its deadly autocannon. The large-caliber weapon roared, hitting one of the *Cicada*s in its lightly armored chest. Taking out the lighter machines would leave him free to deal with the true threats. There was a flash as the 'Mech's fusion reactor lost its shielding and superheated with the cooler air. Then, in a thunderclap of sound and light, the *Cicada* and the *Panther* at its feet simply ceased to exist.

The *Tempest* swept into his field of fire, and Archer juked the joystick to bring it into weapons lock. The *Tempest* beat him to the punch, leveling its gauss rifle and large pulse laser and firing just as he achieved lock. The pulse laser hit his right arm in a green burst of light, stripping the little remaining armor and melting holes in its bundles of myomer muscle.

The gauss rifle slug smashed through the last bit of armor on his chest, knocking the *Penetrator* back so hard that he almost fell to the rocky ground. A sickening groan filled his ears as he heard the internal structure of his 'Mech begin to give way. The last time he'd heard that noise was in the fighting on Huntress, just seconds before his 'Mech was destroyed.

The fusion-reactor warning light went red in front of him on the console, and for a moment, he wondered if he too would suffer the *Cicada*'s fate. His shielding held for the moment, but it had been seriously damaged. All of a sudden, the *Penetrator* felt more sluggish.

Archer wanted to fire his four remaining pulse lasers in a single salvo, but one look at his heat monitor told him the heat sinks were still fighting to bleed off his 'Mech's excess heat. He switched only two of the lasers to the TIC and fired. Both hit the left torso of the *Tempest*, barely marring its paint. The heat inside his cockpit was almost unbearable.

The *Vindicator* had unleashed its fury on Rhonda Snord, its ER PPC tearing into her *Highlander*'s chest. Its medium pulse-laser shot went wild, exploding rocks as their moisture instantly cooked off. Archer knew, in that moment, that they were nearing the end of the fight. There couldn't be too many more 'Mechs left in Feehan's force, and there certainly wasn't much left of either him or Rhonda Snord.

Tasha Snord returned from fending off another attack and leapt to her mother's defense. She fired her ER PPC at the *Vindicator* at the same time that Katya trained her weapons on the other *Cicada*. For a moment, it looked to Archer like the battle was happening in slow motion. Tasha's brilliant blue blast of charged particles hit the *Vindicator* in the left torso, and it sagged backward as its armor flew all over the hillside. The other *Cicada* caught a burst from Katya's medium and small lasers, mostly in the legs. Perhaps the *Cicada* had taken too much damage, or maybe its pilot was disheartened by the field of dead and destroyed BattleMechs all around it. Either way, it had obviously had enough. The 'Mech turned and charged down the hill away from the conflagration.

Archer brought his large lasers up and paused, waiting just a little bit longer for the heat bleed off. He switched each laser to its own trigger to try and balance out the additional heat they would create. There wasn't enough time to do this the way he wanted. He didn't have any frontal armor left. One shot from the *Tempest*'s gauss rifle, and it would all be over. Rhonda Snord was facing the same situation as the *Vindicator* moved into firing position on her.

There was one place where he still had armor. Not

enough to stop the shot, but enough to blunt most of its damage. He glanced out the side of his cockpit, and there was a moment of unspoken communication between the two military commanders—general and mercenary, both of them arriving at the same conclusion at the same moment.

Timing was critical. He heard the tone of weapons lock and torso-twisted a hundred and eighty degrees. From his cockpit, he saw Rhonda do the same. The rear armor of their two 'Mechs was thin, but it just might be enough to weather one more attack.

The *Tempest*'s gauss slug didn't hit him in the back, however, but in the *Penetrator*'s arm, which was attached more by a prayer than by metal. Ripped off at the shoulder, the limb went flying past his cockpit and up the hill, where he could see Katya moving into firing position. Better to lose the arm than the entire 'Mech, he told himself. Much better. Warning lights and alarms went off in the cockpit at the loss of the limb, and he fought to control the *Penetrator,* bleeding off a few more milliseconds of heat.

He completed his turn at the same time Rhonda did. The *Tempest* just stood there on the hillside, seeming stunned by their perfect timing. Archer raised his remaining ER large laser and locked on to the *Tempest* at the same time Katya unleashed the fury of her autocannon. The shots ripped into the stout body of the *Tempest,* pulverizing its armor in a cloud of gray smoke. Archer also saw the *Vindicator* bathed in a blast of laser fire from the mother/daughter team on his flank, forcing it to backpedal down the hill.

The *Tempest* slowed, and Archer thought it would turn on him again and fire, but then he saw a blast hit its rear flank. In the distance was a pair of 'Mechs firing at the *Tempest*'s thin rear armor. The thin haze of smoke from the fight and the dozens of smoldering fires made visual confirmation impossible. Switching to his short-range sensors and scanning the IFF transponders, Archer instantly recognized the call signs on his display as those of Norris and John Kraff. Though Norris was struggling with some leg damage, the pair had obviously succeeded in gaining the *Tempest* pilot's attention.

The Highlander 'Mech stopped and raised its arms straight up in the air. Archer's sensors told the rest of the story as its fusion reactor switched to low-power mode. The two actions were universally accepted gestures of surrender.

"This is Colonel Feehan of the Wolverton's Highlanders," came a voice on the broadband from the *Tempest*. "We surrender. Hold your fire."

"Give me one good reason," came Tasha's terse voice. Archer glanced over and saw that she was still training her weapons on the *Tempest*.

"Because we're better than they are," her mother said calmly. "And no matter what has happened to us, the Wolverton's Highlanders will be nothing more than a memory after today."

Feehan's voice cut in. "This is not about my people. I'm in command, and I alone should be held responsible."

"Not so fast there, Colonel Feehan," Archer said, grateful that the temperature in his cockpit was dropping toward tolerable. "I don't think that's for you *or* us to decide. I think the Mercenary Review and Bonding Commission is going to want a say in your fate— as well as those of your MechWarriors."

Rhonda Snord chuckled. "Yes, I'm sure Jaime Wolf will be understanding. You do know that my father and I served under him, don't you, Colonel?" There was no response from the other mercenary commander.

Kraff continued to move up the hillside past the *Tempest*, flanked by Captain Norris's battered but functional *Masakari*. "General, sir," he said, "Jesus jumping-H Christ, that twist you and the colonel did was about the most beautiful thing I've ever seen on a damn battlefield, sir. Did the two of you plan it that way?"

Archer relaxed for the first time in days. "Not exactly, Captain Kraff," he said. "I think it was a case of the old saying—you know, the one about great minds thinking alike?"

Captain Sherwood held his Blazer aimed at the door of the civilian transport as the prisoners were led out. The first was a tall man he had never met face to face, but who he recognized immediately as Count Nicholas Fisk. It was obvious the Count felt that his capture was merely an irritating formality. Then another man hobbled out behind the count, a look of hatred on his face. That man Sherwood knew personally, having served under him on Thorin for a time. Luther Fisk, a man whose history with the First Thorin regiment was widely known and thoroughly despised.

"You?" Fisk breathed.

"That's right, Fisk," Sherwood said. "This is twice we've had the honor of taking you down. Once on Thorin, once here."

"Captain, I must remind you that I am a member of the Lyran nobility," the Count cut in. "You will release me immediately, or you and your unit will face the consequences of crossing the Archon-Princess." His voice was arrogant, and Sherwood had to suppress a laugh as the infantry under his command led the remainder of the command staff from the captured vehicle.

"Count Fisk," he said formally, bowing his head mockingly, "if Katrina Steiner-Davion wants to come down here and kick my ass, she is welcome to drop in at any time. Until then, you are a prisoner of Archer's Avengers and Snord's Irregulars."

"This is highly inappropriate, Captain," the Count protested.

"Or," Sherwood said, leveling his weapon at the Count, "I could shoot you for attempting to escape and save myself a ton of paperwork. Your call, Count."

Fisk didn't answer, but that didn't keep all the color from draining from his face.

28

Royal Palace, New Bealton
Odessa District of Donegal,
Lyran Alliance
6 May 3063

Archer looked around at the white marble pillars, heavy drapery, and magnificent view, and marveled that people actually lived in such luxury. The Fisk family holdings on Odessa were vast, and all boasted the same degree of grandeur.

His infantry, under Major Alice Getts, had secured the capital city as soon as the Wolverton's Highlanders had surrendered. Thus far, the civilians had not reacted publicly to the fact that the planet was now under the control of Prince Victor and the Armed Forces of the Federated Suns. Katya had suggested that perhaps the propaganda about the Avengers' "atrocities" had actually worked to their advantage. Some who might have protested kept their heads down rather than risk imprisonment—or worse. As soon as the city was secured, Getts had called him in.

Archer and Rhonda Snord had ordered a table brought in to Fisk's throne room. They took seats on one side, while a row of chairs was placed on the other. Tasha Snord took up position behind her mother. Archer's infantry secured the door, while the infantry of Snord's Irregulars provided him and the colonel with personal security. Their armored vests and combat shotguns made it clear that any threats would be dealt with up close and personal.

The three prisoners were led in. Gone were the Count's deep blue robes of rank and privilege. All three wore gray jumpsuits marked with yellow bands on the legs and shoulders to mark them as prisoners. Each also wore two days' worth of beard and sullen expressions. Count Fisk sat down opposite Archer. His son, who limped in minus his cane, took the center seat, refusing to make eye contact with Archer. He turned his cold gaze toward Rhonda Snord instead. Across from her sat a visibly uncomfortable Colonel Feehan.

"We've brought you here to discuss your final disposition," Archer said, setting his elbows on the table and folding his hands in front of him. "You've put both of our units through a lot, but I want to assure you that we will adhere to the Ares Conventions of warfare." He cast a glance at Feehan, who seemed to let out a silent sigh of relief. "Though I might add that there was quite a bit of debate on the matter."

Count Fisk drew himself up to speak, trying to maintain his imperious manner. "As a member of the Royal Court, I must demand that you release me, General Christifori. I believe you'll find that diplomatic immunity applies to members of the royal family."

Archer shook his head. "According to the records we've recovered, Count Fisk, you had direct control of the military assets of the Irregulars and of the Highlanders. That makes you accountable as a military commander, not a member of the nobility."

"Preposterous!" Fisk snapped.

"You can protest all you want," Archer said mildly, "but for now this matter is being treated as a military one. You are formally charged with ordering troops to assassinate me and Colonel Snord, a military commander under your control. More important, you used troops of the same government that employed the Irregulars in an assault against them. You also violated the sanctity of a truce, as the Colonel and I were both riding under the white flag, when you ambushed us. These are serious charges."

"That is only speculation, General," the Count sneered.

Archer nodded to the guards at the door, and Sergeant Gramash and Katya Chaffee entered. Between them stood the sullen form of Erwin Vester.

"As you can see, Count Fisk, I believe I have a little more than speculation." Archer turned to look at Luther Fisk. "Now, as for your son . . ."

The Count cut him off. "Wait a minute, General—what's going to happen to me, to my holdings?"

Archer didn't want to gloat, but he couldn't resist a smile of satisfaction. "Count Fisk, you are now a prisoner of Prince Victor Steiner-Davion. You will be taken to a prisoner-of-war camp until your trial. With the evidence we possess, chances are it will be a long time before you see the light of day as a free man.

"As for Odessa, it is now under the authority of Prince Victor and will be governed according to his law."

"You're a fool if you think the Archon won't negotiate for my release," Fisk said.

"I doubt it, Count Fisk," Rhonda Snord put in. "After all, you cost her this world, the Wolverton's Highlanders, and my unit. Do you really think she'll lose any sleep over you?" The Count seen to sag visibly at her words.

"As I was saying," Archer went on, "Luther Fisk, you were acting in an advisory position as your father's liaison to the Highlanders, but you are no longer in the active military. You will be sent to a prison camp and most likely paroled to a neutral world."

"You can't be serious." Luther looked shocked.

"I may hate you personally," Archer said. "I may think you're lower than the slime on a slug, but I can't pin anything on you directly. For now, I'm not going to press charges."

"You surprise me, Christifori," Luther said. "I never thought you would let me go once you had me."

Archer kept a deadpan expression. "Look in the mirror, Luther. I've taken away your homeworld. Your family's wealth, property, and possessions now belong to Prince Victor because of your father's stupidity. You've been beaten by my forces twice on the battlefield. Honestly, what more could I do to you?"

Archer looked down the table to where Colonel Feehan sat, wringing his hands nervously in front of him. In all of Archer's discussions with Rhonda Snord, they had disagreed most about how to deal with the other mercenary commander. The verdict on his fate belonged to Rhonda Snord and her daughter.

"Colonel Feehan," Rhonda said slowly, "your forces attacked both General Christifori and I with the express purpose of murdering us. You also planned to wipe out both of our units in an attempt to bury your dirty deeds. And your attack on my force was made while you and I were working for the same employer—the Lyran Alliance."

She paused, letting her words sink in. "Frankly, your life should be forfeit. Your unit, what's left of it, is in my possession. Not that it matters—no one would hire you after what you've done. A message has gone out to Colonel Blackstone. I'm sure he will not be pleased when he gets it, since part of the punishment for your crimes will come out of his pocketbook."

Feehan simply stared at her, his face pale.

"I wanted to kill you and save everyone the time and trouble. But"—she glanced over at Archer—"someone convinced me otherwise. So, I've ordered a detachment of my infantry to escort you and the evidence against you to Outreach. You'll be turned over to the Mercenary Review and Bonding Commission for trial. They will strip you of everything you've got and most likely turn over your monies, 'Mechs, and gear to us. Colonel Blackstone is likely to be bankrupted. You will be dispossessed on a world of mercenaries who will despise you. There will be no place for you to hide, no employer who will hire you. And if you ever do manage to get back on your feet, just remember that my Irregulars are out there, just waiting for their chance at revenge."

"It would be better to execute me and spare my people," Feehan said in a low tone. Rhonda Snord had spared his life, but being sent to Outreach was a death sentence nonetheless. He would live the rest of his days as a hunted man.

"Don't think I didn't push for that," she replied. "But General Christifori convinced me otherwise. You've managed to hurt the Blackstone Highlanders so bad that it will take them years to recover. You were the instrument of your own downfall. We don't need to lift a finger to hurt you."

Feehan looked down, unable to face anyone at the table. Archer leaned toward him. "And Colonel, when you get to Outreach, I want you to tell them all—remind them—of what happens when you cross Archer's Avengers."

"Or Snord's Irregulars, for that matter," Tasha put in.

Epilogue

Royal Palace, New Bealton
Odessa
District of Donegal
Lyran Alliance
7 May 3063

Archer looked across the table at Rhonda and Tasha Snord, his chin resting on his hands. They had spent the past few days repairing damage, treating the wounded, and resting. Now the time had come to finish his mission, the one he had been sent to do so long ago.

"So what's it going to take for us to close this deal, Colonel?" he asked.

"What I've been saying for the last hour, General," she said, smiling slightly. "I can't let the Irregulars get drawn into taking sides in a civil war. Look what it's done to us already. I don't want us fighting in battles where you can't tell who's the good guy and who's the bad. We'll be able to rebuild to almost regimental size now that this is done, but that doesn't mean we didn't take a battering. Rebuilding is going to take a long time."

Archer nodded. He'd been rebuilding, too. Stripping the local militia and what was left of the Wolverton's Highlanders had allowed him to turn the First Thorin into a four-battalion unit. Getting the MechWarriors he needed would take time, but he already had volunteers from the Davion loyalists on Odessa. Now, it seemed that he could finally accomplish the mission that had brought him to Odessa in the first place—except for the obstacle of Rhonda's stubbornness.

He sat back, letting his hands fall to the table. "I like to think of myself as a person who can get anything accomplished, Colonel," he said. "Money isn't the issue here. You just don't want to fight Lyran units, right?"

"That's the gist of it," she said, tipping back in her chair and propping up one leg on the table.

He closed his eyes and thought for a second. Prince Victor laid claim to a lot of worlds. Perhaps the solution lay in where the Irregulars were posted. "It's true that you'll need time to rebuild. What if you got a posting that was safely out of the war?"

"Such as?"

"Tukayyid," he said slowly. "The Prince can arrange for you to be posted there to defend against any Clan incursions. It's on the truce line with the Clans, but it's well out of the fight between Victor and Katherine."

Rhonda seemed to consider this for a moment, then nodded slowly and grinned. "Good thinking, Archer," she said. "Can you put that in writing and make it stick?"

"The Prince gave me wide discretion for carrying out my orders here. He thought you were important enough when he gave me the mission. Winning you over will be a coup for him. So, yes, I'll put it in writing. If he doesn't like it, the Prince can fire me."

Rhonda stuck her hand out. "It's a deal."

Archer shook it. "I'll be damned," he said.

"Don't act so surprised," she replied. "Anyone who can walk into the middle of an enemy camp and come out with an ally can handle a little negotiation like this one. My daughter will be in good hands with you." Rhonda glanced at Tasha. She had let her mother do most of the talking till now, and seemed as caught off-guard by her remark as Archer.

If Tasha was going to protest, she didn't get a chance. "I'm getting a little old for all this cowboying around," Rhonda said. "Tasha's proved herself here on Odessa. Besides, I'm not going anywhere yet. We've still got some digging to do out in Bealton to find those jewels."

"Congratulations on your promotion—Colonel Snord," Archer said, extending his hand to Tasha. She took it, and the handshake she gave him was as firm as her mother's. Then he snapped her his sharpest salute.

"Thank you, General," she said, saluting back. "The Irregulars are ready for their new assignment, but I'll have my work cut out for me filling my mother's shoes."

Archer stood, shielding his eyes from the noonday sun, as the technicians hoisted the repaired arm for his *Penetrator* into position and began the task of reattaching it. Their safety lines trailing behind them, the techs moved like spiders across the new armor plating that covered the torso and chest of the seventy-five-ton 'Mech. He watched vigilantly as they repaired the machine he loved almost as much as if it were human.

When Katya came up, Archer turned to her and smiled. He took her hand tenderly, unconcerned at what anyone might say about the public display of affection. After the night they'd shared, he couldn't act as if she was just another member of his unit. He knew enough about women to know that. An intimate relationship between a general and a subordinate officer would normally be frowned upon, but Archer decided that times were not exactly normal.

"We'll be up to strength in a month or two," she said, surveying the busy scene of repair operations.

Archer nodded. "Even with our losses, we're better

off with the gear we captured from the militia and from the Highlanders. Ammo is still a problem, but we've got enough firepower now to hold our own. Most of the new volunteers are Clan war vets. A half-dozen of the former Wolverton boys and girls have signed up as well."

"Speaking of which," she said, "Sherwood and his people apprehended the local militia commander and a lance of 'Mechs earlier this morning. They've been on the run since we took New Bealton. The commander surrendered without a shot. In fact, from what Thomas has learned, he's so pissed at the Count for sacrificing his unit that he's offered to defend Odessa in Prince Victor's name when we leave."

"That's not such a good idea," Archer said. "It would be better to have someone whose competence we're sure of be in charge. Besides, it was never part of our mission to take this planet. It's too close to Tharkad for us to hold. The Lyran Alliance is going to throw a lot of front-line troops to root us out of here. At this stage of the war, I doubt they'll want to commit the resources to hold Odessa, but they'll be running ops trying to tie us up."

Archer had been looking over Katya's shoulder as he spoke, watching the man in fatigues who was headed their way.

Sergeant Anton Gramash snapped off a firm salute, which both Archer and Katya returned. "I take it you'll be leaving us, Sergeant?"

"Yes, General. I wanted to thank you before I left."

Archer was slightly taken aback. "Thank me? For what?" In his mind, the Odessa mission had been a disaster, despite the positive outcome. He and Snord's Irregulars had fought a miniwar here, and the victory he'd barely managed to salvage wasn't the kind he was proud of.

Gramash waved his hand at the flurry of activity

around him. "For everything. That was one hell of a fight. Not just against an elite unit like the Irregulars, but you took on and neutralized the Wolverton's Highlanders as well. And in the end, you handed Prince Victor the planet Odessa, while he was just hoping to hire a mercenary unit."

"What became of that Erwin Vester you captured?" Archer asked, wanting to change the subject. He wasn't sure when he would ever make his own peace with the way things had gone on Odessa.

Gramash glanced at Katya, who avoided his eyes. "Well, General, let's just say he's still a good source of information to us."

Archer winced mentally, but he said, "I hope we have a chance to serve together again."

"Me too," Gramash said. "I've prepared a full report for the Prince, and I'm taking a copy of the draft contract you and Colonel Snord drew up. You'll probably be up for another promotion when word on Odessa gets out."

Archer laughed. "I can't say I hope you're right. It's hard enough dealing with this rank, let alone the next one up." He thought back on all that had happened, of the death of Darius Hopkins and the other losses he and the Avengers had suffered on Odessa. There had been days when he'd been ready to give up, but they'd finally turned things around. And it wasn't just his regiment that was suffering. There'd already been so much pain and loss on both sides since the fighting had begun.

"I'd like to ask you a favor, Sergeant, in case you see Prince Victor before I do. I've got a message for him. All I want is to be there when that sister of his gets taken down once and for all. I want to see her fall with my own eyes and let her see me watching. I want her to know I had a hand in her downfall. I owe that to Andrea, Darius, and all the others who died for her selfish ambitions. Tell him I want to be there when the ax falls."

"Understood, General," Gramash said, flashing another salute. Then he performed a smart about-face and began the long walk to the spaceport, where he would begin his long journey away from Odessa.

Archer and Katya watched him for a few minutes. Archer was silent, and Katya always respected his reflective moods. Their mission was finished on Odessa, but the civil war looked like it still had a long way to go before he would get his wish.

The Red Room, Royal Palace
New Avalon
Crucis March
Federated Commonwealth
10 May 3063

"So, Colonel Lentard, what is so important that you interrupt my gathering?" Katrina Steiner-Davion demanded as she came into the room and slammed the door behind her. The party had been going on for some time, and his audacity in dragging her away was not appreciated.

"You asked that I report to you immediately when we got word of the situation on Odessa, Archon-Princess," the colonel said. "A priority message arrived via ComStar from New Bealton, the planetary capital."

"Good," she said. "I assume Count Fisk has resolved those issues around the Irregulars and the First Thorin Regiment?"

He didn't answer.

"What is it, Lentard?" she asked in a cold voice.

"I have two messages. One from Colonel Tasha Snord, the new commanding officer of Snord's Irregulars. She says that because Count Fisk attacked her and violated her contractual rights as a mercenary, she has signed an agreement with your brother. She is apparently pressing charges against our government."

"What?" Katrina snapped. "That idiot Fisk. He was supposed to make sure something like this didn't happen. He'll pay for this."

Lentard nodded. "Indeed, he already has, your Highness. The second message was in two parts from Leftenant General Archer Christifori. First he wanted you to know that Count Fisk is under arrest. He will not be ransomed."

"Not that I would lift a finger to get that miserable fool back," she said. "What's the rest of the message?"

Lentard seemed to squirm. "The second part . . . he claims that Odessa is in the possession of Victor."

Katrina's face contorted in rage before she quickly got it under control. "What did you say?" she demanded, stepping closer to him. "That planet is practically on the front doorstep of Tharkad, you idiot. Maybe you misinterpreted the message."

Lentard could not help but squirm under her fury. "General Christifori's exact words were, 'If you want this planet, come and get it' "—he paused, wincing at the words he was about to speak—" 'you bitch.' "

Katrina exploded, her shrieks echoing deep within the royal palace for nearly thirty minutes.

But in the end, they changed nothing.

About the Author

Amissville
The Piedmont
Virginia, United States of America
Terra
9 June 2001

Blaine Pardoe was born in Virginia and raised outside Battle Creek, Michigan. He holds bachelor's and master's degrees from Central Michigan University. He works for Ernst & Young's eLearning venture, Intellinex, in corporate development. He lives in Virginia and swears it is the best place to live in the known universe.

Pardoe has written more than forty books, including a number of computer game guides, science fiction sourcebooks for BattleTech and other series, and the best-selling business book *Cubicle Warfare*. He has authored material for FASA for more than fourteen years. He has written several novels for the BattleTech and MechWarrior® series, including *Highlander Gambit*, *Impetus of War*, *Exodus Road*, *Roar of Honor*, *By Blood Betrayed*, and *Measure of a Hero*.

Blaine is a Civil War buff, and when he can he hunts for relics from the war in the old camp and skirmish sites near his house. He also plays the Great Highland Bagpipes when the mood strikes him. He can be reached at BPardoe870@AOL.com for those fans who might want to track him down.

DEEP-SPACE INTRIGUE AND ACTION FROM
BATTLETECH ®

❏ **LETHAL HERITAGE by Michael A. Stackpole.** Who are the Clans? One Inner Sphere warrior, Phelan Kell of the mercenary group Kell Hounds, finds out the hard way—as their prisoner and protégé.   (453832 / $6.99)

❏ **BLOOD LEGACY by Michael A. Stackpole.** Jaime Wolf brought all the key leaders of the Inner Sphere together at his base on Outreach in an attempt to put to rest old blood feuds and power struggles. For only if all the Successor States unite their forces do they have any hope of defeating this invasion by warriors equipped with BattleMechs far superior to their own.   (453840 / $6.99)

❏ **LOST DESTINY by Michael A. Stackpole.** As the Clans' BattleMech warriors continue their inward drive, with Terra itself as their true goal, can Comstar mobilize the Inner Sphere's last defenses—or will their own internal political warfare provide the final death blow to the empire they are sworn to protect?   (453859 / $6.99)

Prices slightly higher in Canada

Payable by Visa, MC or AMEX only ($10.00 min.), No cash, checks or COD. Shipping & handling: US/Can. $2.75 for one book, $1.00 for each add'l book; Int'l $5.00 for one book, $1.00 for each add'l. Call (800) 788-6262 or (201) 933-9292, fax (201) 896-8569 or mail your orders to:

Penguin Putnam Inc. P.O. Box 12289, Dept. B Newark, NJ 07101-5289 Please allow 4-6 weeks for delivery. Foreign and Canadian delivery 6-8 weeks.	Bill my: ❏ Visa ❏ MasterCard ❏ Amex_____(expires) Card#_____ Signature_____

Bill to:

Name _____

Address_____ City _____

State/ZIP _____ Daytime Phone # _____

Ship to:

Name _____	Book Total	$ _____
Address _____	Applicable Sales Tax	$ _____
City _____	Postage & Handling	$ _____
State/ZIP _____	Total Amount Due	$ _____

This offer subject to change without notice.   Ad # ROC3 (4/00)